DARKE

DARKE

Rick Gekoski

CANONGATE

Published in Great Britain in 2017 by Canongate Books Ltd,
14 High Street, Edinburgh EH1 1TE

www.canongate.co.uk

1

British Library Cataloguing-in-Publication Data
A catalogue record for this book is available on
request from the British Library

ISBN 978 1 78211 936 4
Export ISBN 978 1 78211 937 1

Typeset in Bembo by Palimpsest Book Production Ltd, Falkirk, Stirlingshire

Printed and bound in Great Britain by Clays Ltd, St Ives plc.

For Sam Varnedoe

Part I

I wasn't sure of the right word. *Builder? Odd-job man? Repairman?* Or perhaps I needed to see a specialist? *Carpenter? Joiner? Woodworker?*

I looked at the keyboard intently, as if the letters could Ouija themselves up, and reveal the answer.

Handyman? I typed it into Google and added my post-code, hope congealing in my heart. Most builders, handy or otherwise, are incompetent, indolent and venal.

I will not pay unless the job is done perfectly, on time and within estimate. I do not provide endless cups of PG Tips with three sugars, ta, nor do I engage in talk, small or large. Preferably no visits to my WC, though a builder who does not pee is rare. Tea makes pee. But if that is necessary, only in the downstairs cloakroom. Afterwards there will be piss under the loo.

I also wanted one who is taciturn. I loathe the inane chatter of workmen hoping to ingratiate themselves while simultaneously padding their bills. A handyman who cannot talk? Bliss. Somebody should set up a company that supplies them. Tear out their tongues or sew up their lips, that'd do it.

I added *taciturn* to my search options, but unsurprisingly

nothing turned up, though one chap described himself as 'tactile' which gave me the creeps. I tried various alternatives: *Quiet?* Nothing. *Unobtrusive?* Chance would be a fine thing. I eventually opted for *Thoughtful,* which provided two alternatives: one pictured in a string vest, who I suspect offers a variety of distinctly odd jobs, the other with a few recommendations affixed to his entry, which lauded his reliable service.

Mr Cooper, he is called, but I did not ring him, as that would provide evidence that I can hear, whereas I intended to feign almost total deafness. I emailed him, enquiring if he might be available next week. He responded immediately, which is a bad sign: shouldn't he be out handy-manning his way around town?

Yes, he replied, he was free next Wednesday and Thursday. What can he do for me?

My requirements of Mr Cooper concern the entry to my house, which has a handsome Georgian door, which will need to be removed and 'amended' – I believe this might be the right term – in five ways:

(1) Remove the brass letter box, and then fill in the resultant hole, prep and paint in Farrow and Ball Pitch Black gloss. (There are a variety of blacks, some of them greatly preferable to others, and black is one of the few colours (or absence of colours) in which doors should properly be painted. One of our neighbours, a recently arrived Indian family, decorated theirs in a Hindu orange so offensive, so out of keeping with the tone of the rest of the street that a petition was discreetly and anonymously raised by 'Your Neighbours' (guilty as charged) asking him and his wife to reconsider. They did, and repainted it bright turquoise.)

(2) Install a doorbell that rings once only, no matter how many times you press it, and which issues a melodious, inoffensive tone which can be heard clearly inside the house, but not outside the door.

(3) Install a Dia16mm-x-200-Degree-Brass-Door-Viewer-Peephole-with-Cover-and-Glass-Lens, which I will provide.

(4) Install a new keyhole and change lock.

(5) Remove the brass door-knocker, and make good.

The jobs I have outlined will take a day and a half, according to Mr Cooper, 'unless something goes wrong', plus an extra visit to put on a second coat of gloss. Mr Cooper's hourly charge is £35, plus materials, which, when I compare it to others offering similar services (though without extra thoughtfulness), is pretty much standard.

We agreed that he would arrive at 10 a.m., and that I would have a parking permit ready for his van. He seemed untroubled by my announcement of my deafness.

'No worries, I can get on with my work. Not very talkative myself.'

I considered asking him to bring his own tea, but if he finds himself in desperate need (which he will, he will), he can always pop out to the neighbourhood café, a few hundred metres down the street.

James Fenimore, as I have inwardly designated him – his site, curiously, only describes him as Cooper Handyman – arrived right on time, which was a good sign. Had he been more than fifteen minutes late, I would not have answered the door. He looks reassuringly like a handyman. Stocky, uncombed white hair that manages to be both lank and frothy at the same time, florid face pockmarked like an autonomous wart. The details don't matter. But the smell did: cheap cigarettes, stale beer, decaying teeth, wood shavings and something acrid that burned my nose, about which I didn't wish to speculate. He was disgusting, and I could barely resist the impulse to send him away: *Shoo! Off you go!* Like a stray dog.

My senses are out of control, imperious, undermining. I can smell the decomposing bodies of the flies on the windowsill, the morning light burns my retina, the residue of the morning's toothpaste coats my gums, my fingertips tingle when they come into contact with hard surfaces. It's like having a migraine without the headache.

After I opened the door, gingerly, he took a careful builderly look at it, its solidity and sheen, the perfect proportions, depth, weight.

'Don't make doors like that any more,' he said. 'Shoddy rubbish nowadays.'

I held my hand to my ear to remind him of my deafness, and made a quizzical face, as if he were speaking Mongolian.

He spoke louder, and stepped forward, which I instantly regretted. 'Shame to muck it about. Security problems I'm guessing? Lot of burglaries round here!'

None of his fucking business, is it? 'No, not security. Just some changes. I'll leave you to it. Let yourself out when you finish for the day, and I will see you tomorrow.'

At 5 p.m. I heard the door close, and went down to see how he'd got on. I was pleased – and surprised – to see that he had cleaned up after himself, and the reinstalled door closed with the same satisfying clunk as ever. It now had some new wood, undercoated and primed in dark grey, set where the letter box had been, and the area where the former door-knocker resided was filled in, sanded and painted as well. The new keyhole had been installed, and a set of three keys was on the table in the hallway. There was a newly drilled hole at eye level – he and I were much the same height so I didn't have to be measured for it – where the peephole would go tomorrow. James Fenimore had carefully taped over it with black masking tape. Altogether, a distinctly workmanlike job.

He arrived at ten the next morning, clutching a takeaway paper cup filled, I presumed, with builder's tea and lots of sugar. He put it down carefully on the hall table, remembering to put something under it. Keeping the door open, he inspected yesterday's work and tested that the undercoating was dry.

'OK so far?' he asked, in the kind of slow, loud voice one uses for foreigners, recalcitrant children, the stupid and the deaf.

I nodded, trying not to get too close to him. His smell was so invasive that I had not dabbed but sloshed some of Suzy's L'Air du Temps on my upper lip. When I opened the tiny bottle, it released a painfully sharp memory, not visual but somatic, of my head cushioned between her breasts, her original breasts, smelling of a trace of scent, as blissfully content as a boy can be. And a girl, all those years ago, before we were lost, both of us, lost.

'Will you do one thing for me?' I asked James Fenimore. 'Please go outside and shut the door, and then knock on it as loudly as you can. Maybe five or six times?'

He wasn't an inquisitive chap, or perhaps he had already marked me down as not merely deaf but barmy. How likely was it that I would be able to hear the door-knocking if I couldn't make him out at eighty decibels over four feet?

He closed the door, and gave it a few almighty wallops with his knuckles, which must have been severely tried by the experience. I listened carefully, having walked down the hallway into the kitchen. There was a distinct but muffled thudding, to be sure, but it was tolerable at that distance.

From upstairs I would hardly have heard a thing. Well-made door that. Don't make them like that any more.

Greatly reassured, I readmitted James Fenimore, only to find that he recoiled as he passed me in the doorway, stepping back, alarmed, and checking an impulse to raise his hands. His nostrils quivered noticeably, he sniffed. I was wearing scent! And as I hadn't done so yesterday, I must have put it on just to meet him!

It explained everything. The eccentricity, the fussy taste, the fancy clothes, the fastidiousness. A poofter! And I fancied him! I could see this line of thought pass slowly over his features, as he added one observation to another. He stepped back, and leant against the wall, ready to defend himself. I had a fleeting urge to kiss him on the cheek, just for the fun of it.

'When you have installed the peephole, send me an email. I'll be online, and then I can come down and see if it works properly.'

Queer as a coot.

Just after 2 p.m. my email 'ding–ding' sounded, as I was making some notes on my current concerns, composing myself in painstakingly extracted bits. I have no job and no life: no occupation, just preoccupation.

My Inbox revealed that Cooper Handyman would be finished in twenty minutes, and reminded me that I had promised to pay in cash, to save VAT. I had ordered an extra cash delivery from American Express in anticipation of this, because my usual fortnightly £400 would not leave enough to cover the bill.

I had purchased the very expensive peephole instrument for $200, when you can get perfectly serviceable ones for a tenth of that, because this top-of-the-range model alters the laws of nature. Your Mr Cooper fits it in your door, and it claims to give you 200-degree coverage. Now I am no mathematician, but even I know that from the flat surface of a door only a 180-degree arc is visible. So, as far as I can make out, the new magical instrument will allow me to see into my own hallway, presumably 10 degrees on each side, through thick brick walls. For the extra $180 I am longing to see how it works. Thus if I stand in the right position, I should be able to see myself looking at myself.

'It don't do that, it can't!' says James Fenimore scornfully. 'Just trying to sell it to idiots. Might work if you just held it to your eye, but it's for a door! Not worth the money you paid for it!'

'Shall we test it? If you go outside and close the door, perhaps you could stand in various positions while I look though the peephole.'

'No problem.'

A moment later I was looking through the new peephole directly into Mr Cooper's face. He smiled uneasily, perhaps concerned that this might be seen as a come-on. And then, with his back against first the left-hand wall and then the right, waved a hand gently, as if the Queen from her carriage.

I cannot imagine what I have done to encourage this skittishness. Does he think all queers like waving Queens? Next thing I knew he would want us to have a cup of tea together, pinkies in the air.

I think he has had enough of me too, and clutching his small cache of £50 notes, shakes my hand, with firm masculine pressure. I allow mine to melt into his. I will wash it thoroughly when he leaves.

'You take care of yourself now,' he says warily.

'You too.'

I tried to suppress a fugitive feeling of gratitude from my tone. After all, he was a good workman, unexceptionable, scratching out a living.

The new door, as I stand on the step to look it over, is stripped of both grace and function without its knocker and letter box. Black, bare, blank, beautiful in its stripped-down brutality. Just spyhole and keyhole. A bit sinister, as if it were guarding a fortress of some sort.

I hope it works. It locks them out, and me in. It gives me a – might I call it a window? – on the world. Or maybe just a way of peeping, unseen.

The next morning I woke early, and after my showering and coffee rituals, arrived at the door at 7.58. I rolled up a newly washed, fluffy hand towel and placed it above the eyehole, leant forward so that my forehead rested on it, comfortably adjusted it until my eye was perfectly aligned. The world came into focus. Across the street, just on 8 a.m., right on time like the Bombay Express, the Singh family left their house. Doctor and young son, top-knotted, turbaned. Mother and daughter in immaculate saris. You could set your watch by them. Sikh and ye shall find. Every morning both parents walked the children to the primary school before making their way to the Tube: he to the Chelsea and Westminster, she to her accountancy offices. Deloitte's, was it?

They were wonderfully presented, less disgusting than their English equivalents. Stripped of their ethnic accoutrements, their turbans, suits and saris, they would be the colour of lightly toasted Poilâne, redolent of cardamom and ghee. If you were a cannibal, you'd toss aside a pallid smelly Cooper – the colour and consistency of uncooked bread – and have a bite of these tasty Oriental morsels.

★

I've composed a list of further world-proofing chores. I like lists. You think of every contingency, plan for it, cross it off. It gives the impression that everything is controllable.

It's going surprisingly well, the elements falling into place. First, the essential communication – I hope it will be the last.

Dear George,
It was good, all things considered, to see you last week. As I intimated, I have a small request. I am going to be taking some time off, and I need to redirect my mail. If you will be so kind as to receive it, all I ask is that you throw it away. All of it. Please. I do not want to be disturbed for the foreseeable future, for any reason. I will be out of touch.

I am most grateful for this.

I have also changed my email address, as you can see. I do not want this divulged to anyone. Indeed, I would rather you did not use it yourself, once you have confirmed you can help me in this minor way.
Thanks,
James

George is as close as I came to making a friend amongst my fellow schoolmasters. He is a harmless, good-hearted duffer, and a passionate enthusiast for all things Victorian. He kits himself out in fancy dress: silken cravats or bow ties, itchy tweed suits, waistcoats, flouncy shirts, shoes with buckles. And a bushy beard, of course. He is idealistic, staunch, sentimental, hearty, blinkered, patriotic, and hopeless with women. I suppose – there was speculation about this in the Common Room – you might have mistaken him for a repressed homosexual, but he is not. He is one of that virtually extinct species, the bachelor. He visits friends in the country at the weekends, is a reliable walker for widows and spinsters, has godfathered half the children in Gloucestershire, and is keen on travel, amateur theatrics, cricket, and especially on the works of Alfred Lord Tennyson. Every 15th of September he celebrates the death-day of Arthur Hallam, the poet's lost friend and only true love, with a select dinner at Boodle's, at which he insists on declaiming the entire text of 'The Lotos-Eaters', a poem that, like Hitler, should never have been born. He acts it out, waving his arms like a drowning fairy, sensuous, mellifluous and slinky.

But, comic figure though he is, I can count on him. I'd solved my incoming mail problem. Brilliant. I have also cancelled my landline, got a new mobile number, and made a database of essential providers: handyman, plumber, electrician, doctor, dentist, optician, nurse, cleaner, ironing and laundry service, computer and telly fixers. I can order cash, coffee, cigars, food from Waitrose or Harrods, wine from Berry Brothers if I outlive my cellar. I have enough clothes and shoes to last a lifetime.

I will never go out again. If I am incapacitated by severe illness or a heart attack, I will abjure the emergency call, suffer and die. If the house catches fire, I will go down with it, perhaps put on some smothering and sizzling music – Stravinsky perhaps, can't think what else he's good for – and smoke and barbecue like Joan of Arc.

Of course the price of my enforced isolation will be a regular invasion of both house and self by a succession of strangers, none of whom will be congenial to me. Of course I dislike a chippy chippy, but I'm equally hostile to the charming, the well spoken or well read, the interesting, the beautiful, the whimsical. Next thing I know they will be smiling and waving at me from their carriages.

Anyone who enters this house does so as an instrument of my will. I am not here to meet people, but to use them. If they could be replaced by machines, I would do so without compunction, and if they were robots they would be programmed to listen but not to talk.

Only four days after its installation, the doorbell rang. I ignored it. Either it was someone who didn't matter or, much worse, someone who did. I cannot say what time it was. I have renounced my watch, drawn the curtains. It is dark amid the blaze of noon, a total eclipse without hope of day. I am become a thing of darkness.

I do not follow the news, hardly turn on the telly or wireless. My computer wants to tell me the time and date, but after some searching I turn off that function. The house is still, timeless. Eternal in its way.

I drift off in my chair, resolve to drink my way through the wine cellar, nibble smoked oysters on cracked wheat biscuits. The oysters are delivered (on Thursdays) from Scotland. They do not come in tins. Anything that is tinned, tastes tinny: baked beans, tuna in oil, white asparagus, all similarly contaminated. No, my oysters are plump, recently smoked, and come in plastic packaging that hardly affects their taste.

I eat grapes, though it is hard to source decent ones. But if I eat too many, or drink too much, I am sick, sick at heart, vomiting, bereft. The nausea rises out of me like a metaphysical force. It is in the walls, it is everywhere around me, it is the air that I cannot breathe. But I carry on with my grapes, both liquid and solid. I don't wish to die of scurvy. I don't wish to die at all, not yet.

I feel as if the house is under surveillance, staked out, as

I am staked out within it. Crucified. But behind its blank façade, there are few signs of life, as I have few signs of life behind mine.

The only vulnerability is on Thursdays. If you were a weary gumshoe slumped over your steering wheel, eyes propped open, in need of a shave and a toothbrush after a sleepless Wednesday night, in the morning you might observe someone walk up the path confidently, open the door and go in. You might try to confront them, or more likely advise your employer to do so.

When the doorbell rang again a few days later – just once, that was a good idea – I snuck into the hallway, my footsteps muffled by the thickness of the carpet, and surely imperceptible outside the door. I looked through the peep-hole. It was just as I had anticipated, and feared. I retreated upstairs, my restless heart threatening its cavity, and a few moments later the knocking started, first a regular rapping, followed soon by a robust banging, less loud than burly James Fenimore had produced, but surprisingly vigorous nonetheless. I closed the door to my study.

It happened again the next day, the hammering, and a more protracted and furious banging. When I opened the door a few hours later, having ensured that the 200-degree coast was clear, there was an envelope taped to it, obviously with a letter inside it. Perhaps four or five pages thick. I took it inside, tore it up without opening it, and threw the many pieces into the bin.

From the outside, with the curtains closed, the house might well have looked uninhabited. The only tell-tale sign, ironically, was the change to the door. Why would someone who had left a house for a protracted period feel a need to reinforce its entrance in such a way? No, the unwelcoming black door signalled that someone was inside, who would

not welcome the presence of an intruder. I steeled myself
– not a cliché, just the right metaphor – to expect further
visits, further knocks, further entreaties. I will ignore them,
steely in my resolve.

The air is stifling, humid, it feels as if I could drown in it.

> Here I lie where I need to be
> I am the sailor home from the sea

I choose the darkness because I hate it, and I loathe the
sea, it's so bloody insistent: whoosh whoosh, drown. No,
my adventures are over. Save this one, which I am writing.
   If – God forbid – I had to go outside now, I would wear
a sign. I could print it on the computer, on heavy gauge
paper in Gils Sans typeface, and attach it with a string
around my neck:

> **Do not talk to me, or come near me.**
> **I am not interested in your opinions.**

Thinking this gives me a warm feeling. I can no longer
bear to be in the presence of my fellow man, even to dismiss
them. I will not go out, though sometimes of a morning
I fold my towel and lean against the door, peeping at my
fellows on their daily rounds. The sight of them fills me
with hatred, disgust and contempt. This feeling comes upon
me with the buffeting terror of a tsunami. I am swept away,
hardly able to breathe, in danger of extinction. The thought
of wandering into the streets, bumped and jostled by these
acrid creatures, makes me retch.
   I have lost my capacity to avert my eyes, or my nose.
They stay open, however much I blink and flinch and turn

away. I keep thinking those thoughts which, if we can only cast them aside, allow us to live tolerable, satisfied and self-satisfied existences. To make do. Reality punches you, pummels you into bruised submission, except that there is no way in which you can throw in the towel, wave a white flag, mutter 'No más' like that poor boxer once did, and retreat to the safety of your corner.

Or perhaps to your house? Reality: out there. Aversion: in here? If only it were so simple. If only it worked. How can we bear to be ourselves? How can we bear our children, whose lives begin in pain and terminate in agony? Enough. Too much.

> O dark dark dark. They all go into
> the dark.

Fucking T.S. Eliot. All of them? Damned? Surely somebody gets to go into the light, don't Christians think like that? The source, the beginning, the brightness at the end of the tunnel, the soft fading dribble of final consciousness, the ethereal infinite. In his end is his beginning, like a snake with its arse up its head. Welcomed by the heavenly hosts and hostesses. Pearly gates, genial chat with St Peter, try not to push in the queue, get your individual destination. Not very efficient. More sensible to suppose some quick trans-formation from person to angel. The soul leaves the poor just-dead remains and *Swoosh!* like that sound mobile phones make when they send a text (better than *Quack! Quack!*). The soul shoots away and finds itself in the clouds.

What do you do up there? What are you going to do tomorrow? Next year? Next millennium? What sustains and nourishes them, the angels of the dead? In pictorial accounts they are corporeal in some faded, washed-out way, like threadbare cotton nighties left to dry in the sun, softly flapping, drained of essence.

Yet they have human features. Faces, chests, wavy hair, noses, arms (wings, anyway), something sort of leggy. In heaven there are no signs or vestiges of what got you there. No swollen tumours, no bullet holes or crushed skulls, no filled lungs or ruptured appendixes. No shrunken cadavers. Every body filled up and filled in. Reformed, reformulated, returned, retuned, resurrected. Good as new. Better.

Does this celestial self retain its humanity? Does it get cystitis or haemorrhoids? There is no testimony that it gorges and disgorges, excretes or sodomises. Do angels have arse-holes?

Do they examine themselves, these freshly minted angels, wonder at this shimmering new essence, this new freedom from weight and care? Might they, before they morph into pure angeltude, do an anxious inventory of what is, astonishingly, missing, as if they had survived some terrible bomb blast, and in a hectic, final shocked moment checked to see what was left of themselves? Lips? Check. Legs? Hard to tell. Eyes? Functioning. Ears. Nothing to hear. No viscera at all at all. No stomach: nothing to eat. No lungs: no air to breathe. No blood: no menstruating angels, no cut fingers. It's enough to make you scream with laughter. Dead and not dead. Body and not body. It makes me hysterical.

Angels are the riddles of heaven: dead things with feathers. Only the damned remain fully alive, cursing and writhing, bleeding and bruising, smelling and excreting, in agony and despair. Bit like life really.

Later in his dreadful poem, Mr Eliot assures us – can you fucking believe it? – that you are damned according to your *profession*. The Great and the Good go to Hell, along with the usual haul of cowards, narcissists and murderers. Plenty of arseholes in Hell. Mr Eliot includes himself amongst the damned. I like that in a poet.

Heavenly reward is only for the meek, the humble, the unostentatiously kindly: dinner ladies, scout masters, carers, primary schoolteachers, nurses, cleaners, rubbish collectors, gardeners, college scouts, curates and handymen. The worthies who, in their finest hour, are offered an MBE by the Queen, and are charmingly and naively delighted. And after that they become angels!

And here we have him, ladies and gentlemen! T.S. Eliot: classicist in literature, royalist in politics, the most pompous form of the Jamesian American ex-pat. Worse yet: as from his religious conversion, a Believer! It horrified his friends, his erstwhile friends. That frigid snitbag Virginia Woolf was so distressed that she virtually sat shiva with her husband Lenny the Jew to signal the passing of poor Tom, no longer a member of the atheist tribe.

Unlike Leonard's, her nose hooked up, not down, it sniffed, she was a great sniffer, a terrific bitch. Her letters and diaries are fastidious, superior, deadly. So much more enjoyable than all those girly hyper-sensitive novels. Mrs Shalloway. To the Shitehouse. Beyond reprieve or comprehension, poor Tom, sighed Virginia, 'may be called dead to us all from this day forward. He believes in God and immortality, and goes to church . . .'

Of a sudden, he's all public pious, intellectual, and – how ghastly, how utterly uncongenial – a seeker after wisdom. We are told his poems have spiritual quality. What an oxymoron. Worse! He would be an imparter of wisdom, another failed-priest poet. Like them all.

Like that dreadful gasbag Kahlil Gibran, the archetypal fakir, whose platitudes informed the weddings of a whole generation. Lucy produced two of his 'poems' at her ceremony: one read with doleful earnestness by her soon-to-be husband Sam the other intoned by herself:

> Sing and dance together and be
> joyous, but let each one of you
> be alone,
> Even as the strings of a lute are alone
> though they quiver with the same
> music.

Christ! This ghastly humbuggery was enough to make me yearn for Mr Eliot. Perched in the front row on a hideous plastic chair wrapped in a floppy gentrifying serviette, I suffered mightily, and (I gather) let out a discernible groan. Lucy glared at me. She was still angry from our disastrous conversation two days before.

I'd thought I was helping, like a signalman on the tracks diverting a runaway train. She'd been at the house, sitting on the bed doing something with a pile of clothes. She and Suzy had been assembling her 'going-away outfit' – which I gather is what your change of clothes after the wedding is called – and Suzy had announced she was popping out to buy some suitable garment or other. Lucy was turned away from me, her shoulders hunched, shaking gently and regularly.

'Lucy, love, are you all right?'

'It's Mummy, she's driving me crazy. This whole bloody farce is down to her. Just because she had to endure a big wedding, she's inflicting it on me. She says it's one of a woman's rites of passage, like childbirth, you just have to bear it.'

I hate weddings, especially this one, for which I had to pay. Why does the bride's family have to shell out? Though we would have had to anyway, for Sam's worthy parents didn't have two beans to rub together. Though if they'd had them, they would have.

Give me a good funeral any day: some happy memories and encomia rather than fatuous hopes for a dodgy future. No drunken rowdies, no idiotic dancing till early morning, no ill-dressed maids of honour losing theirs with best men desperate to shuck their formal clothing and get on the job.

Lucy's eyes drifted downwards again, and she selected a cream blouse, pressed it against her chest, looked into the mirror, put it back down. She tested another blouse, rejected it, frowning. Her displeasure was directed more at the activity than the various garments. There were only two days until the wedding, and (as Suzy insisted) *choices have to be made.*

Lucy had been suborned into compliance. Left to her own devices, she'd have put on a frock, gathered a couple of friends as witnesses – *not* her parents, nor Sam's – trotted off to the local registry office, had a celebratory nosh-up with some pals, then gone back to work the next day, a wife.

'Lucy? I've been thinking . . . Can I say something?'

She put down yet another blouse, and sat on the bed. 'Sure. What?'

'I just wanted to say, you know, while there's still time . . .'

'What?'

'You don't have to do this, you know.'

She nodded her head in agreement. 'I know I don't! But I got hassled into it by Mummy, and somehow once you agree to a proper wedding you end up with all sorts of stuff that you don't need or want.' She leant sideways and began to flick through various items of clothing.

I was determined to persevere, though I had nothing to fall back on emotionally. Suzy told me I needed to 'work on my relationship' with Lucy, but I never thought we had one, not quite, which was rather a relief. She was unaccountable to me, and I cannot recall many sustained personal conversations between us. I was rarely alone with her adult incarnation, and vaguely ill at ease when I was. She had made, it seemed to me, a set of uninspired choices, the consequences of which – work at a desk in some down-at-heel centre of worthiness – were no doubt admirable in some abstract way. Sam was another, and far more dangerous, example of her bad judgement.

'No, love. I'm sorry. Do come over here and sit for a moment.'

Lucy looked up, puzzled by my request for enhanced proximity, and came to sit beside me in the twin armchairs in the alcove by the window, her body turned slightly away, as if shielding herself from unaccustomed intimacy. 'What's this all about?'

'I just want to have a little chat, you know, before the day.'

'Day? What day? You're being awfully mysterious.'

'I'm so sorry, I'm not very good at this. Your wedding day, of course. Saturday.'

She turned to face me squarely. 'What about it?'

'Well, I was wondering, perhaps you might be getting cold feet? You seem on edge. And I just wanted to say it isn't too late if you want to reconsider. I – Mummy and I – would quite understand . . .'

'Let me get this straight. Are you asking me if I have cold feet, or advising me to have them? Because if you are . . .'

I knew there was some risk involved, but was determined to pursue the thought. 'It's just that people often marry in spite of the fact that they have misgivings. They just get carried along with the flow, and are too timid to say "hold on a minute, I'm not sure I'm ready for this".'

She stood up from her chair, until she was only a few feet away from where I was sitting, and I was looking up at her angry face.

'How dare you! First Mummy hassling me about clothes and stupid fucking details, now my father is trying to call the whole thing off! That's it, isn't it? That's what you want!'

'No, love, not at all. It's just that – '

'You've never liked Sam. You never gave him a chance, did you? You never met him halfway, sat down and talked and tried to get to know him?'

That was true enough. From our first acquaintance, when he came to dinner to meet the parents, uncomfortable in a new jacket and tie, I'd spotted him as the sort of earnest working-class Northern boy who would have benefited from a decent education, had his sharp edges and broad vowels polished and regularised.

She was leaning down now, her face close to mine. 'And you know what is sad? You don't get it at all. Sam is his own man, and he has wonderful qualities, you just can't see them.'

'Tell me what you mean.'

'It's hardly worth bothering,' she said, standing straight and backing away, making a curiously operatic gesture with her hands. 'You'd find it hard to recognise his virtues.'

'Oh yes? Tell me about them. I'm genuinely interested.'

'Goodness,' she said. 'And integrity.'

'I'm glad you feel that way.'

'I do. I only wish you did too. And I do want to marry him with all my heart. It's the only thing in this whole ghastly mess that I'm certain about.'

I stood up to comfort her, though reassuring cuddles are well outside my normal repertoire.

She turned away. 'Let's leave it,' she said.

'I'm sorry,' I said, 'perhaps it was ham-fisted of me. But I meant well.'

'Did you now?' she said.

This always seems to happen when I try to be fatherly.

Lucy's stare, as I perched on my plastic, was a rich amalgam of triumph and warning, and I turned away, unforgiven. I stifled myself, clenched my cheeks.

Suzy elbowed my ribs, then clasped my hand firmly in tacit reassurance. The sleeve of her silk blouse, that we'd bought in a market in Rajasthan fourteen months before, made a shocking contrast with the pallor of her wrist, where the veins traced their purple trails in a manner that should have felt ominous. The royal blue of the silk shimmered, startlingly lit by a tribe of crimson parrots, beaks slightly agape, dangerous and moronic, yearning to squawk or to nip.

She'd been uncertain, in that stifling market smelling of turmeric and petrol, cooking curries and cow dung, urine and the waft of human shit. I gagged with humid disgust. She held the blouse in the air to inspect it, then placed it across her chest.

'Very nice lady! Very nice! Parrot most lucky bird. I give you good price!'

A tiny boy and his smaller sister, dressed in rags, had followed us around the market, importuning, holding onto Suzy's skirt and attempting to grab hold of my trouser leg.

A quick slap put paid to that. The little boy pointed to his slim but by no means distended stomach, and groaned piteously. The little girl looked up – at Suzy – beseechingly. At first glance – I didn't take a second – the lower half of her face was composed entirely of snot.

'Hungry, sah!' He put his hand out, and his tiny sister mimicked the gesture. Suzy patted them on the head kindly, already thinking of a way to slip them a few rupees without causing an urchin storm. She took out a piece of Kleenex, wiped the girl's nose, and threw the tissue into the dirt with the other detritus. I shuddered. I know nothing of caste systems, but these children were verily untouchable.

'For pity's sake,' I said, 'just buy the damn thing! How much can it cost? You can always give it to Lucy if it doesn't suit you. Let's go!'

'I give you best price!'

'Yes! Yes! She'll have it. How much?' I offered half the amount.

'Hungry, sah!'

'Are you sure?' Suzy held the garment uncertainly. I had confused her by switching categories. Was it for Lucy? Would it suit her?

Back at the hotel, after a revolting walk of some fifteen minutes, beseeched by beggars of the heat and dust, the children paid off by the front gate, I made straight for our room, convinced that the stench of the market followed me across the marbled foyer, carried subtly on the jasmine-conditioned air. I spent the next ten minutes in the shower, soaping and gelling and scrubbing. I sniffed my hands, and they carried still the odour of dung and spice. I washed them again.

The ritual of changing into freshly laundered clothes was soothing, and with each layer – freshly ironed socks and underwear, a crisp cotton shirt with a touch of starch, and finally the careful donning of my mushroom linen suit – I felt as if I were being reincarnated. I put my filthy clothes in the hamper, ready for the hotel butler to pick up and return – pristine – tomorrow. Draped over the chair were Suzy's nightgown and bathrobe, and on the floor lay discarded underthings, for she had changed, God knows why, before we went to the market. Getting clean to get dirty.

The unshowered Suzy was standing on the veranda, her rumpled carrier bag with the silk shirt in it on the recliner beside her, looking over the gardens and the water below. The late afternoon air was freshening. I opened a bottle of wine from the fridge, and poured a glass for each of us.

My box of cigars was in the safe in the wardrobe. I opened it ceremoniously, spirits already lifted by the anticipation of my evening treat. The hotel had a humidor in the bar, next to which a stagey turbaned gentleman with silk robes and silkier moustaches stood at attention, whose sole employ was pompously to facilitate the choice of a cigar for anyone willing to fork out the hefty price for importation from Havana to a five-star palace in Rajasthan. That didn't bother me. Good for them. But the cigars – I was informed before coming – might not withstand the travel, and would deteriorate further languishing in an inadequately moisturised humidor. They would be brittle to the touch, crack and crumble in the mouth, and shed outer leaves in the hand. I saw a florid gentleman, the evening before, expostulating furiously as he peeled the dried outer leaves off the Bolivar Churchill for which he had paid the equivalent of £65.

Forewarned, I'd brought a box of twenty-five Montecristo No. 2s, opened it in London and smoked three cigars – just enough to create room for two peeled halves of a new potato – and resealed it firmly, tapping the nails back into place. The cigars would stay moist for our full three weeks, allowing my usual one a day. Twirling it between my fingers, I snipped the torpedo end, and gradually heated the tip, turning it slowly and regularly, until a red glow showed across the entire area, blew on it gently, then slightly more firmly. I took the first, the most highly anticipated, the perfect first draw, held it in my mouth, exhaled slowly, allowed the smoke to surround my face – indeed, stepped right into it – and took a deep breath. Richer than a glass of great claret: earth, cinnamon, cream, perhaps a hint of vanilla, also some chocolate, perhaps a homeopathic trace of manure. Even in the morning, when the smoke would have settled and infused the curtains – and as Suzy would remark (again) her clothes (I like it when it infuses mine) – it would still, in its lingering staleness, be one of the great smells of the world. And quite enough, just then, to get the filth out of my nostrils as effectively as the water had expunged it from my pores.

Joining Suzy on the veranda, I offered a glass of wine to her unresponsive hand. She looked out over the lake, unmoved, sucking at a cigarette. Why the smoke did not penetrate her clothing, while mine did, was one of the unexplained mysteries of our marriage. Her claim, which had no merit that I could detect, was that her Sullivan & Powell tipped cigarettes emitted only the mildest and least penetrative of odours. Unlike my Montecristos.

'Never again,' I said. I may actually have shuddered. I remember some involuntary movement, a full body tremor. 'I'm happy to see the sights. I like our driver. But keep me off the streets. They utterly disgust me.'

She half turned, and took a long drink of the wine, lips

pursed as if against excessive acidity, some crass grapefruity
sauvignon perhaps. It wasn't. Along with my box of cigars,
I had imported an adequate supply of Meursault, which
had travelled better than I had.

'Tell me about disgusting,' she murmured, not meeting
my eye.

I came up behind her and put my arms around her. 'I'm
so sorry,' I said, 'this is all my fault.'

'I know,' she murmured, 'you're doing your best. It was
asking too much of you . . .'

I kissed her neck, which smelled of the market and humid
air.

'There's still time before dinner,' she said. 'Let me have
a quick shower.'

She 'felt at home' in India, she said, though this was our
first trip together. She'd been determined to save me the
discomforts of such a visit, but eventually I had insisted: if
she felt that India was (in some idiotic way) 'her spiritual
home', then the least I could do, before we both dropped
off the perch like dead parrots, was to accompany her there.

She would happily have abjured the palaces and luxury
hotels with which India is now so amply provided, and
stayed instead in simple hostelries, or – more desirable yet
– with 'real Indian families', as she had on previous visits
with various friends. (I don't know what 'unreal' Indian
families would have been. Except, of course, for her own.)

Her parents Henry and Sophia – latterly Sir and Lady
– lived in a Georgian rectory in Dorset, which they
purchased in their late-thirties with money gouged out of
the City. They proceeded to reinvent themselves as stereo-
types, took up country pursuits with the idiotic enthusiasm
only urban refugees can generate. They hunted (fox), fished,

went on bracing walks in wellies, planted a kitchen garden, were active in the local church, and provided occasional jobs for a number of locals, whom they, not entirely discreetly, called yokels. Their only deviation from the county norms was in their choice of governesses for the children, Suzy and her older brother Rupert. Not for them the sulky and hormonally hyperactive au pair – 'trouble on wheels, my dear' – nor indeed, did they look for the sort of nanny self-advertised in *The Lady*. No, they wanted only Indian women, of mature age, to look after their children. They wanted an ayah, and indeed a succession of them were called just, and only, that. The local gentry sneered, but Sir Henry was triumphantly unrepentant: 'It's what they would have done, if they'd thought of it first. Too late now.'

And so Suzy grew up, in their Dorset idyll, a foster child of Empire. Sir Henry encouraged Ayah to read Indian stories, sing Indian songs, draw pictures of tigers, elephants, and parrots, make Indian sweets, and otherwise indicate to the children that there was something other – if not something more – than the long tedious days of West Country life. He could hardly wait to catch the 6.50 train from Dorchester to London every Monday morning and spending the week at his set in Albany. He had some grand times there, and Sophia left him to it. It was rather a relief, she said.

On the raised dais, slumped next to the couple as they exchanged rings, was their dog Bruno, an ungainly slob-bering half-breed, tarry black, bleakly unappealing, intermittently dangerous. He'd twice bitten their postman, and their mail now had to be picked up at the local post office. The ring had been attached to a string around his neck, and the wedding celebrant, who to my surprise wore neither beard nor sandals, had some difficulty getting it off the beast's neck, and into the hands of the increasingly anxious groom.

Further noxious blather ensued. Suzy's crimson parrots seemed to mock and threaten me, as her hand released the firmness of its grip, and became still, coolly resting in mine. When the groom, finally, kissed the bride, with more enthusiasm than I thought seemly, the pleasure on Lucy's face soothed me. Next to me Suzy wiped her tears. Our daughter was married.

I presume it should be a happy memory, but its edges are frayed and foxed by sadness. Happiness is fragile at the very moment of pleasure-taking, so easily defeated by a toothache or an itinerant virus. And past happiness? That lovely weekend at Lake Garda? The week that Suzy's first novel came out? Delicate, easily bruised, soon rotten, evanescent. Do we lie on our deathbeds remembering such nonsense? Who cares? Who cared?

I was undelighted by Lucy's choices and prospects, though I am unsure, as things developed and she entered fully into her life as wife and mother, whether I was right to worry so. And now worry seems a pallid, almost desirable state of mind compared to my daily dose of helplessness, desperation and withdrawal. Oh, to have some worries! School fees. Recalcitrant teenagers. Marital disharmony. Any of the above, please. All of the above. Anything, rather than this.

When Lucy was three, I recall her slight and wispy in a favourite cotton dress, white with tiny pink hearts perhaps – I can't remember – but in the story I am constructing she looks dreamy in it, worn unfashionably long for one so tiny, floaty and ethereal as an angel. She would walk alongside as we went to the local shops, reach up on tiptoes and, if I leant down, put her hand in mine. We weren't holding hands, hers was too slight to grasp mine, yet, but I would enfold her tiny fingers in my palm, and squeeze them as gently as if I were testing a downy apricot in the supermarket, anxious to avoid bruising.

I found myself whistling quietly as the song drifted through my head: Johnny Mathis's 'Misty', a sentimental ballad that I had always scorned, though when I was sixteen my first girlfriend found it moving, though not moving enough. *I get misty, just holding your hand.* The metaphor felt surprisingly appropriate, for such a rotten song. Love fills every available space, soaks, suffuses and diffuses like a sea mist filling a room. Distances recede, all you can see is what is in front of your face. It makes you feel soggy. Nothing is better than love.

It was striking, only a year or so later, when Lucy had gained a couple of inches and no longer had to tiptoe, nor I to lean, that we could walk hand in hand, she giving me an answering squeeze, as firm as she could. We were both aware, I felt, of some new dimension to our relations, something grown up, reciprocal but diminished. I had stopped singing 'Misty' by then – you had to lean down to feel that way.

Her childhood reappears, now, only in cloudy vignettes that I rather suspect I have invented, or at least elaborated considerably. I suppose it doesn't matter. We reconvene what time allows, and the arc of our stories is drawn from the few incidents that we recall, or make up. Most of my memories of her as a tiny girl are set in the summer. In the winter she was a demon, felt the cold terribly, shivered and sniffled, and resolutely refused to wear warm clothing when she went out. One Christmas Suzy bought her a chic olive green duffel coat with wooden toggles, which Lucy loathed from the very moment it emerged from its wrapping paper and refused to wear.

'No buttons!' she would howl. 'No! No! No buttons!'

I was inclined to struggle and to confront, hold her steady and force her arms into the sleeves, to insist on doing up the dreaded toggles.

'Not buttons!' I said, trying to keep calm. 'Toggles! Toggles good, buttons bad!' I pushed her little arms firmly into the sleeves and commenced toggling her up. If she cried, too bad. Children have to be taught to stop crying. 'Do hold still! How are you going to keep warm without a coat?'

'Don't you say that *to me*! No buttons!'

What was so objectionable about buttons was unclear. She hated them on a blouse, on pyjamas, on a coat. We eventually capitulated, for Lucy was amenable to zippers, which she liked to play with, and (particularly) to Velcro.

'Velcro! For fuck's sake. I have a daughter who loves Velcro . . . Kill me,' said Suzy, initiating a lifetime's disappointment with her daughter's tastes. She even disapproved of Lucy's Laura Ashley phase: 'all those cutesified anodyne patterns, the awful pastel colours, the sheer drab mediocrity of it. She's Welsh, you know.'

'Who is?'

'Laura Ashley. All you need to know.'

Call me a damn fool, but I loved it, at least on Lucy. Her mother would have looked soppy swanning about in all those flowery garments, but on a three-year-old they looked peachy.

I want to remember Lucy's dress as it was, that summerised day walking to the newsagent's. I scrunch my eyes up to replay it, to see us walking so slowly and happily up the street, hand in hand. Some sort of little girly dress, wispy and delicious. I can make one up if I want to. I try a variety of colours and patterns, of the kind that she loved. Pink? For sure. Polka dots against a cream background? Or perhaps white? I try them on her. She looks — we're in the present tense all of a sudden — she looks gorgeous in it — cream is better! So delighted and free, aware of herself.

That was the past, then: not immutable, oddly biddable, malleable. There was no one to object, and it no longer mattered. The past is something we make and remake, remember or disremember — same thing, almost. You can polka-dot it, change times and seasons, rewrite the dialogue, rearrange the cast of characters. There is no dissembling in this. Most is lost, the vast percentage of what we have been. This is what it is to be a person, and it gets worse as you get older.

'Worse?' Not that, not quite. As we age, our stories are reduced until the constituent flavours are enhanced and concentrated. And sometimes, as in this story of little Lucy, too great a concentration gives not pleasure but something closer to pain, as a reduction of the essence of sensual pleasure, say, would produce something unendurable. As my recollection of my little daughter causes me to smile and to wince.

I am reduced to this. I live in reduced circumstances, left with the unendurable intensity of wormwood and gall (whatever they are), with fading hints of honey. There is something both inevitable in this, as we move towards the final telling of our final stories, the last version of ourselves, and something moving.

This journal? A coming-of-old-age book, dispirited, hopelessly knowing. For what happens, faced squarely, is loss. Loss of what we have been, loss of the history of our dear loved ones, loss of the incidents and narratives that have defined us.

I cannot locate much by way of gain in this process, save

that most of what I have forgotten wasn't worth remembering. Good riddance really, like clearing the attics before the house is sold.

So what? I can't even remember the plot of the novel I read last week. Or its title. I struggle sometimes to remember what the names of common objects are, I keep losing things. A fork, a sofa, the Prime Minister. I am still a master of adjectives and verbs, and pretty damn good at summoning adverbs, but I am losing my nouns at an alarming rate.

I would worry about early onset Alzheimer's, only I'm not young enough for it. But you can get away with a lot when there is no one to talk to but yourself, and you know you are 'misty-fying', like one of those fade-out images in a film, but you are watching it by yourself, and can turn your head at the scary bits, whine a little and put your paws over your eyes.

How do I remember myself? Or Lucy? Or Suzy? Why should I?

I cannot bear dogs, they disgust me. Why would a civilised person welcome such a creature into an otherwise orderly home? No matter how cunningly disguised by fluff and fealty, all I see is a shameless slobbering arse-sniffing leg-humping scrotum-toting arsehole-flaunting filth-spreader: as profligate a shitslinger as Kahlil Gibran, only closer to the ground. If I presented myself like that I'd be hauled away, no matter how much I licked your face or howled on your grave. No dogs in heaven.

I particularly detest my neighbour's dog, whose hideous noises are sufficient to awaken the dead, or at least the dying. I gather it is called Spike, and it looks the part, with a face composed of overlapping layers of fat mysteriously transformed into muscle. Hard blubber, hideously prophylactic: not even his proud owner could have stroked that face tenderly.

I don't know what sort he is. Are they called breeds? I can't tell one from another. I'm not even very good with people. When I taught, I would make up a class physical appearance list on the first day, correlating physical characteristics to names in my desk diary. It was ever so helpful, and within a couple of weeks I wouldn't need it any more. But for the first days, it gave me a sense of intimacy with my new charges that I could recognise them so easily, as long as I could take a peek at my list and their faces.

One day, leaving the teaching room with a surprisingly pressing need for the loo, I left my (closed) diary on my desk, rather than putting it in the top drawer as usual. On my return, five minutes later, Fatboy Linus was crying at the back of the room, Cross-eyed Charley had exacerbated his disability so radically that he can have seen nothing but his own nose, and Acne Andy – I was told – had run out of the room, scratching himself madly. I didn't see him again for a week.

The next morning I received a brusque note from the Head:

Dear Darke,
I have had one or two parents on the phone, regarding an unfortunate incident in your classroom. Could we have a word about this? I will be free between 4.15 and 4.40.
Best,
Anthony

He was a pacific fellow, liked but mildly mocked by his staff, and he hated confrontation. The very word 'parent' made him anxious, and if you attached 'concerned', or even worse, 'irate', he reached for the Panadol and drew the curtains.

I entered his study at 4.15 on the dot, to find him pacing in front of the fire. His room was over-heated, as if some objective correlative of his state of mind, and he had never been known to open the window. He smoked a pipe of some noxious Balkan mixture (not Sobranie) to add to the fug. It was hard to see, and harder yet to breathe. The idea, I presume, was to make the place uncongenial to visitors, while he himself was inured to it, smoked as a kipper.

'See here, James, we have something of a to-do about some damn book of yours . . .'

'Book, Tony, what book?' I called him 'Tony' when I wanted to irritate him, for he much preferred 'Anthony' or, better yet, 'Headmaster'.

'Apparently you have a book that you use to write insults about the boys, and you left it for them to see. I must say − '

'You are referring, I presume, to my desk diary, and to the unpleasant incident in which the boys opened it in my absence?'

'And uncovered the most appalling descriptions of themselves! I have two sets of parents threatening not merely to remove their boys, but to sue for damages. For trauma, humiliation in front of their peers. It's just dreadful.' He pulled at one of the few strands of what was left of his hair, which resides largely on the lower left side of his bald pate, somewhat further down than anatomically plausible.

'Guilty, Tony. And innocent.'

'How is that?'

'I do keep such a diary, and at the start of term it helps me to remember which new boy is which. To do this, you fasten on the single defining characteristic: curly hair, very tall, that sort of thing.'

He looked down at some notes jotted on a pad next to his telephone: 'Acne, cross-eyed . . .'

'Very defining characteristics, wouldn't you say? I learned their names in only one lesson. Most of them I still can't remember. I'm always grateful for ugliness, or better yet disfigurement.'

He was sufficiently agitated that he could not be further provoked. 'But what,' he asked plaintively, 'am I to say to the parents?'

'Tell them the truth. Tell them that one of the boys, wholly without permission and entirely dishonestly, contravening every law of privacy and good behaviour, opened my diary, and – what is worse – read the contents to his fellows. I have some idea of who that was, and I suggest that he be expelled, and that the angry parents assault him with sticks and rocks.'

'I really don't think your levity appropriate here.'

I have no time for the schoolmaster's pastoral role, which most use as a way of cosying up to the gentry and currying advance favour with the soon-to-be celebrated, rich and powerful. I will not do this. 'I'm a teacher, not a damn curate.' In spite of my insouciance, I never managed to say 'fucking' to the Head. 'Let them move on to pastors new.'

The headmaster winced. 'Must you, James?'

I was dismissed. Not from my position, but from the study. The Head would no more fire me than rusticate the culprit. I'd have respected him more if he'd done both. But, as often happens in schools, the matter blazed merrily for a few days, and then was forgotten, though attendance in my class diminished somewhat.

Only a couple of years later, to the not entirely secret

pleasure of his staff, he died of a cerebral haemorrhage, rather than the emphysema he had courted so assiduously. He should have drowned in his own Latakia-infested sputum, lungs burbling like a hookah. Instead, he was found slumped over his desk, looking rather peaceful (according to the school secretary, who found him), that smirk of wimpish sanctimony wiped finally from his features. Lucky bastard.

Spikedog, sadly, was more reliable in his attendance than my former pupils, and I don't need any mnemonics to remember him. He had a thick black collar with fearsome nails sticking out, which, had he aimed properly and generated the right momentum, might have crucified a toddler. I didn't know his owner's name. Spike too, probably. Ugly enough, though without the muscles, but equally dangerous. He bore more than a passing resemblance to his brutal pet, and if he lacked the neck-nails, he had various bits of steel protruding from his ears, nose and lips. I suspect many other bits of him were also highly metallic. God knows how they got him through security at airports. Though proud of his doggie – he tended to simper at the mutt – he never did anything as normal or desirable as taking him for a walk. Instead, every evening he would let the dog loose in the garden for a crap, and leave him there for an hour or so, while he retreated to his flat to receive his conjugals from his visiting girlfriend. I never heard her name. She was a Gothic, dark, black-clothed, steely, pale, skinny, silent, miserable.

Spikedog hated being excluded from the fun, and would first yap, then whine, and finally howl at the back door, demanding to be let in. He never was, and he never learned. He knew enough to do his business on what passed for a lawn – a bit of uncut scrubby grass – before returning to demand readmittance. Every now and again Spikeman would open the bedroom window, which overlooked the garden, and shout 'Shut the fuck up!' First asked to stifle the mutt, then begged, then severely admonished by neighbours leaning out of the windows of the adjoining flats, he soon said the same to them.

Considered as an exile, it might have been possible to see something representative in Spikedog's abject misery. Had he merely whimpered, I might have pitied him, felt some fellow creaturely feeling. But he had no restraint, no consideration for the feelings of others, sunk in his howling canine narcissism. I could do that too, I recognised in him a shadow self, *mon semblable, mon doggy frère.* But I am not a brute, I howl not, though I've been known to whimper.

From my first-floor window I had a perfect view of the scene. By the end of the week the garden would be replete with piles of dog shit, until at the weekend a resentful crop-headed teenager – a gristly leftover on the plate of divorce – would appear with a handful of plastic bags to clean up the mess. The first time he was required to do this, he vomited copiously, and was ordered to clean that up as well, which is less easy. He didn't do that again.

There is no use arguing with such a dog, or such an owner – both more anxious to bite than to placate. No, to influence the behaviour of such animals, you have to attack before they do, get in the first blow. But I am a pacific fellow by nature, most distinctly unmartial. When I was ten, the class bully punched me on the nose, I daresay not very powerfully, but I recurrently find myself feeling it to make sure it isn't bent out of shape.

But what I lack in courage I more than make up for in

cunning. If the dratted hound would not shut up, I needed him to develop a fear of the garden, to associate it so thoroughly with pain that he would refuse – whatever the punishment – ever to go there again.

In my next Waitrose order I included three bottles of tabasco sauce, and a pound of Aberdeen Angus aged fillet steak, an extravagance I justified on the grounds that its tenderness might make it sop up more of its lethal marinade. On its arrival, I cut a piece an inch and a half square (saving the rest for a celebratory dinner), pierced it with a knife and hollowed out the centre, which I filled with half of the bottle of sauce. The tabasco had a pungent aroma that teased the nostrils, and would have brought tears to the eye if I'd got too close. But I never cry. I do not approve of it. Once you start, it would be impossible to know when, or how, to finish. I have observed this in infants and women. There is nothing agreeable about the process, which is largely used to wound or to manipulate.

That evening I waited until Spikedog ascended to his highest pitch of declamatory desolation, so that he would associate that noisome activity with the punishment to come, and tossed the meat into the garden next door, hoping he wouldn't be put off by the smell. The dog saw it land, not so many feet away from him – I was rather proud of my aim, it's not that easy from a half-opened window – and sniffed it expectantly. As I had hoped, he ate the piece in one slobbery bite, leaving no trace of my malign intervention in his life.

A few moments of blessed quiet followed, as he stood stock still and interrogated the new sensation burning his mouth. He whined a little, but exhibited no signs of the extreme distress I had anticipated. The tabasco did quieten him for a few moments, during which he paced the garden, returned to the patch where the steak had landed, and sniffed it with what seemed — could this be possible? — a sort of longing.

He wanted more. When I repeated the trick the next day, he couldn't eat the meat fast enough, and the following day I could swear that his howling was directed not at his copulating owner, but at my window, demanding some hot stuff of his own.

I'd made a friend.

We oldies are almost without exception narcissists and bores, until the blessed lapse into silence in the corner armchair in the old folks' home, unvisited by relatives and ignored by staff. If you asked the elderly what they really want to talk about — after all of the stuff about the weather, what's been on telly, how rotten the food is, and by the way how are the grandchildren? — what were their names? — most pressingly what the old want to talk about is the state of their bowels. Dutiful daughters will listen sympathetically, but not for long; their husbands will find a reason, screaming silently and metaphorically plugging their ears, to get a coffee, talk on the mobile, or even visit the WC, which is a bit hostile really.

The sad irony is that, if a human (like a Spikedog) is a machine for producing shit, it is not a reliable long-term mechanism for expelling it. I've gone three days without a visit this week, which is my normal pattern. Eaten the statutory fruits and vegetables, ingested my revolting mixed seeds, like a parakeet, for my breakfast. Indulged my favourite ritual, more delicious than efficacious: the making of the morning coffee.

One of my little treats, a few years back, was the purchase (almost £5,000, I didn't let Suzy know) of a restaurant quality – and size – Gaggia espresso-maker. And, also essential if I was going to get the best out of my new machine, a Super Caimano burr grinder. Coffee beans arrive once a month, made to my own recipe (two thirds dark roast Ethiopian and one third Blue Mountain beans) by Higgins and Co. of Mayfair, labelled Special Dark Blend, which rather tickles me, though they always forget to add the final 'e' to my name.

Suzy did not begrudge me the foolish indulgence, and grew used to the diminished space, but what she couldn't tolerate was the fuss. The grinding of the beans, just so, the full but delicate pressure as you put the coffee in the professional filter holder, the heating and frothing (by hand) of the milk – press the plunger one hundred and twenty times at a steady and regular pressure – the gentle stirring of the resulting liquid with a spoon, the slow and even pouring onto the one-third full cup of crema-rich espresso. The unhurried process is soothing, though the resulting coffee is anything but.

'For fuck's sake,' Suzy would say, 'it's like a religious ritual.'

'Better. If Jesus had blood like this, I'd go to church.'

In the mornings Suzy drank hot water with a slice of lemon. I was so in love with her, I forgave her the sheer insipidity of this, for she was distinctly sipid in many other ways. During the day she would drink some herbal tea or other – boysenberry with extra digitalis – the kind of tasteless stuff imbibed by vegetarians, Buddhists, neurasthenics, homeopaths, organic food faddists, faith healers and members of the Green Party. Stupid tea for stupid people.

And this is the worst part: her bowels were as reliable as a clock. Hot water with lemon, piece of sourdough toast with her home-made Seville orange marmalade, off to the loo. And I would drink my double-shot flat white (the only great invention to issue from the southern hemisphere), eat my seeds, and continue to swell inwardly, discomforted and discomfited, morose.

The poor old body can hardly keep running. Sooner or later there will be a Tube strike: the tunnels get blocked and the trains can hardly get through. And when they do, they're more and more likely to have suicide bombers within: tumours, viruses, bacterial infections of every sort, so intent on mayhem that they willingly kill themselves too.

It's not just the bowel that is a reluctant worker. Arteries fur up, the large intestine grows polyps and muddy protuberances, the throat will not disgorge, the nose ceases to release its blockages. Even my penis, such a reliable ejaculator for so many decades – I once got sperm in my eye – can hardly be bothered to release its pitiful discharge. Having indulged myself with a very occasional wank – Think! Reminisce! Fantasise! Pray for Rain! – I am aware of having come, however mildly, only to notice that the tip of my penis bears no sign of the release of the (previously) essential body fluid. If I give it a post-orgasmic squeeze, upwards and firm, sure enough a little trickle of semen will appear at the tip, hardly enough to wipe off with my finger.

I can accept that. It's in the natural course of things. Ejaculations are for the young and pious. But I can't even piss any more. Unless I constantly top myself up with water, making sure my kidneys have something to work with, charged like a tank of petrol, all I can release, however urgent the imperative, is a series of effortful dribbles.

It's not just my pants and trousers that I stain. I bleed. I get blood on my socks, the cuffs of my shirt, my pants, the insides of my trousers. My face bleeds, and I put tiny swathes of tissues to mop and staunch it. It comes from my scratching. I bleed less but more frequently than a woman, and I scratch more often than a baboon. I have eczema on my psoriasis, my skin itches as if infested by insects. I scratch and scratch, apply ointments and then scratch in the wetness, humid furrows plough my skin, and when they dry, patches of red sores mature into tiny scab fields, which I pick, which then bleed, and itch.

But my scratching of my multiple itches is also recreational. The satisfaction of this has to be experienced to be credited. I moan, I prance, I gibber – though I am not entirely sure what gibbering entails.

My pants, my shirts, and most of all my sheets bear the brown – again! – residue of this frantic activity, and the stains are hard to shift. Though she was in charge of laundry matters, Suzy finally refused to clean up after me somatically: if I was going to ooze into the sheets and shirts, she said, I'd have to deal with the consequences myself.

I cannot send the sheets to the laundry, for they come back still stained. When the laundry lady returned the ironing and washing, I could feel her regarding me peculiarly. That bleeding man . . . No, I need to put stain remover onto the offended garment before putting it in the wash myself. I've never done this before. I'd say it was therapeutic, creating cleanliness where there was dirt and disorder, but it's not. It's just another choreful humiliation.

It's enough to break your heart, life. It breaks it, the sheer ghastliness of decline, best not to speak of it, as women do not tell expectant first-time mothers of the pains of childbirth. What's the point? Which brings me back to Mr Eliot, doesn't it? Youth, fleshiness, emptiness, loss. Waste:

Electric summons of the busy bell
Brings brisk Amanda to destroy the spell . . .
Leaving the bubbling beverage to cool,
Fresca slips softly to the needful stool . . .

Needful? Shit will out. Consider Spikedog, who was once handsome and tall as you.

I'll be damned. Is there a book lurking in this? *The Needful Stool: Sitting at the Feet of the Master.*

I had begun our first session for this select group of boys – before they sailed through their A levels and Scholarship exams – begun by making a plea. I enjoined them like a vicar intent on saving souls, only employing an unpriestly lightness of touch (I hope) and mild irony designed to penetrate the carapace of their cynicism, begged them as we read our literary texts, only to *listen*. To wrench open – it takes an effort of will – the port-cullis to their teenage hearts for just a couple of hours once a week, to humbly admit another, and better – a Yeats or Shakespeare, a Crazy Jane or Hamlet – and to welcome them, to allow for those tiny spots of time some vibration in the jelly of being, that makes, once it has settled, a subtle new mould.

Boys are not unregenerate monsters of solipsism. There is hope for them – some of them at least. I could sense at first some interest, then a sort of attention, however grudging. I am not sure, recovering this now, whether they were listening because they were moved by my ideas, or because I was. Why would someone feel so passionately about books, and the act of reading?

Otherwise, I would observe tartly (a number of them rather resented this), you are merely going to become a product of your family, the few friends you might make and the few lovers you may garner – a product of a good London address or of an estate in the West Country, nothing more than a function of your upbringing – a type. Whereas, if you will only read, and listen, you will admit a multiplicity of voices and points of view, consider them with some humility, allow them gracious entrance however strident or discordant some of them may sound, then you will grow and change, and each of these voices will become a constituent part of who you become, an atom of growing being.

It is literature and only literature that can do this. The Church can't help us, not any more. (I got a visit from our rather aggrieved chaplain the first time I said this, when one of the boys snitched on me.) But good reading of good literature, I insisted, both to him and to my boys, interprets life for us, sustains and consoles us.

Whatever even the most cynical of those boys might have felt, none could deny that I said so with a full heart. I might have appeared a zealot, a wanker even – I rather hope not, even all these decades later – but I was not being teacherly, this was not by rote, it was sufficiently real to be embarrassing, rightly, to many of them, and year after year, to myself.

We met once a week, my chosen group of boys, slouching to Oxbridge to be born. I gave them their head, which was dangerous, for a couple of them loved showing off their literary wiles, trying to amuse and to subvert. But any form of engagement, I counselled myself – and them – is better than sitting there looking bored.

'Next week, choose one of Yeats's poems,' I suggested, 'and then read it aloud, and we can discuss it.'

The first couple of boys, biddable and unimaginative,

wanting to please by a demonstration of sensibility, came up with the usual suspects, and I made the usual responses:

'The Lake Isle of Innisfree'? Boring! Sentimental. Stupid. Sounds like a yokel.

'The Second Coming'? There was some sniggering from the rough beasts, which I expected, and ignored.

Which led us to Golde, who had been lying in wait with 'Crazy Jane Talks with the Bishop', which he read ponderously, until he got to the final lines, which he smothered in lascivious relish.

> I met the Bishop on the road
> And much said he and I . . .
> 'A woman can be proud and stiff
> When on love intent;
> But Love has pitched his mansion in
> The place of excrement;
> For nothing can be sole or whole
> That has not been rent.'

There was a silence that I would hesitate to call pregnant.

'Please, sir,' he said, 'I find this very intriguing, but I'm not sure I understand entirely. Could you guide us through it?' The class closed ranks in quiet expectation and for a moment I had their full attention.

'What exactly is the nature of your problem, Golde?'

'Well, sir, I'm not sure whose problem it is. It might be that Jane is just crazy, like it says, and bishops are only bishops, aren't they? But perhaps Yeats was a little confused about such matters? Wasn't there a bit of a problem with that woman he fancied?'

'Maud Gonne.'

'Ah, sir: Maud today, and Gonne tomorrow. It's no wonder

she ran a mile if he told her he wanted her in the – ' He pretended to consult the poem. 'Oh yes, sir, "the place of excrement".'

'Wanted? I see no mention of desire.'

'What do you see, sir?'

'I see a reference – perhaps you might think about this – to pitching a mansion.'

He was ready and waiting. 'Oh I have thought and thought, sir. It seems a very uncongenial place to build a house.'

There was a mass guffaw, which I allowed to peak and settle down.

He wasn't finished. 'After all, sir, there's plenty of arseholes in mansions, but there can't be many mansions in – '

By this time I had joined in the laughter. For a schoolboy, it was a masterful act of deconstruction, and his comic timing could hardly have been improved.

'I must admit, Golde,' I said, 'that I've always had my doubts about that line. There seems something unparsable about it, something personal perhaps. But I agree with you – '

'In what way, sir?'

'It's crap.'

He looked proud, but humble.

'But Golde, perhaps you and Jane have something in common?'

'Are we both crazy, sir?'

'No, you are both fools. But she is a wise fool, like the one we studied in *King Lear*, if your memory stretches back to last term. Whereas you are just as foolish, and not at all wise.'

'Tell me why she is wise, sir, and I am not.'

'Because she is trying, in her way, to assimilate the tragedy of getting old, and inhabiting a body that was once luxuriant and is now decaying. Whereas you are just being a smart arse.'

It was a bit unfair. He'd done very well, and the exchange had left me with an increased respect for him, and a diminished admiration for Yeats. Funny old Willie.

Respect for Golde was rare, and unlikely to abide. He was physically unprepossessing – small, weak, whey-faced, curdled as a bowl of yoghurt left in the sun – and his fellows tend to turn on such creatures with a ferocity that makes you think William Golding underplayed his account. But my description makes him appear insignificant, whereas Golde was as memorably repellent as Tolkien's Gollum, given over to obsessional nocturnal habits, stroking his Precious, fingering and fondling his ring. You could imagine him trailing a spool of viscous liquid behind him, like a snail.

It was reprehensibly easy to turn against such a boy, who was universally despised, teased and diminished. If there had been keystrokes to do it, the boys would have reformatted his disc. I ought not to have colluded in this, but the temptation was irresistible. I consoled myself that, like many boys who are relentlessly bullied, the poor chap found an identity in his victimhood: being the butt of jokes and worse was presumably better than not being noticed at all.

I carried on with my evangelical enterprise for years, too many years, indulged the recurrent Goldes, allowing Crazy Jane her yearly pilgrimage into instructive madness. The premise was clear, obvious, and unchallenged by man or boy: reading exposes us to the experiences and minds of others, makes us challenge our own provinciality, deepens and widens who we are and what we can become.

It was an inspiring notion, and I tried to live by it, and to teach my boys to do so as well.

Unfortunately it was wrong.

I cannot go on, like this. I cannot go on. Passing the dying days. Remembering, thinking, justifying. Assembling bits of stories, making stupid jokes – logical, scatological. For what? Nothing assuages the pain of being. Faced squarely, it unmans and unmasks; evaded, it undermines and casts a shadow.

Sitting in my study, thinking. I think, therefore I am not.

All you can truthfully say, anyway, is that thinking is going on. But who is doing it? I'm the last person to say, or to know. Silly old fool, gorged on the saturated fatheads of philosophy, putting Descartes before des horse.

Thinking is the opposite of being. And it is so boring. Thoughts are the dullest things, they leave a funny taste in the mouth.

It is impossible to say just what I mean. There is nothing to be done. I shall do nothing. Nothing will come of nothing, it lies coiled in the heart of being – like a worm. Nothing is what I am used to, what I have, *what I choose.*

Nothing is better than love.

> Do not go gentle into that good night . . .
> Rage, rage against the dying of the
> light.

Dark, doubly dark.

The boys did not understand this. Understandably. Everyone gets this wrong. This is not a poem about death, though that blubbery piss-artist's father is old now. That's a metaphor, and this is literal – his father is going blind. That's worse. Bang! God curses him with blindness, but he is going to die soon anyway.

When I imagine being blind, a groan involuntarily escapes me and I shudder. Not figuratively. I am a claustrophobe, the sort who begins to claw at the door if the Tube gets stuck – pauses even – in a tunnel for more than fifteen seconds. In a foolish desire to see if I could train myself into slowly increasing tolerances of discomfort, I once asked Suzy to lock me in a darkened closet, and to stand outside and count to twenty, loudly. By the time she reached seven I was banging desperately on the door. She knew better than to tease me, even for the extra thirteen seconds. When I emerged, I had somehow managed to cover myself in sweat.

I cannot bear movies or novels in which someone is buried alive, perhaps by a sadistic kidnapper who entombs his prey underground in a coffin, with only a tiny duct of air to breathe. Or perhaps she – it's always a she, isn't it? – is locked in the boot of a car for hours, or days. Annihilated in the dark, helpless, stripped of air and movement and light. I wouldn't rather be dead – I would be, soon. A heart attack perhaps? Or merely a fright paralysis so crippling as to stifle life. The triumph of the darkness.

He is the Prince of Darkness. Not Satan, who has been given rather a bad name in this respect. He is a man of integrity, the Devil: if he promises your bowels will boil, get ready to burble. What you see is what you get. Yet his is merely High Octane Badness. Evil is not so simple. To do evil you have sometimes to promise good, and willy-nilly keep your promise, but sometimes break it: build up expectations and satisfy them, or outrageously deflate that which was confidently expected. To be genuinely, heart-breakingly wicked, you have sometimes to do good, both satisfy and disappoint, and you have to ensure that your anxious subjects – your Abrahams and Jobs – can hardly tell what sort of being they are engaged with.

He is supposed to protect us.

The LORD shall preserve thee from all evil:
He shall preserve thy soul

Either He can't, or He can but He won't. Or perhaps the evil from which He is supposed to protect us is integral to His nature, unruly and ill-controlled? I need Him. He is the focus for my indignation, a bull's-eye for the rage that our poor sad predicament – lonely, desperate and perilous – causes in me. I need someone to blame.

FUCK GOD

Fuck Him and His angels and archangels, fuck the Heavenly hosts and hostesses, fuck the saints and the sainted, fuck their priests, and most of all, and at long last, fuck the Virgin Mary.

My eyesight is deteriorating. Particles float across my field of vision, when I read, the print gets blurry and my head begins to ache, I get shooting pains in my eyeballs, and itching around my eye sockets. My glasses no longer clarify or magnify, and sometimes I abandon them and press the book close to my face, anxiously scanning the text until the pain gets too bad, and I put my book down, full of dread.

I summon my visiting optician, who arrives reluctantly,

bemoaning the absence of his most treasured and necessary instruments, which are too large and too delicate to make home visits. We begin, like Vladimir and Estragon, with him moaning and me telling him to shut up. Then I moan, and he tells me to relax.

I call him Dr Karlovic, though I suspect he has no such qualification. But he has never corrected me, and the glint of pleasure when I proffer the D-word is presumably a sign not so much that he has hoodwinked me (his business card has no mention of a medical qualification or PhD), but because he takes it as a form of respect.

He changes my prescription, and next visit brings me my new glasses. They work. I should email him to say thanks. It's a blessing to see clearly again.

Hand in hand, we walked round the corner to Khan's, the local newsagent's, which was one of Lucy's favourite places. Better than the park, the swimming baths, or even the beach. From her earliest months she'd had a craving for sour things, and Mr Khan stocked a particularly mouth-puckering lemon super-sour ball, for which Lucy was, I suspect, his only customer. Not that she was allowed to buy one. Nor was I. As we entered the shop most days, in search of the newspaper and perhaps a magazine, he would open the large plastic jar of lemon sours that sat on the shelf behind him, and pick one out.

'Goodness me,' he would say, looking at the ceiling, where the fan was circling lazily, 'I wonder if anyone likes these nasty sour things?'

'I do! I want one!'

'Now who could that be?' he would enquire, for her head didn't reach above the counter, and he would pretend to look around the shop to see who was talking. 'There is nobody here, is there? Except you, Dr Darke. Good morning, sir!'

'No, no! It's me! I'm down here! I want one!'

Mr Khan loved this game, but Lucy had only a limited toleration for it, before her desire for the sweet became overwhelming and she would start to cry.

'I'm down here!'

'Where is that voice coming from?'

'Me! Here! I want it!'

With practised timing, he looked down to spot her head, inclined backwards as she tried to look over the edge of the counter to catch his eye.

'Oh,' Mr Khan would say, 'it is you, is it not?'

'It's me! It's me!'

He would have gone on for another few minutes – he loved it – but the ritual ended here, with the transfer of the sweet. Lucy grabbed it and stuffed it into her mouth, her fingers already sticky with the white sugar covering.

'Ooooh,' she said, puckering and slurping, 'it's sourlicious!'

'Shall I have it back?'

'No! No! It's mine!'

'What do you say?' I enquired from my news rack, unable to choose between the stodgy *London Review of Books* and the high-falutin' *New York Review of Books,* neither of them likely to occasion a smile, much less any laughter. Perhaps I should buy *Private Eye*, and have a good sneer, but I cannot abide that sanctimonious midget, its editor.

I occasionally buy one of the literary magazines, prey to the stale fantasy that they represent a view of the world, of reading and writing, that can still move me. But they don't. If I find even one article or review that amuses me, I feel blessed. Why is literature become so dull?

The magazines are curatorial. Run by curates, marching

off to war: improve the unimproved, wash the unwashed, enlighten the heathens. *Literature improves you*. I believed that for God knows how long, ever since being brainwashed by Dr Leavis and his gang of Cambridge acolytes. *The improved!* Poor fucking Frank and his ghastly and appropriately named wife Queenie. I wonder if they thought of him as Kingie?

'Thank you, Mr Khan!' said my slurping girl, her face a rictus of received sourness, her attention now on a young African who had selected an ice lolly from the freezer, and was approaching the counter.

Lucy stared at him intently. 'Daddy,' she said, 'why is that man so dirty?'

I think it is American cowboys – or perhaps Bugs Bunny? – who *skedaddle*, a word I've always fancied using, though actually doing it is not all that different from the (weaker) English locution 'beat a hasty retreat'. You turn as fast as you can, passing the enemy (who glared not at tiny Lucy, but at her reprehensible father) and head for them thar hills.

As we made our way home, she sucking away industriously, I tried to explain. It's not easy. To her innocent eye the poor African had looked distinctly odd, and other. 'Darling,' I said. 'I'm afraid you hurt that poor man's feelings.'

She looked up at me, bemused, sour-mouthed, puckered. We lived in a largely white, middle-class neighbourhood, and I'm not sure she'd ever noticed the few West Indians or Africans who occasionally drifted by.

'You see, darling, the man is not dirty. He just has brown skin. You have white skin, he has brown. But both of you are people.'

She looked up at me quizzically.

'You both have faces, and noses and eyes and arms and legs, don't you?'

I expected some response, some acknowledgement that there was, if not a problem, at least a mystery to be explored. But she wasn't interested.

'You know Amarjit and Sanjay at the crèche? They have brown skin too. And you know they're not dirty.'

She laughed. 'That's silly. They're the same as me.'

'Everybody is the same, but sometimes we just look different.'

Poor. And untrue – or true in a way that it would take her many years to assimilate. How to explain things to a three-year-old, who was now staring at me with the wide-eyed fixity of a barn owl?

'I have a good idea,' I said, in what was intended to be a breezy and assured tone, 'let's go back to Mr Khan's. Shall we say we're sorry?'

'No.'

Relieved, I took her hand once again, and we walked home, quickly.

The new cleaner will come on Thursdays. I couriered the agency a key so that she could let herself in, and the first week I left detailed instructions on the kitchen table – not detailed enough, as it turned out, for she was curiously selective about which she chose to follow – telling her where the cleaning materials and Hoover were. On the first day she arrived, as promised, at nine in the morning and I heard the front door close as I sat upstairs in my study, with the door locked and a yellow Post-it sticker on its door (and the one across the hall), saying 'Do not clean this room'.

For the first couple of hours she busied herself emptying

the dishwasher, putting the clothes in the washing machine, and doing the ironing. I heard her hoovering the drawing-room and dining-room carpets. But what I also heard, sometime just before noon – she must have brought a wireless with her – was the sound of music, blaring, inane, peace-destroying. Pop music, accompanied by the grating voice of an adenoidal presenter whose every utterance required an exclamation mark.

I had every intention of hiding away. I had no desire to meet, only to evade her. I did not even, at this point, know her name. Or perhaps I had forgotten it. But she had been sent to try me and I rebelled. I unlocked the door and shouted down the stairs. 'Will you turn off that bloody wireless!'

This may have been a bit loud, and sounded, well, demented, perhaps. I needed to be heard above the din of both Hoover and music, and perhaps I bellowed. It must have given her a considerable fright.

Both of the offending objects were soon silenced. She started up the stairs, determined to meet and presumably to pacify her new employer. Her footsteps sounded sturdy.

She soon appeared on the landing, flushed and unembarrassed, martial, facing the enemy. I must have frightened her, and I had spoken to her rudely. She had every right to be cross. I didn't care.

'I cannot abide loud music in my house. There is to be no wireless playing.'

'I did not know. They say no one is here.'

'Well, you know now.'

'I return now to cleaning.'

Her face had the oval quality of the Slavs, without defining planes, with a pronounced forehead that did not suggest extra brains – a face that in repose looked vacuous, but animated when lit by feeling, as it was now, simmering with irritation. She was probably in her mid-forties, tall and slim, her bare arms wiry with sinewy muscle that ran from her shoulders down to her wrists. Some sort of athlete, perhaps, or a gym rat, or perhaps just designed that way. She turned to descend the stairs, with an oddly graceful whirl, as if she were about to throw a discus, and made a quickstep retreat. Her smock, vulgar but not unclean, swished around her waist, and her too-tight jeans, quite inappropriate for cleaning duties, showed off a bottom crisp as an apple as she descended.

Anxious to re-establish my supremacy, which had slipped alarmingly, I followed her downstairs into the drawing room, to be met by another horror. The curtains and windows had been opened wide. There was a soft breeze blowing, and outside the sun was shining as brightly as ever it can in this godforsaken country, the skies were pretty well unclouded, pretty much blue.

I've never been a great admirer of weather. It has no integrity, it teases and promises and disappoints. You can't count on it in England, and in those places where you can, it's even more irritating and oppressive. I have exiled weather, and the relief is palpable. Fuck it. I don't much like natural light either. Give me 150 watts any day.

Which is to say I hate nature? Not at all. I couldn't do without it. I just don't want to be plunged into its unregulated midst. I commend my fish and my fowl, praise my beans, leaves and grapes, transformed by human ingenuity into a well-cooked Dover sole or roast pheasant, a demitasse of dark roast espresso, a Montecristo No. 2, a bottle of Bâtard-Montrachet or glass of Krug: nature still and sparkling, nature methodised.

'Close those windows and draw the curtains please!'

'But,' she remonstrated, 'is hot and dark. Not nice to work. And dusty. Bad smell. How you say – ?'

I can't resist a word game. 'Stuffy?' I suggested.

She looked puzzled. 'No.'

'Yes! Stuffy! I love stuffy!'

She looked mildly alarmed. Was I propositioning her?

'I clean some more now,' she said firmly.

I went on a tour of inspection. The curtains in the kitchen, dining room and downstairs study were pulled back, the windows opened wide. The sunlight infiltrated my interiors alarmingly. I went round hastily, closing and drawing, re-establishing the gloom. You can't study the darkness by flooding it with light.

She followed me, puzzled. 'I am Bronya,' she said. She did not offer her hand, thank God.

'I am – '

'I know. Mr Dork.'

'Darke,' I said.

'Yes, Mr Dork.'

When I'm not desperate, I'm bored.

I spend a lot of time in bed on the desperate days, and in my comfy armchair on the bored ones.

But I am not inflexible with regard to my emotional states and sites, and can make do in either place in either mood. But then I get bored being in bed, or desperate in the awful comfort of my chair.

Being bored makes me desperate, and being desperate is boring.

I am a double helix of human emotion, and its absence. Over-filled, then empty. Up, then down. Only without the up.

★

The pleasure of my daily rituals is that I have no one to share them with. I wake slowly, make my first cup of coffee and return to bed, read for an hour or so before showering and shaving. Though I have no one for whom to look good, I take care with my appearance, as I never feel whole unless I am dressed well. I am aware that this sounds foppish, or foolish, or perhaps just sad, but I wear a clean white shirt every day, and a casual cashmere jacket. My moleskin trousers are pressed, my shoes shined. My scruffy colleagues – most schoolteachers lose their self-respect quickly, and end up mooching about, whiffy and rumpled – teased me about my fastidiousness. I didn't mind. I looked better than they did.

I feel imposed upon by the mere ringing of the doorbell, much less by the person that it may herald. And so I have – I thought rather cleverly – made Bronya's regular Thursday hours (between 9 a.m. and 3 p.m.) the time at which my various deliveries appear. She can then receive and unpack whatever shows up. The Waitrose order comes in the morning delivery slot, and Bronya has been instructed never to accept substitutions. They once offered a jar of pickled Jewish cucumbers when I ordered cornichons!

She turns out to be competent in many ways, and I am delighted that her English is too rudimentary for sustained conversation, else she would no doubt impose her life history on me. I pretend to be very hard of hearing, though I slip up too often. She has proved biddable in all respects save her insistence that the curtains be opened while she works downstairs, and having admonished her about this, her innate intractability set in and she threatened to quit.

'Is not healthy. I rather work someplace else.'

You have to pick your issues with Bulgarians, and had she resigned, who knows, I might have done much worse. A surly Latvian perhaps, or a talkative Pole. After all, I could stay upstairs – as she was quick to point out – while she worked downstairs. And when she came up to do my bedroom, bathroom and study, I could retreat to the drawing room and close the curtains.

This small domestic tiff having been settled, we are consequently getting on adequately: she knows how to programme the dishwasher, do the week's washing and ironing, and (which took some time) learned where everything goes: wine glasses here, dinner plates there, silver – not to be put in the dishwasher! – in the drawer in the sideboard, sauces on this shelf, seeds on that, pickles and chutneys on the second shelf at the rear of the fridge. I like things in their places. I am by nature what I call orderly and Suzy deemed obsessional.

I'd come into the kitchen to make a second cup of coffee, though Bronya had offered to make one and bring it up to me. I interrupted her search for the Nescafé (!) and said I would do it myself. She'd seen Gaggias in cafés, but was astonished that a private person could own one, and watched me carefully as I made my cup.

'Smells good!'

She peered into the cup, her face intrusively close enough to attempt a quick slurp of the contents. I pulled it away, rattling the saucer. It would have spilled, but a double espresso only fills half the cup.

Bronya pointed to the contents. 'What is that?'

'What is what?'

She pointed again. I was for a moment alarmed that she might be about to dip her finger in.

'Oh, that. It's called crema.'

'Is cream?'

'No, is oil from coffee bean. Is very delicious.'

Why is it that, faced with a person with limited English, we end up talking in this pidgin variety, rather than setting a good but simple example of right usage?

'You make like this – ' She searched for the right word. 'Purposely.'

She nodded. She was a quick study, and I suspect could have produced a passable cup if I had allowed her to try. I did not. I do better than passable, and I already resented the invasiveness of her desire to please, to know, and to participate. If I wasn't careful, next thing I knew I would be making coffee for her, and then we would be having companionable lunches together. I needed her presence, but did not want it. Did not like the thought of her using even the downstairs WC, and had instructed the agency that she was to bring her own lunch.

I was making my way out of the kitchen – it was dangerous to linger – as Bronya began unpacking a bag of heirloom tomatoes, in their muted purples and greens, yellows and oranges.

'What this?' she asked, holding a large purplish one in her beefy hand, and thrusting it towards me aggressively, as if I had brought something dangerous into the room.

'A tomato.'

'Is not. I know tomato. Red.' She looked at it again. 'Is wrong. Gone off.'

I do not discuss vegetables with my cleaner.

'Just put over there. On basket on table. Not in fridge!'

Lucy had a new best friend. This had already happened several times in her young life, for her feelings were both intense and shallow, like most children's. Attached to a playmate, she was ferociously monogamous, but it rarely lasted. One year, propinquity bound her to a flaxen-haired waif called Jenny, who had joined the playgroup at the same time as Lucy. The two were as inseparable as five-year-olds can be, visited each other's homes and begged to stay overnight, went to the park together in the afternoon and swimming at the weekends.

'I love her so much,' Lucy would enthuse, holding Jenny's hand. 'She's my best!'

The next autumn Jenny was taken out of the group, because her mother could no longer afford it. Lacking its support, both mother and waif were desperate for Lucy to visit as before, or more than before. But Jenny was out of sight and nearly out of mind. Lucy had a new playmate called Gloria.

'She's my best!' said Lucy.

At which point, clear that some response had to be made quickly, or Lucy would be forever lost to her daughter, Jenny's mum – I never quite mastered her name, it seemed to come and go as frequently as she did, and on each of her reappearances I would have ask Suzy sotto voce what her name was – came up with a master-stroke and bought a puppy, a Shih Tzu called Milly, a bite-sized fluffball of vulgar gorgeousness, with a shaggy little face and an insatiable desire for company. It looked as if it had come straight from Hamley's Cute as Fuck Dog Department.

Milly was wholly promiscuous, it even approached me skittishly on its sole visit to our house. I took an instant dislike to the creature, as tricky and licky as a schoolgirl on heat. I measured its stature, how far its stomach passed above the ground, and reckoned – the calculation was inexact, to be fair – that if I got my foot squarely under it, I could kick it at least three metres through the air.

'How cute,' I said, though even the besotted Lucy could sense my reservations.

'She's my best!' she said happily.

The puppy ploy worked a treat, and Suzy was distinctly irritated by how easily manipulated her daughter was. 'That bitch, she knew exactly what she was doing! Of course Lucy would fall in love with the mutt. Who wouldn't? It's like a paedophile offering sweets to kiddies, it ought to be illegal!'

Nothing to get heated up about, I counselled. Surely the dog was bought for Jenny, not Lucy? And why not? The little girl was now at home a lot, her best friend had abandoned her without a wave of farewell, and she needed a treat. It was quite the right thing to do.

'Mummy,' said Lucy, 'I want to go to Jenny's to see Milly. Please can I go? Please?'

'But darling,' said Suzy severely, 'you don't like Jenny any more, you said so.'

'I don't, she's boring. But I LOVE Milly!'

It shouldn't have mattered so much, but Suzy couldn't reconcile herself to her daughter's new obsession. Lucy visited Milly, dreamt of Milly, begged to go to Milly's. One evening, as I read her a bedtime story, I noticed that she had a picture of Milly Blu-Tacked above her little desk.

She saw me looking over her shoulder. 'Isn't she dear!' she said. 'Do you want to see the pictures of her and me?'

'Have you shown them to Mummy?'

'I did,' said Lucy. 'But she doesn't like Milly.'

'Why is that?'

'She says she's too small. And she doesn't like her name.'

'Her name? What's wrong with "Milly"?'

'Not that name, silly. You know, her rude name.' She giggled.

Lucy had quickly discovered a joke lurking there, which could cause a potent combination of merriment (hers) and irritation (her mother's).

'Don't you just love her, Mummy?' she'd say. 'She's a real Shih Tzu.' A well-timed pause between the syllables of the dog's breed, and you had: 'She's a real shit, Sue!'

Suzy found this mildly amusing the first time she heard it, but she was oddly prudish about our daughter's language, and believed children ought not to swear, apparently forgetting that she'd been a foul-mouthed child herself. The fact that she swore constantly was an adult prerogative, which Lucy might look forward to. 'That's enough of that, young lady!'

'A shit, Sue! Get it? Like a shit! And Sue! That's funny, isn't it?'

Later, I overheard her on the phone, apparently talking to the dog. 'It's me. It's Lucy! I'm coming to see you soon. Did you miss me?'

She made some kissy sounds. 'I do love you,' she said, 'I'll see you soon.' Before Jenny could regain control at her end of the call, Lucy hung up.

'This has got to stop,' Suzy said to me.

Only a week later it did. The sort of narcissist who thinks that everything that happens involves *them* would have felt responsible for the disaster. But neither Suzy nor I felt remotely answerable for Milly's death, much though we had wished her to go away. Neither of us had warmed to the pooch, but it was quite impossible not to be moved by the tragedy.

Not Milly's tragedy. There's plenty of dead dogs out there, but I save my regrets for the demise of (a very few) members of my own species. No, this was Lucy's drama, her first encounter with the death of anything more dear to her than a goldfish, and she – if I may be allowed an unfatherly thought – wallowed in her misery, indulged herself so utterly and so publicly that there was something luxuriant and performative in her grief. When she retreated to her room to be alone, for one reason or another, she fell silent.

She had no idea of death, of the brutal finality of it, the tearing physiological degeneration, the erosion of functioning, the inexorable return to dust. The unmitigated, unmanning awfulness of it. No, what Lucy – like all small children – reacted to was not death, but absence. She hated parting with something that she was used to, that she needed fiercely in her fickle way, and was shaken when it was taken from her. Her feelings were not grief, if that may be supposed (commonly but mistakenly) to involve feelings for the deceased. No, her feelings were for herself alone. She was outraged. Milly was *hers*, her *best*, and now she was not. There was something shockingly arbitrary about it.

'It's so unfair!'

She'd exhibited the same reaction when a redundant piece of furniture was taken from the house, to be replaced by something better, more beautiful and more useful: the kitchen sofa with its tatty brown William Morris loose cover full of holes, with springs beginning to worm their way through the seat, to one's occasional acute discomfort. It had to go, and Suzy found something prettier, less dated and more comfortable to take its place.

On the day it arrived, the delivery men agreed, for a tenner, to take the old one away. They grabbed an arm on each side, and hoisted it up to be transported out the back door, through the garden, and into their lorry at the back of the lane. But they hadn't reckoned on Lucy, who burst into tears, screaming 'No! No!' and clung first to the sofa, and when that became precarious, to the leg of one of the removal men.

Her outrage had two distinct and equally felt components. First, she was used to her sofa, she had grown up with it. It was part of her world, yet another *best*. But more profoundly and oddly, her feelings were actually for the thing in itself, as Kant put it. The poor sofa would be devastated to be taken away.

She was the last of the animists. At the supermarket she searched through the tinned vegetables to find those with dents in them, and made sure that Suzy purchased them – otherwise no one else would, 'and they'd be sad'.

'It's so unfair!' she howled.

I detached her from the man's leg and held her in my arms, screaming, as the funeral procession of the sofa wended its way down the garden path. The gate opened, and it was gone.

Lucy stopped crying and sat on the new sofa, sucking the little rag of cloth that she carried with her at that age. She looked pensive, and settled down into the undoubtedly more comfortable new surroundings. 'Can I watch Sesame Street?' she asked.

Milly's death, little as I regretted it, was both sudden and shocking. Most days, after school, Jenny and her mother, accompanied by their new mutt, went for a walk in the local park, a play on the swings, and a choc-ice at the café. An intelligent and biddable little creature, in no time Milly was let off the leash and able to sniff about at her leisure. She was far too gregarious, and needy, to wander very far, but liked making the acquaintance of the other dogs, large or small, young or old, male or female. And one day she chose the wrong dog.

You couldn't have seen it coming, I gathered. The wrong 'un was not a Spikedog with a Spikeman, swaggering bundles of danger, from whom you needed to avert your eyes and move to safer ground. Onlookers later described it as medium-sized, with curly dishevelled brown hair. It was over in a moment. Milly approached her assailant in her usually friendly manner and, for whatever reason – perhaps she nipped it, or just pissed it off by being small and friendly – in an instant Milly's head and shoulders were clutched between the dog's jaws, being tossed about, both of them making frightful noises. Within a few seconds the Shih Tzu was thrown back onto the grass, broken and bleeding, howling, then silent.

I had no wish to imagine the ensuing drama, though it was hard not to. The problem was how to tell Lucy, in some suitably restrained, edited and untraumatising manner. Milly'd been attacked by another dog in the park. She was in the doggy hospital and was very poorly.

'But Milly wouldn't fight with anybody! Milly loves other dogs! Milly loves everybody!'

'Maybe the other dog started it, I don't know.'

'Poor Milly! I want to go and see her!'

'I'm afraid we can't. She's not allowed any visitors.'

'But she's going to come back soon, isn't she?'

'We'll have to see.'

But there was nothing to be done. Sometime the next morning, Milly, on the vet's unambiguous advice, was put out of her misery.

Lucy took the news badly. 'Why didn't the doctor fix her?' she asked tearfully.

'She was too poorly to fix, darling. She lived for a little

while, but she was never going to get better, and was in a lot of pain. So they thought it kindest to put her to sleep.'

'Sleep?'

'She's in Heaven now. That'll be lovely for her, won't it? With all the other doggie angels?'

There was a very long pause. 'You mean they killed her?'

'No, darling, I don't. I mean they ended her suffering, because there was no way she was going to get better. That is a kind thing to do.'

'But I need to see her again!'

'I know, love.' Suzy picked her up, resisting, for a wriggling desperate cuddle. 'So do I.'

'You don't! You're lying! You hated Milly!'

Anyone with sufficient emotional or narrative sense might have seen it coming. I am living alone by both choice and necessity, but in spite of my many talents for both self-indulgence and self-deception, I continue to need another voice, if only to project mine against, another visage, if only to register what I have to say.

In my enforced isolation is an accompanying solipsism: it is intermittently enjoyable, being the only person in the world, like God, free to torment the odd dog. But, not to put too fine a point on it, and I resist even writing these words, I was getting lonely.

I do not want the company of Bronya, but I have come, appallingly, to need it. A bit, perhaps a little bit. This is more than surprising to me, I feel abashed by it. Bronya? Like many Eastern Europeans, she is both blunt and insensitive to a degree that, to an English sensibility, is shocking and easily mistaken for crassness. I can be rude to her, dismissive, angry, domineering. Equally, her approaches to me are not so much tactless – which somehow suggests someone who, knowing what tact is, eschews it like a Yorkshireman – but utterly without consideration of how her words might sound to someone who isn't similarly disabled by having come from Sofia.

Bronya is abrasive without knowing it. She has no sense of humour, is as capable of irony as an armadillo, takes everything literally. Lightness of touch? Not even with the dusters. I am surprised that the paintwork on the ceilings survives her attempts to clear the cobwebs. Should I point out these manifold truths, she would not know what I was talking about.

I feel invaded and bruised by her company, but she is all that I have. And, to be fair, she is also bright, hardworking, cheerful, inquisitive and anxious to learn. When she wormed out of me that I had been a teacher – of literature! – she wouldn't let go of it. She was apparently well read in the classics of Bulgarian literature, and reeled off a list of -*ovs* and -*ics*, none of whom I had heard of.

'I want to read books,' she said, 'improve English. Who is good writer?'

'I'm frightfully sorry,' I said, holding my hand to my ear, and making my voice louder. 'Bad day for hearing. Not getting you at all.'

'Want to read! You tell me books!'

'I'm so sorry,' I said, 'you're not getting through to me at all,' and left her to my ironing.

Suzy had history with cleaners. She'd collected them over the years, bonding with one after another, though they frequently disappeared without notice or trace. You can't count on cleaners. Not in London anyway. I think she was unconsciously nostalgic for country servants, like bleached

69

ayahs, but instead all she got were unreliable refugees from old countries. She enquired of agency after agency for robust Indians or sturdy Bangladeshis – even Pakistanis at a pinch – but they were never on offer. Presumably most of them were employed by the NHS. They probably run the damn thing by now.

Fortunately I met almost none of them, as I was teaching on the days when they came. I made sure of that, staying late if necessary. But I heard their stories, which Suzy collected assiduously, as if they were raw material. I can remember, in no clear order, a Czech with herpes, a Polish mother of a toddler who accompanied her on her jobs, making a mess at one end as she cleaned at the other (she was fired when the brat started colouring in the Leech illustrations in my first edition of *A Christmas Carol*), a Sicilian with dodgy relatives, and a Ghanaian who claimed to know the location of a lost gold mine, needing only a few thousand pounds to mount an expedition to rediscover it. Very good investment, missus!

She rarely met a cleaner she didn't like: she approved of cleaners, admired them, sucked their stories out of them ruthlessly.

'The fact that some poor woman is working for a ghastly London cleaning agency for minimum wage guarantees there's a compelling backstory. If you listen sympathetically and ask the right questions, they are anxious to talk about their lives. Telling ameliorates suffering, it helps you to right yourself.'

I think it ameliorated hers as well. She worked from home much of the time and was always grateful to be distracted from writing a review or editing a manuscript – tasks that she found increasingly stressful and uncongenial – to share a cup of tea, make a light lunch, or hunker down for a short gossip before Lucy came home from school.

She had a notebook in which she described each woman in detail. She was good at faces, practised looking with the intensity of a portrait painter, made notes on skin tone, nose formation, eye setting and colour, blotches, wrinkles, pimples, dry patches ...There were notes about funny phrases the cleaner might use, anecdotes about their troubles. Further notes on how they dressed. Quite a lot – for God's sake! – about their shoes. More and more and more.

The material just sat there in her notebook, gestating away as she was inwardly assimilating it, and eventually some of it made its way into a modest book of short stories that, according to a review in *The Observer*, 'heralded a welcome return of a distinctive voice, and eye'.

Few of the cleaners lasted more than a year. When the anniversary of their coming loomed – which was rare, as most moved on within a few months – Suzy encouraged them to go. 'It's bad for these women to stay too long with one client,' she maintained, though she never said why. What she meant was that it was bad for her to keep up a (one-sided) relationship with a poor woman from whom she had already extracted whatever might be useful to her, who then needed to be discarded like a squeezed lemon or pot of coffee grounds.

This sounds unsympathetic. To be fair, the cleaners liked and admired her, and were delighted to be the focus of her interest. Suzy was uncommonly decent to them, those wretched souls who were inured to being bossed about or ignored by their clients, or to cleaning empty homes, listening to the wireless, weary and demoralised. And there was Suzy – she hated being called Miss Moulton or, worse,

Mrs Darke – who was genuinely and warmly interested. I'll bet they missed her after she, mystifyingly, seemed not to need them any more.

I remonstrated with her about this, the arbitrariness of it, the unkindness.

'A lot you know about it,' she said tartly. 'You hide in your study, never even make a cup of tea, don't bother to learn their names. At least I engage with them.'

'Exactly!' I said. I may have pointed a finger in the air in triumph. 'Just what I mean: you eat them up and then you spit them out!'

'They'll be fine,' she said, 'they're survivors. I take something from them, and they get something from me. We're good for each other for a while, then we both need to move on.'

At nine years old, Lucy announced she was a vegetarian, in the tone that a zealot might employ to say they had been born again. The Lord be praised! I don't know who converted her. That cartoon girl on the telly with the star for a head, didn't she give up meat?

'It's so unfair! Animals have rights same as we do!' She glared across the table at the roast shoulder of lamb with braised leeks and roast potatoes in goose fat, that Suzy and I had cooked together, and attacked her tofu patty with moral fervour.

'That's fine, love. You don't have to eat them.'

'Neither should you! You're a murderer! You eat innocent little lambs.' Her eyes watered with grief and indignation.

I couldn't resist teasing her. 'Mmmm, lambs are the best. With gravy!'

'I hate you!' she cried. 'I'm never eating with you again if you keep eating meat. My tofu is so delicious.'

'I don't think I've ever heard of tofu? What is it?'

'It's pronounced to-fu, not toffy! It's made from soya beans. It's ever so good for you! Mummy and I made it into burgers.' She showed me her bun, which was filled with something crisply fried and brown – like some sort of bhaji – with ketchup on it.

'Darling, I'm glad you like it. But we are all going to eat together, you in your way and us in ours. What are you going to do, have your own dining room?'

'I'll eat upstairs. I'm not going to sit with a cannibal! It makes me feel sick!' She clutched her stomach dramatically, summoning a vomit.

'Sweetie, cannibals eat their own sort – like a man eating a man.'

'That's better than eating a poor cute lamb! Who cares about men?'

'So. You'd rather eat man-chops? Maybe Mummy could rustle some up!'

'You're not funny! You're horrible!'

When Bronya took her lunch break the following Thursday, she unwrapped her sausages and pot of Russian salad, reached into her bag and took out a paperback. Ignoring me ostentatiously, she opened it, halfway through. I glanced at the title – how could I not, it was as if she were flashing her privates at me. Bronya was reading *Oliver Twist*.

Dickens! She had cleaned the study, Bulgarianed her way in, tut-tutting as she dusted, vacuumed and resisted the temptation to open the curtains.

'You are not to touch the books,' I said firmly.

'Dusty!'

'I prefer them dusty. Leave them alone!' I had an absurd

desire to gather them all, the many hundreds of volumes, into my arms, to hold them to my chest, muttering 'my Precious' – protective, obsessional, crazed.

I was pretending to write in the burgundy crushed-morocco folder in which I keep my journal, but really I was monitoring Bronya, counting the minutes until she left me alone. The Hoover made a frightful noise, and the dust swirled. It was intolerable, but captains do not abandon ships when they fill with water and become uncongenial. I stood fast.

I had no reason to suppose she would have noticed my *Collected Works of Charles Dickens*, much less the double- and triple-decker first editions that filled a shelf and a half in the early Georgian break-fronted bookcase next to my desk.

They were collecting books, not reading books. More useful were my paperback Dickens novels, copiously annotated and underlined over the years, which were the building blocks for my longstanding, fruitless little project.

She lowered the book an inch or two, to meet my eye. She had a lovely smile, and I was seeing more of it as she relaxed and got used to my grumpy ways. God knows she would be used to such responses. All Eastern Europeans are grumpy. Bronya probably mistook my recurrent surliness for normal intercourse. I might soon become an honorary Bulgarian.

'Is a little hard to understand,' she said. 'But funny!'

Bulgarians do funny? And Dickens? Surely the dialect, often difficult even to a modern English ear, twisting syntax and exuberant run of sentences, much less the critique of English Victorian values, would be impenetrable to her? But, now I thought of it – and I sincerely did not wish to, the thoughts simply came unbidden, as my old teacherly reflexes kicked in – there was a lot there to which she might easily relate. Dickens is a champion of the poor, he gives them stories and voices and entitles them to respect. And *Oliver Twist* was a reasonable choice: the children, the poverty and need, the pathos of the workhouse, the clear-cut distinction between good and bad, innocent and depraved.

'Well,' I said, 'tell me what you like about it.'

She had neither the language nor any familiarity with the period, but she was engaged and comfortable in the company of a book.

'I like,' she said, 'very much. Good stories, and he is on right side. Is good man.'

'Yes, he is. Very good.'

She paused for a moment. 'You too, I think. You are good man also.'

God knows why she should have thought so, but I was alarmed none the less, and during her next few visits kept my distance.

A month later it was *Hard Times* – 'I go to school like this, bad teacher,' she said.

'When you were a girl?'

'Of course.'

'Was that in Sofia?'

'Yes.'

We were both uncomfortable, entering this mildly personal new ground.

'Your parents live there now?'

'Yes.'

'What do they do?'

'Father university teacher. Languages. Retired now. They have no money, pension in Bulgaria only £40 a month. Not enough. I help them.'

She can hardly have made £10 an hour from her agency. If she was sending money home, it was hard to imagine how she lived on the rest.

'Hard times,' I said.

'Always,' said Bronya. 'What else?'

Some weeks later she was reading *Bleak House*, as if seeking legal redress for the many problems of the world.

I approved, it is my favourite Dickens text. 'It's a wonderful book! It shows that justice is a farce, and the law is an ass.'

She looked shocked. 'Is an arse?'

'No, like a donkey or a mule: slow, plodding and stupid. Human life is too complicated to be governed by such a blunt instrument. It shows how absurd the legal system is, and how cruel.'

She nodded, as if forgiving the crudely mixed metaphors. 'Is like Kafka,' she said.

We were eating quail's eggs, which she initially supposed to come from a miniature chicken, and wild smoked salmon, which I slice with my Yanagi sashimi knife. Bronya asked to try, and I was reminded again, with increasing alarm, that once you lower your guard and ease your boundaries, an intruder comes storming through.

I repeated my mantra – 'he who forms a tie is lost' – but I was in danger of capitulating. It was curiously agreeable to talk about Dickens again.

'Perhaps the other way round,' I said.

She looked puzzled.

'Kafka is like Dickens. Because Dickens came first.'

'All books,' she said, 'come at same time.'

It kept me awake, that line. I don't know, quite, why it should have intrigued and irritated and astonished me that Bronya should make such an observation. Perhaps I was embarrassed not to have made it myself?

She was right. We teachers and students of literature consult our chronologies, map out influences and continuities, talk about the periods of literature as if they were discernibly distinct. But in the very reality of reading and of talking about books, it is all glooped up together. Chaucer side by side with Dickens, Shakespeare with Ted Hughes. Like with like-ish, one text, or moment, or sentiment, stimulated by the other, like passengers on the same train, however disparate they look, moved by the same impulse, heading in the same direction.

That's not quite right. I'm not sure I can get this right. T.S. Eliot said something similar, though not so elegantly or concisely as Bronya's single phrase, which she tossed off without ceremony, as if wishing me a good afternoon. It was something she knew, about which she didn't need to make a fuss. Surely everybody knows that? All books come at same time.

It was worth losing sleep over. Anyway, I can't sleep, and Bronya's aperçu, and my vain attempt to generalise from it, were welcome replacements for my usual, harrowing night-time obsessions.

I sit up much of the night. I can't be bothered to read any more, and most of the time I can't write either, though I try, strain, and produce little lumps. It makes me feel worse – bloated and unreleased. I thought I could write my way out of this, but I'm just writing my way further in.

Suzy said sometimes you have to hit rock bottom, but bottom for her wasn't all that low, she had no aptitude for genuine misery, her former depression now seems thin and histrionic.

I'm a lot lower than that. And still descending. The earth

is over my head, the light dimmed, the suffocating void descending.

'Tell me about him. Is married?'

Bronya was becoming more and more interested in Dickens the man.

'He had a poor background, hardly any education. His father went to debtors' prison.'

'What is that?'

'If you did not pay your debts, you were sent to gaol until you did. Often your whole family went with you. It was a most appalling institution, because it treated debt as if it were a felony and not a civil offence.'

It was not clear if she understood this, but she nodded for me to carry on.

'Anyway, he married too young, to a rather simple woman named Catherine, who bore him ten children . . .'

'Ten! Is a Catholic?'

'No, most Victorians had large families. A compliant wife was very useful to Dickens, for a time. He had his work to do, travelled widely, worked like three Trojans, supported charities, gave public readings of his works. He was amazing. But after they'd had all those children – he only ever wanted three – he got fed up with Catherine, who was often ill, never very good company, and had grown fat and indolent.'

'So what? She had hard life.'

'He eventually left her, and carried on with a girl actress, though very discreetly. He was in the public eye, but Victorians were good hypocrites and dissemblers. He couldn't be seen in the company of an eighteen-year-old.'

'Eighteen!'

'There's no need to be so rigid. He was a genius.'

I was astonished to be talking so frankly with her – indeed, to be talking at all. Of a sudden the barriers were if not down, at least eased. I was anxious to educate her, and she was proving surprisingly recalcitrant and provocative.

'Now who is stupid? I know mens . . . He leaves childrens and fat mother. Is wicked behaviours.'

'Is not! Needs a little understanding. He was a man of remarkable and relentless encrgy. No doubt he had his faults . . .'

She nodded. 'In Bulgaria we say, "there are no heroes without wounds".'

'Exactly!'

'But he is causing wounds, not receiving them. Is no hero!'

It was more than exasperating having Dickens – Charles Dickens, for goodness' sake! – abused by my semi-literate cleaner.

'Perhaps your not being English makes all this a bit difficult?'

'What? What you say? Bulgarians don't know good from bad? You are crazy and rude and stupid.'

'You're right, I'm sorry.'

'I go now!' she said, and walked from the kitchen, slamming two doors on her way out.

The next week the agency emailed to inform me that Bronya had called in sick, and that they could send a substitute if I wished. I did not. I wanted Bronya. I was not fond of her, I was used to her. I knew more or less how to use her, and had no desire to train someone else, even for a day. Unlike Suzy, I don't trade in my cleaners for new models.

And here's a bad sign, or perhaps it is a symptom, though

I don't know of what. In her absence I started reading Bulgarian poetry. Or, not to be entirely alarmist, I Googled 'Contemporary Bulgarian Poetry in Translation', and was offered more of the stuff than I would have thought possible. But people, even Bulgarians it appears, will go on writing their poems, no matter how hard their schoolmasters (if they are any good) attempt to dissuade them. Composing verses is a reprehensible and self-regarding activity, likely to lead to the most appalling psychic inflation: *I am a poet!* As if the moniker established a kind of wisdom, or enticed more partners into your bed.

If you must express your feelings, I used to counsel my boys, much better to keep a diary than to write a poem. Write poetry as a last resort, and only if you have independent confirmation that you are reasonably good at it. People should need a licence merely to write poems, and to pass an advanced test before they take them on the road.

This goes for Bulgarians as well. Why shouldn't it? I am offered the following, by one Ivan Borislavov − perhaps he is one of the *-ovs* she first mentioned? − who, like Bronya, is from Sofia and is about my age, so we share him across space and time:

Odyssey

We are the illegitimate children of
    freedom,
we are the fallen angels with broken
    wings.
We were the boatswains of the
    cursed frigate
damned to sail in the impenetrable
    fog . . .

If there were a contest for how many risible metaphors you can squash into four lines, we have a possible winner here. Saying so – even in the privacy of this journal – makes me feel guilty, though I am not clear, even, who I might be offending. Not Mr Borislavov. Bronya? I will never mention Mr B to her, under pain of death by a thousand clichés.

I feel no compunction about belittling these verses. That's often what criticism is for, and much pleasure is to be had from caustic exercise, sharpening one's discriminations, learning ruthlessly to distinguish between the good, the less good and the excremental. And this is a pile of the latter unless: (a) Might it be badly translated? Or perhaps (b) Maybe it is too foreign? Maybe a Bulgarian might swoon on reading it, as metaphor piles on metaphor and thickens the goulash?

I don't have enough to do, and my control over my thoughts and feelings has slackened – since Bronya came into my home. I will not say my life. She is not in my life. And she is rarely in my home. And even that, it is becoming clear, is too often.

When you feel a lump developing, cut it out. It may hurt a bit, but it prevents the spread of something potentially deathly.

Dear Sir or Madam,
I have, for the last months, employed a weekly cleaner from your agency, who comes every Thursday. Except for last week, when she was apparently ill. I believe her name is Bronya.
    I write to say that I no longer have need of her services.

Might I add that she has been reliable, and I have no complaint to make of her services?

Yours sincerely,

Dr James Darke

I had developed an irreversible antipathy to Golde, as his fellows had, but I did not indulge and refine it as a boy might, instead reminded myself, again and again, without any diminution in my dislike – no, dislike is wrong, what I felt was a kind of exasperated abhorrence for this boy who was so wilfully and so cleverly resistant, and undermining – of everything that I had been trying to do for – and with – him and his Friday afternoon set.

There was a rumour that he was Jewish, though my enquiries suggested a more conventional upbringing, distinctly unHebraic. Anyway Golde, as I remarked to one of my colleagues, is hardly a Jewish name.

He raised his eyebrows. 'Goldberg, originally, I'd bet. They used to change it to Gold, but now people see through that one. Trying to pass. They often do.'

I was mildly irritated by this. Just because a boy is clever, attention-seeking and physically uncoordinated doesn't necessarily make him a Jew.

Golde was not a member of the tribe. He was descended from rather a grand Catholic family. The English – the Church of England, white, proper English – have a proud tradition of hostility towards both Jews and Catholics. But Jews, though recognisable and easily parodied, are more a danger to themselves than to others. Catholics, on the other hand, are a murderous lot. Inquisitors and torturers, to this day they would deny the starving poor the benefits of contraception.

Golde was one of us, almost. Not merely because he was some sort of a Christian, bless his soggy socks. It was impossible, if you made some effort of sympathy – and making efforts of sympathy is, after all, supposed to be what reading is about – not to see that he represented, in some extreme form, a regression to our common human ground, to our childish ways. After all, what is this creature of Tolkien's, this Gollum, but the figure of the inner child, twisted and distorted – defined, really – by greed and need, an embodiment of something universally repellent about us all?

It was only when I had a child of my own – the dear, the often very dear Lucy – that I understood for the first time what those Catholics mean by original sin. For the very dear Lucy was, often, too often, a hellion of demand-ingness. That's what little ones are like. If God had not graced them with the smiles and beguiles, we'd throw them out the window, and nobody who'd had a child would fail to understand.

Stinker and Slinker – two of Gollum's many names. All babies are stinkers and slinkers, nappy-fillers and self-interested seducers, ready with a smile to get their ways, or a howl in case that doesn't work. What a piece of work is a child, these Gollums of the night, somatic baskets of need and ruthless manipulation.

Many of the boys knew their Tolkien, though unlike the boys of my own generation, they had outgrown him by their teenage years and looked back on their former enthu-siasm with amused disdain. They cared no more for him, in their mature schoolboy incarnations, than they cared for Winnie the Pooh or Ratty and Mole. When that awful trio of films came out a few years ago, done by that bushy Australian chap, one of the boys remarked to me that it was basically just like a video game, only too long and boring.

'All it consists of, sir, is the same battle over and over again, with the volume increased each time.'

I wasn't clear, not having seen these movies, what he meant.

'Well, you start with a small group of apparently peaceful little creatures, and all of a sudden they face a threat. Surprise! They overcome it. And then they face even bigger threats. And they overcome them! End of first film. Two more films, loads more threats. Orcs in their tens of thousands! And the Hobbits win again!'

'It sounds a bit stupid, like most epics.'

'By the end, sir, I felt really sorry: it was a slaughter. Orcacide! Those Hobbits are killing machines!'

'A useful lesson about the English, do you think? Our mild exterior is only a mask. Provoke him sufficiently and your average Englishman is a cauldron of darkness, with unsuspected depths of aggression and audacity.'

He was too young to recognise the truth of this, but nodded wisely, thinking, I suppose, of drunken yobs and football hooligans.

Most old people can't sleep, they wake in the night, get up and eat toast and marmalade, go back to bed, sleep fitfully, dream a little. In fact, we sleep more than we know, for Suzy often shook me to stop my snoring, when I was perfectly clear that I was wide awake, and thinking.

'Snoring!' she said. 'Out like a light. Would you turn the other way? That might help.'

I also have an analogous problem, a sort of shadow sleeplessness. I can't stand being awake. I pace the house, read a bit, but hardly remember any of it, drink another glass of claret, and begin to feel the wrong side of agitated, though still the right side of panicky. In this middle ground, as my anxiety thermometer rises, I get into bed at tea-time, more able to nap than to sleep in the evening, even when that damn dog starts barking.

The bedroom was hot, stifling, humid. Dust filled the air, or perhaps it was those floaters on my retina? I could hardly distinguish what was actually out there from what I projected into it. It was impossible to sleep. Perhaps that was to be expected, I brought it on myself. I eat too little, and sometimes vomit when I do, now smoke three Montecristo No. 2s a day, which make me dizzy and toxic, drink coffee rather than water before going to bed. Add a bottle of Berry Brothers best ordinary claret with (often instead of) dinner, and you perfect the insomniac mix.

I turned out my bedside lamp. Not in anticipation of sleep – fat chance – but in order to feel, however futile the gesture, that I was orchestrating the proceedings. I turned onto my right side, pulled the Egyptian cotton sheet up to my chest, scrunched up my goose-down pillow, adjusted and readjusted it until comfort was perfect, and there was no tension in my neck. Breathed deeply and slowly, trying to clear my mind. And then I lay there, with my curtains closed, no light whatsoever penetrating the darkness, and tried *not* to will myself to sleep. That wouldn't work. Neither meditation nor masturbation would get me off. I would have turned onto my other side, but if I did I would hear my heart beating, and I get enough trouble from that sad recalcitrant organ anyway. I preferred to pretend it wasn't there. Sometimes it's not.

I was feverish, nauseous with the smell of six-day-old red lilies, their water stinking of death, a begloomed ruminant of the entropics. I longed for even the briefest of naps, even dreams, distressing though they are, were still preferable to this roiling agony. I took ten milligrams of Valium, usually enough to guarantee an hour of rest, if you could call it that.

Once I begin to think, I am full of sorrow, and I can do nothing but think. In these desperate hours, re-reading works best. I worked my way through the Sherlock Holmes stories once again. If someone were to quiz me by reading aloud a single paragraph, I could have named the story from which it was taken.

The tales have a lovable simplicity, and like Dr Watson I was impressed by Holmes, though not by his ratiocinative powers, which are shallow and showy, but by his self-confidence, his capacity to invent himself. But I knew the stories too well, the Valium began to work and the book dropped from my hand.

But a drug-induced nap is also a watchful one, and I woke with a start. Something was wrong. I wondered if I might have had a nightmare. But that wasn't it – it wasn't a dream, someone was inside the house. I was quite unable to move, struck down with terror, I looked about the room for possible implements of self-defence. In my wardrobe there were shoe trees – though they had shoes in them – and wooden hangers . . . No golf clubs. Or shotguns. I was defenceless.

It was hard to say how many minutes had passed. The intruder – please God there was only one – must have been aware there were people in the house, and been anxious not to stir them. I lay like a corpse, rigormortised with fright, my breathing harsh and strained, my heart scrabbling in my chest, desperate as a hamster in a handbag.

And that third step on the stairs made its tell-tale creak.

My wallet was on the bedside table, and thank God had

over a hundred pounds in it. I had my vintage Cartier Tonneau watch, some gold Dunhill cufflinks. Bargaining chips perhaps, assuming that my intruder was a mere burglar and not also a lunatic.

I wanted to shout – I tried to shout – 'I know you are there! I am calling the police!' but my voice was a strangulated croak, like a frog singing Wagner. Even if I could have summoned a human voice to make my complaint, I had no phone at the bedside.

I tried to sit up, to look less a victim, and tucked the sheet around me. I had an absurd desire to comb my hair. My eyes were fixed on the doorknob. Time passed, seconds perhaps, even minutes. I thought I could hear tiny footsteps, but the carpets in the hallway were thick wool, installed to muffle any sound. The doorknob began to turn.

Summoning my will and freeing the paralysis of my vocal chords, I managed to murmur a protest. 'I have money. Don't hurt me!'

The door opened fully. 'You shush yourself,' said her voice. 'Is only me. Is surprise!'

I sat up abruptly as she entered the room. It astonished me how quickly my fear transformed to rage.

'You stupid fucking woman!' I tore off the sheets off and shook myself, as if the residual terror could slip away like raindrops from a tin roof. 'You break into my house, you scare me to death, and you call that a surprise? Are you totally insane?'

'I rang bell, no answer. Is not middle of night, is only six o'clock. I call you from hallway, but no answer, so I come upstairs . . .'

I glared at her.

'Sorry, am very sorry.' She waved her hand in the air as if conducting the orchestra of regret. Tears formed in her

eyes. 'I know,' she said, backing away slowly. 'I make tea.'
She turned and went out of the doorway, descending the
steps quickly, trying to put an end to our frightful, inappropriate, embarrassing episode.

I pulled myself together, straightened the bedclothes and
joined her in the kitchen, where she was pouring the boiling
water into the teapot.

'Stop that right now! I want you to leave my house.
How dare you break in like this?'

She had the temerity, or self-confidence, to laugh. She
was no longer apologetic, nor even sheepish, entirely
self-composed, and infuriatingly, inexplicably proud of
herself. 'Not broken in. Is impossible for me. I made copy
of key after you fire me.'

'Go!'

'No,' she said, carrying the pot and a jug of milk to the
table. 'Sit down. We talk.'

It was quite impossible to persist in my indignation. And
I owed her, I thought, as I sipped the restorative tea – how
sad and predictable we English are – both an apology and
an explanation.

'Bronya,' I said hesitantly, suppressing an impulse to take
her hand, 'I am so sorry to have treated you so badly.'

'No worry, worked out good. Now on Thursday I do
tutoring, got pupils from Bulgarian Embassy.'

'Tutoring? Surely you don't . . .'

She laughed. 'Not English, stupid. A level Chemistry and
Biology. Pay is good. I like very much, maybe soon no more
cleaning. Maybe I give thanks to you!'

'No,' I said. 'You don't. Not at all. But I need to tell you
some things . . .'

'Shush!' She stood up from the table, walked behind me
and placed her hands on my shoulders, massaging them

gently. The firm feel of the silk against my skin was indescribably nostalgic, and though not aroused, I felt as if I might swoon.

'But I know.'

'What? What do you know?'

'Everything. For smart man you very stupid,' said Bronya. 'Maybe you go back to bed now?'

She paused for a moment.

It was my own bloody fault. I should've known better. It's built into the structure, irresistible. We teachers experience it all the time. You offer yourself modestly as an example of high intelligence and refined sensibility: urbane, knowledgeable, cultured. Is it any wonder they want to be like you? And *with* you?

But teaching eventually left a bad taste, and the efforts of the boys – now grown men, bless them – to keep in touch felt regressive to me. Both for them – give it up, for pity's sake! – and for me. I was no longer their schoolmaster, nor did I wish to garner their belated gratitude for having subjected them to a regime that may have done them more harm than good. All that reading and listening and second-hand seeing, storing up and deploying the voices of others, whose life-experiences – if you can have such things in literature – are different to their own. A widening of sympathy was supposed to ensue and accumulate. It didn't. Not for me.

Of course I answered their letters, but I soon weaned them off the fantasy that I might become their friend. After a time the clipped quality of my responses ensured that no correspondence, much less meeting, was likely to ensue. I don't have many friends, thank God, and plan to have even fewer as I get even older. And they will not include ex-pupils, though every now and again they crop up, as boys from a great public school are likely to. I sometimes wish I had taught at a comprehensive: you are unlikely to encounter the successful career of your former charges in quite the same numbers.

Yet I have to admit there was something fascinating about it, having known the child, to map him onto the public figure that he was to become. One boy – I never taught him – did A level Art, plus two other subjects just to fill in the blanks, for he was relentlessly set on a career in the vanguard of contemporary painting – and he made it. I vaguely remember him, dressed according to some laughable sixteen-year-old idea of what an artist is supposed to look like: baggy trousers, filthy cravatty scarf, leather jacket and boots, wild hair. Lots of black. Cigarette (hand-rolled). He had decided to call himself S. Rimington, instead of the Oxbridge norm of a double initial, or his full name, which was Sebastian.

For his A-level project he created a 'construction' made entirely of tobacco rolled into various coloured papers, and then assembled into buildings based on the School Hall and Library. The idea was that they should be set on fire in public, but the Head was unwilling to sanction such a conflagration. No reasons were given, but they would certainly have included the dangers of passive smoking and insurance problems, as well as critical acumen. It was rumoured that a generous amount of the tobacco was wacky baccy. The idea was symbolically to burn us down while getting the whole school stoned. Even without the public conflagration of his construction, though, S. was given an A by the examiners, who were not required to justify their decision.

He later made his reputation with an installation, as I

think they are now called, at the Whitechapel Gallery, which was entitled *Jigsaw: Puzzle*, and consisted of a room with boxes full of variously coloured 'pieces' which the visitors to the exhibition were invited to arrange into one of the frames set on tables around the gallery. Like Mondrian, only even stupider. The key to this – according to *The Guardian* it was a 'brilliant and ironic conceit' – was that all the pieces were square, but of different sizes. Consequently there was not – as art properly insists – some overall pattern, some authorial or artistic control. There was simply a multiplicity of possible shapes and combinations of colours. No inevitable shape, which is what artists impose, just a bunch of inter-changeable pieces. Put them together like this, or that, or the other! It doesn't matter – each to his own, every arrangement a new form of art, every arranger his own artist. No form. No content. Just whatever pattern of colour the individual 'artist' might choose.

The result of this risible rubbish, this unwillingness to take seriously the role and function of the maker, is that S. Rimington (having made his name) made his name, and was quickly annexed to that category of Young British Artist, that brainless bunch who have abandoned entirely the imper-ative to make something coherent, organic and satisfying in itself (never mind beautiful), rather than the enactment of some half-arsed idea. Or 'concept' as it is called. They are, all of them, the products of art colleges in which eighteen-year-olds were encouraged – indeed obliged, drawing and painting having been abandoned as hopelessly outdated crafts – to express themselves, develop their ideas, explore new concepts. But teenagers are callow and self-important, cannot tell a concept from a condom, and have no skills whatsoever in the transmission of ideas (if they had any) onto paper (not) or canvas (certainly not) – but onto some floor, or open space, or treetop, or boudoir. Tracey Emin's bed! Did her mother never teach her to make it, and to straighten up after a night of debauchery? Are there no well-brought-up artists any more?

I had an invitation to the opening party, at which Rimington (S.) was going to give a little talk, after which the gathered throng would be invited to make and to solve their own Puzzles, while being videotaped as they worked. The resultant variations on a theme would then be streamed live for the rest of the show, on an enormous wall at the rear of the gallery.

It was a prospect that I found resistible. I sent S. a brief note, and signed it J., regretting my incapacity to attend. I didn't add any details. Suzy, on the other hand, decided to go, I suspect to spite me. God knows she had been exposed to my views, and knew that I would regard her visit to the opening as an act, if not of treachery, at least of provocation. The treachery itself was exposed a few weeks later, when an 'original' artwork, which she had constructed dutifully on the night of the opening, and then purchased, arrived at the door, delivered by an android gallery boy of the standard sub-Armani type.

Suzy being out at the time, I opened the box and took out whatever you wish to call a Rimington, other than horseshit. A picture? A sculpture? An installation? Not only was the category unclear, so was the maker. Suzy had put it together herself. But as S. observed in the printed notes to the catalogue, the work in (t)his show was collaborative. He supplied the shapes, the sizes, the colours, the frames, the occasion. His co-equals put these given pieces into a new shape of their own. 'Thus,' S. concluded, 'deconstructing the autonomy of the artist, producing a work of art which can be traced to the dialectic between artist and onlooker, in which the latter becomes an artist and the former himself an onlooker. The artistic gaze is irrevocably dual.'

Rimington (S.) apparently believes that if the term 'artist' has to be used at all, we have to erase or cross it out at the same time. I'm not clear what this means, though it's much how I feel about him.

I hate the telly. Stupid stuff. But occasionally, in a weak moment, I turn on the *News at Ten*. On one such foolish evening, I was informed that the Prime Minister, blessed be his name, had reshuffled his dog-eared pack and come up with a new Minister of Education. And there, staring down the screen like a demented adult child, was the egregious Golde.

'Gollum!' How bloody marvellous! He looked – Foetus Hague is another example, and Gummy Millipod, who killed his brother – like someone whose inner child persists in the visage of their outer adult, whose grown-up manifestation is unnatural, macabre and mildly alarming. A confirmation, if one was needed, that we are indeed being led by a gang of incompetent schoolboys.

Why can't other people see this too? Or is it sufficiently common in politicians of the most thrusting kind, this regressive self-centredness, accompanied by an adult capacity to mask it in the phony voice of concern, and the learned facial tics and grimaces that are supposed to pass for compassion? Think: Margaret Thatcher, showing sympathy. It's no wonder every politician needs spin doctors and image-enhancers. They change their views, alter their voices and bodily carriage, and the more they do so the less convincing they are. The mere desire to run for high office ought to disallow holding it.

And there was old Golde, Golluming away about his Precious Education!

I have had an impertinent email from George. There was no need, so far as I could anticipate, for him ever to initiate contact, but it was my own fault. He alone knew how to get in touch.

And today, this:

My Dear,

Do forgive me this, because there are, I believe, two formidable reasons to disobey your injunction to leave you alone for a goodly time. The first of these, I think you will agree, is not unamusing. The second I am initiating with some trepidation. On moral grounds, as we used to call them at school.

I recently received – or you have received, to put it properly – a letter with the embossed seal of the House of Commons, delivered by Registered Post. Though the postie was reluctant to allow it, I signed for it on your behalf, explaining that you were out of the country. I must admit to opening it. How could I not? And can you credit this? – It was from Golde, recently installed in a rather grand position in the government. A walking embodiment, one might call it, of the Peter Principle, though I always had a lurking respect for the boy. Unlike his fellows, he had a voice of his own. Sly, to be sure. But neither entirely disagreeable, nor stupid. I sometimes found him amusing, when I wasn't repelled by him.

I suppose I still feel the same, encountering him in his adult incarnation. Are you aware of this? I have no idea how you live now, whether you have severed your connections to the world so thoroughly that you have abandoned the news, and the new. Our new Secretary of State for Education is forming an Advisory Board on the Arts in Secondary Education, to consist of ten carefully selected worthies, and writes to ask if you would do him the honour of serving on it?

I presume you will not answer this request, and unless you tell me otherwise, I will inform the Minister that you are not available for public service.

My second reason for writing, though, is more pressing, and I apologise for raising the matter. You/I have received, over the months of our agreement, a series of letters from Lucy – she always puts a return address, so I know it to be her – and I have not thrown any of them away. The most recent have notes on the envelopes themselves. Typical: 'DAD, FOR GOD'S SAKE READ THIS, I NEED TO SEE YOU! WHY ARE YOU DOING THIS TO ME?'

I find this heart-breaking. I am chagrined that you should be so adamantine in your withdrawal. Surely some sign, some glimmer of response, some acknowledgement is called for? It is a cruel and unusual punishment for her, and I am aware that you have always adored Lucy. Why would you cause additional pain, after all that you both have gone through?

Can I beg you to answer her in some way or other, however slight, and however strong your reasons – I cannot, quite, fathom them – for remaining so cruelly aloof.

Forgive me for saying so.

Your old chum,

George.

I was sufficiently astonished and distressed by this to turn off the computer and to walk away. I may have been hyperventilating, but I'm not sure what that entails. I cannot recall being so angry since my battle with Spikedog. I will not be bullied in this manner. I cannot bear being the focus of George's interest. Or anyone else's.

Or indeed my own. I do not write in this journal because I am interested in myself. I bore myself silly. These notes and evasions and snippets are mere distractions: I am rummaging in my effects, reduced to this. It's rather agreeable actually to have something to do.

Dear George,
I am sorry you have felt obliged to disregard my clear instructions. But as you have done so, and in the spirit of marginally diminished curmudgeonliness, here are my answers:

    1. Write to the Minister. Say NO. Perhaps you might convey to him my view that 'The Arts' ought not to be taught at secondary level at all. Better to teach young persons to enter trade, or to learn one.

    2. Throw Lucy's letters away.

Never write to me like this again. If you cannot avoid doing so, for your moral reasons, then do not write to me at all.

Yours,
James

MAN SAVED BY FUCKING THE CLEANER!

Was I tempted? Not at all. Better than that, I was flattered, and better yet, touched, and best of all, momentarily breathless with sensuous pleasure. I held onto her hand fiercely for a few moments, but quickly repressed the impulse. Give in to that, and lips are next. I remember the drill. It escalates, it rises. I didn't.

I may not have fucked the cleaner – God forbid! – but it was well nigh time to fuck the dog. Revenge is a dish best served hot. Hotter. It was time to do some serious research! I love the internet, that library of information and misinformation, the hunting ground of thieves and butchers. What surprises me is not how much malice I find there, but how little.

And so useful when you need something, if like me you have retired from the world. If you Google 'What is the world's hottest sauce?' you get a number of links. I chose 'Chilliworld's Top Ten Hottest Sauces'. The third was distinctly promising:

ChilliPepperPete Congealed Dragons Blood. This is a [sic] even hotter version of the bestselling Dragons Blood. Pete says that the concentrated flavours and heat makes this bad boy over 5 million scovill. £19.95

A 'Scovile', I gather, is a scale named after Wilbur Scoville, who calibrated chilli hotness in 1912. Sixteen million is as hot as you can get: 'Pure capsaicin and Dihydrocapsaicin'. But, persevering, I found ChilliPepperPete's apparently lethal concoction was but a strawberry milkshake compared to:

Blair's Collector's Reserve bottle contains 16 million Scoville Units of Pure Capsaicin. The tiny 1-ml vial inside contains pure capsaicin crystals, hottest element known to man. Nothing in the world could get hotter then [sic] this 16 Million Reserve. Be among the few to get one of these limited edition bottles. No more the [sic again] 999 of Blair's 16 Million Reserve will be produced.

The reviews were promising: 'Back when I was in my frat phase and dinosaurs roamed the earth a frat bro dared me to dump a tsp of this on my tongue. Lo! The earth was covered in magma for forty days and forty nights! Hell had released all fury on my bowels!'

Sounded good to me. I dislike frat boys almost as much as Spikedogs. That the amount of hot stuff was so minuscule, and the price so extravagant (£245), reassured me. This was just the bad boy for my bad dog. Anyway, it's always better to buy the best. I'm not rich enough to buy cheap things.

My only fear was that Blair's Reserve would not just teach Spikedog a lesson, it might kill him. That's the problem with employing your nuclear deterrent. You can't learn anything if you are dead. Death is not a punishment, whatever the proponents of its capital variety may argue. Prison is a punishment. Misery and pain and despair and solitary confinement are punishments. Blair's Reserve is palpably a punishment. I should recommend it to the good ol' state of Texas, it would save them a fortune in hangings, or however they execute their villains. They only need to incinerate their tongues, and bowels. That'd learn 'em.

The tiny well-wrapped vial arrived six days after I sent my order, accompanied with the direst warnings about overuse – which meant virtually any use at all – and especially about getting any of the devilish stuff on your skin. This would apparently be exceedingly unpleasant, and the resultant hole would end up in Peking.

Perfect. That very evening, wearing two pairs of rubber gloves, I inserted the crystals into a piece of fillet steak, which I then coated with Tabasco, to make sure it looked and smelled the same as Spikedog's accustomed hotty treats.

It wasn't. After I lobbed the napalm accurately into his chosen locale, he approached it with barely repressed delight, like a drinker in a bar who orders his Bloody Mary extra spicy. He gobbled it down, and looked up at my window with as grateful a look as could sit upon his hideous features. Dumb mutt.

There ensued a short pause as he began to feel something new, and different. And worse. And then – trust me on this, it is not fanciful – he levitated like an overfilled but unknotted balloon suddenly released, you could imagine him spiralling upwards making rude noises, diminishing as he got further away and the air ran out, then tumbling back to Earth as a soggy bit of rubber.

As he landed, his legs splayed out, in imitation of the sort of tiger-skin rugs Sir Henry would have placed in Ayah's bedroom, if he'd been allowed.

Furious activity ensued at both ends of the wretched creature. If his previous howls, at their most piteous, were, say, 500 on the Scoville Howling Scale, of a sudden he was at 5,000 and rising. If a dog can scream, he was screaming. Windows opened above his garden, and in the adjoining houses.

'Shut up, you fuckin' mutt!' the neighbours chorused. Spikedog screamed louder. His tongue hung so far out of his slobbering mouth that you would have supposed him trying to rid himself of it entirely, to excise it at the junction with his throat.

At the other end, my chilli pepper was proving a catalyst

for the universal organic truth: the body is a mechanism for producing shit. It is inexcusable of me to mix metaphors like this – I can be quite strict on the subject – but he was mixing his. He was an open fire hydrant of sewage. He howled like a demented banshee (whatever that is), whirled like a dervish, trampolined up and down again, spewing as he bounced.

Spikeman hurried out, bare-chested, buckling his belt. 'Oy, darlin',' he said. 'What's up?'

Watching carefully from behind the curtains, I would have laughed, had I any laughter in me. Instead I gloated, a richer sensation by far.

Part II

It was dictated by her physical grace, the confidence that nothing could ever go wrong with her body. She'd suffered recurrent bouts of depression, whether caused by her inability to write, or the other way round. But through it all the physical glow was maintained. She kept up her tennis, joined Queen's Club after we moved to London, and actually improved as the years went by, until she had established herself as a high-quality club player.

Though she'd scorned doubles at Oxford – 'if I am going to lose I want to be responsible for it myself' – in middle age she came to enjoy it more and more. Less physically demanding, more tactical. And anyway, most clubs do not allow singles play at peak hours. Yet another reason, Suzy remarked tartly, why this country cannot produce good players.

One afternoon, when they had a roll-up mixed doubles – you simply got matched up with whoever was hanging about – she was paired with a portly, middle-aged doctor named Lawrence Weinberg, a former Cambridge blue, who was genial, encouraging and possessed a solid all-court game. They teamed up, got on and became a regular partnership.

Too regular, I thought. Soon he – they – were Suzy's

major topic of conversation, for I had long since silenced her on the gossipy inwardness of London literary life, which I despised: who was likely to lose their job as literary editor, who'd switched agents or publishers, who'd be shortlisted for the Booker, who was fucking whom. Hah.

Suzy found more and more time, and excuses, for her new passion for mixed doubles. She was out a lot – didn't he have any doctoring to do? – and came home smiling, triumphant, and late. A shower after the match, a few drinks to wind down, home just in time for supper, which I was expected to provide, and would not. Often we went out, or without. I was aware that she would have liked some acknowledgement of her exalted state, some suspicion, some confrontation. Something dramatic.

I suspected that she had chosen him because he was Jewish – appetitive, highly educated, over-confident – because she thought it might provoke me. She would have been delighted if I'd put framed Hamas posters in my study, or added *The Protocols of the Elders of Zion* to my bedside table. Something to show that I cared. Anyway, I could hardly accuse her, could I? She had an affair. So what? I did too, more than once. People make such a fuss about the odd casual insertion. We had dinner with Lawrence and his perfectly adequate wife on a couple of occasions, but we were playing at being civilised, and I put an end to it.

I suspect that the sexual partnership ended within a year or two, but the tennis one went on and on. In the event what really mattered was that he was a doctor, and he was worried about her health. She and I had both noticed that she was low on energy, and that her throaty cough was less sexy, more insistent than it had been. Suzy shrugged it off. Illness was something that happened to other people, a sign of physiological imperfection that didn't pertain to her. An organic category mistake. If she was going to be ill, it would be mental, never physical. I cannot remember her having so much as a cold. Her increasingly husky voice, she insisted, was merely an attractive by-product of her cigarette smoking, not a symptom of some malady.

She didn't consult a doctor, maintaining that they were for the needy, seedy and weedy. But it was finally the doctor who consulted her. As she walked off the court, after a strenuous final rally, having twice successfully chased down a lob, only to lose the point and match to a drop shot, she stood by her chair gasping.

'Sit down,' Lawrence commanded, 'you've gone pale. I don't like the look of you at all.'

'I'm fine. Do shut up,' said Suzy, taking the courtside chair, coughing harshly, handkerchief to her mouth. 'You fucking doctors are such scaremongers.'

'Are you coughing up blood?'

'No, it's nothing. Hardly anything. Nothing. I just cough so much it makes my throat bleed.'

That evening Suzy got a phone call, and went into that hushed I'll-take-this-in-my-study mode that often indicated that something was up. I ignored it, and didn't ask who it was when she returned to the drawing room.

'That was Lawrence,' she said.

'Oh yes.'

'He's concerned about me. He thinks I need to get a check-up.'

'So do I. I've said so a lot. Why are you listening to him and not me?'

'For fuck's sake, this isn't a pissing contest! He's a doctor, and he says he would be grateful if he could set up an appointment for me.'

'With him? That's a bit rich . . .'

'Why? It isn't improper or unethical to use a friend as your physician.'

'Inappropriate comes to mind.'

'Not to me it doesn't. He just wants to oversee things, keep a doctorly eye out, pass me on to the right people. He wants me to see a specialist he knows, and have a chest X-ray and some tests.'

To my surprise, she made the appointments the next morning, a sure sign that she suspected something was wrong.

The tests took almost no time to organise. Good old private medical care. Suzy spent a few hours at the Chelsea and Westminster having blood tests, X-rays, CT scans, being prodded and poked about, which she despised, having no experience of it save for the processes associated with Lucy's birth – which she also had not liked. She had a monarch's relationship with her body: if anyone was going to examine it, she would have preferred to be covered by a sheet, aloofly modest and aristocratic, not because she was bashful, but because she was physiologically snobbish. She never forgave the hostile nurse at Lucy's birth, and vowed never again to allow herself to be handled by lesser organisms. The injunction, by now, often applied to me as well.

Lawrence's rooms were on Wimpole Street, which he regarded as smarter than Harley Street, which is an address designed to attract Arab hypochondriacs. Wimpole Street was more discreet, soaked in the medical tonalities of that neighbourhood, classy and understated, like living in Chelsea rather than Knightsbridge. Rather to my surprise, Suzy asked me to come with her, anxious that she might forget to ask the right questions, or remember their answers.

A smoothly tailored receptionist, middle-aged and impeccably banal, showed us to the waiting area, which looked like the drawing room of a house in which the owner had no taste but some money, with soft sofas, upholstered chairs, soothing and meaningless landscape paintings on the walls, stacks of newspapers and back issues of *Country Life* and *Tatler*.

Suzy gave it a quick glance with her usual disdain, turned down the offer of coffee and biscuits, and settled down with the latest novel by Teddy St Aubyn, the fashionably grungy society novelist whom she liked disliking. 'All that fine writing wasted on a bunch of shits,' she'd written in a review somewhere. 'Henry James would have been appalled.'

Lawrence came out to meet us personally – you get all the social graces with private medicine, especially when it was once conjoined with ongoing sexual care – shook my hand warmly, gave Suzy a studiedly brief hug, and ushered us down the corridor into his rooms. Sitting behind his desk, he looked at his computer screen and read for a moment before saying a word.

'It's bad, isn't it?' Suzy said.

He looked up quickly. He wasn't used to being pre-empted, and did not allow his patients (or friends) to make their own prognoses in their own words.

'I wouldn't put it that way . . .'

'How would you put it then?'

'I'd say we have a problem, but that it is – '

'Don't beat about the bush, for Christ's sake. What is the problem?'

'The biopsy shows that you have a growth on your lung.'

I had a notebook and pen to hand, and made a quick note. I was studying his suit jacket, as he sat with practised calm behind his reproduction Sheraton desk. A fine worsted material a shade darker than navy with a slightly lighter stripe, a black silk lining, the shoulders hardly padded: it fitted him well but not too closely, with none of that slightly larger than necessary off-the-peg looseness. The buttons were lustrous ebony secured with very fine thread, the lapels designed with his slightly portly build in mind. I would have bet a hundred pounds that it had either no label on the inside pocket, or something entirely discreet. *Not* the name of the tailor. Schneider of Golders Green? Never. The suit was like his Wimpole Street address: not Savile Row, probably better than Savile Row, and less expensive.

Suzy was unresponsive, and I hardly dared ask. 'A . . . growth? Do you mean a tumour?'

'Well, that's a blanket term, there are all kinds of growths and tumours.'

'Is it malignant?'

He smiled, patronisingly. 'Not a term I'd use. But it is cancerous, and I suggest we start treatment as soon as possible.'

I made a useless note.

'Now. Suzy, do you want the details?'

'Of course we do,' I said, pleased to take control, and her hand, establishing a spurious supremacy in the face of his overwhelming competence. And power.

His shirt was fine white cotton, hand-tailored perhaps, but I was unable to tell at the distance. It wouldn't have surprised me if he saved a few shekels by having them made a dozen at a time in Hong Kong. But his tie, the only piece of his apparel that he would have chosen himself, the key to how discriminating he really was, was quite wrong. Expensive to be sure, Zegna, I suspected. But it had too much of the wrong shade of red, in a pattern without aesthetic conviction, lacking both style and gravitas. Vulgar, as Italian designers frequently are.

He'd been talking on and on. Suzy looked blank.

'. . . sometime next week?' Lawrence looked at his computer screen, made a few adjustments and looked up. 'Chelsea and Westminster still OK with you?'

Suzy nodded.

'I'll send you an email confirming the details.'

He paused, and looked at her directly, personally. 'There's no reason not to be hopeful.'

'Hah!' Suzy snorted. 'Double negatives always give the game away! You think I am going to die!'

Lawrence laughed, with a hearty confidence. 'Of course you are.'

I made a note.

'. . . but not yet. We've got a lot of tools at our disposal. The prognosis with your kind of cancer is quite favourable. You've got a lot of tennis matches in you yet.' He smiled at her. '*We* do.'

We left his rooms soon after, ushered directly to the door, Lawrence standing between us (spoiler: meaningful metaphor), and giving us a reassuring hand on arm as we left.

'See you soon. And remember what I told you!'

'What was that?'

'No looking on the bloody internet!'

'Oh, that. Of course I will. Goodbye.'

We strolled down Wimpole Street for a few minutes, taking things in.

'What next?' I asked.

'Fat lot of use you were. Did you listen at all?'

'On the contrary. I looked. I was very unimpressed by his tie.'

She laughed, and took my arm. 'Bit of a disaster. He's so concerned to get things just so, but there's always the telltale sign, isn't there?'

'Always.'

'Anyhow, let's ring and book a table at the Wolseley. See if you can spot a taxi. I fancy some caviar and a bottle of Taittinger. Then let's go home and make love.'

This was ominous. She usually said 'fuck', not that we did it much. When I had recovered from being startled, I got frightened. She knew she was going to die.

At the Wolseley, I told Suzy I was going to retire from teaching.

'Good for you. I've finally given you an excuse. Left to your own devices you would have been carried out of that place feet first. At least now something good can come out of this.'

It was inexpressibly kind and brave of her, and I resented it very much. 'For goodness' sake, darling, I hardly need you to get cancer to make my decisions for me!'

'Of course you do. Don't you even know that?'

After we'd got home and made stately love, I wrote a post-coital letter to the Headmaster, announcing my retirement. I did not feel it necessary to give reasons, though they were more complex than Suzy's forthcoming decline, which was no business of his.

I ought to have done a bunk years ago. School-teaching was entropic: energy faded, differences distilled and normalised. The boys, clever and less clever, agreeable and less agreeable, began to merge into each other. This was not, I think, because after the passage of the decades one's memory simply congealed them into an undifferentiated adolescent mass, but because our college rules and traditions, strictures and structures, our common fund of history and anecdote, set texts and exams, sporting fixtures and cultural endeavours, produced a type. Most of the great public schools do.

By the end, as passion faded, I was a type as well. For a

time I resisted the process, but we masters were congealing too, and sometimes, in the Senior Common Room, I got the surreal and discomfiting impression that one of the others was me, or perhaps it was the other way round. Here we are, I observed, drinking rotten coffee and being witty and dismissive in a fond and bitchy way. Quoting, referring, citing, attaching Greek and Latin tags, self-satisfied, as individuated as a bunch of carrots – second-rate, second-hand.

I was inhabited, I could recognise – though a good deal of this becomes imperceptible over time – by the voices of others, in both high and low registers. By the internalised sentiments of the poets and novelists, by my mother's shrill homilies, and my father's hearty fatuities. I was the filter through which they passed and into whose mouth they issued. And the result, which is called ME, is little more than a melange of competing voices, a cacophony, unmelodious, often wracking and discordant, which, if we smooth and censor and rearrange, could be mistaken for something coherent.

A self? Forget it. Behind the façade of even the most orderly-looking of selves, the benign vicar or the cheerful butcher, is a maelstrom of opposing voices and forces, dark rumblings and regrets, yearnings to be elsewhere, other, and someone else, free and wild. Everyone is a moon, and has a dark side.

Those boys, had they followed my passionate admonitions, might have ended like me now – as a chamber in which everything and nothing echoes. I imposed on them the myriad voices of others, recommended them as constituent parts of developing being, suggested that such voices are easily assimilable, and even more dangerously suggested that they might become an authentic element of the developing self.

Why assume this? Why is the voice of that miserable

stringy Hamlet, wracked by guilt and indecision, or that dopey Wordsworth retreating into his gloomy lakeside cottage, to be recommended to the young? What do they know of such things? Their life experiences neither promote such musings and choices, nor recognise them as real. Literature is dangerous. You can define yourself in and through it, make yourself, try to become someone cultured, well read and referenced, big yourself up like a dentist's receptionist.

Literature doesn't mediate or explain our experience, it replaces it. I should have taught them that they have to choose: between the philosopher's silence or the shitslingers jabbering away. But I didn't know it at the time.

I am overcome by chagrin, contemplating this. I wonder if those once-innocent boys might forgive me? I wonder if they have even noticed? I rather hope not.

Suzy had cancer. Following the habit of a lifetime, I sought consolation in my reading – fading nosegays of wisdom to sniff when the life ordure became overpowering. Like that poor Joan D'Idiot after her hubby dropped dead at the breakfast table. Probably never felt more than a few cornflakes up his nose. Lucky him. And she, poor shocked thing, did what she could: consulted the great and the good, the sages, the geniuses on whom she – we – have been raised.

But let's face it, citing is the opposite of thinking: all this splashing about in the hot tub of literature merely appropriates the emotions and thoughts of others. You don't have to think or feel for yourself, just to pick and choose, like magpies assembling shiny trinkets of discarded verbiage.

We don't have God, so we have literature, with its associated proverbs and allegories, its received wisdom. We quote and genuflect and defer and pay homage, as if in a holy sanctuary. But just as God failed us, so too will reading. We will turn against it as certainly, and rightly, as we did against Him. Nobody, and nothing, can explain life for us. It's not a mystery, a problem or a puzzle, it doesn't have a meaning or a solution. It just is, make of it what you wish. Or better yet, just get on with it and hope for a modicum of good luck.

Reflexively leafing through my internal pages, I revert to Yeats, repair to Eliot, return to Dickens – and am disappointed in new and surprising ways: their lines have atrophied from insufficient exercise, or gone stiff with overuse. My rancid touchstones. The better known the sentiment, the less likely it is to retain its power. It will have turned into one of those homilies that we mistake for wisdom, from which we seek comfort:

> Consume my heart away; sick with desire
> And fastened to a dying animal
> It knows not what it is . . .

Wrong! Wrong again. Is there a poet who isn't a D'idiot? Not a dying animal, a dying *person*. Persons are dreadful at dying. Animals drop off the perch, fall asleep on the hearth, slink off into the woods feeling poorly. They have nothing to reflect upon, or to make a fuss about. Poor Josef K. in *The Trial*, whose pathetic final thought before he is executed is: 'like a dog'. Wrong! He'd be lucky to die like a dog.

Something's going to kill you. Why make a fuss? But we do, we do. We try to understand. I have to remember this in order to disremember, before it dismembers me. But I am not deluded, or fortunate enough, to expect consolation from scribbling. There is none, neither from others nor from oneself.

> Do you imagine you can exorcise what oppresses you in life by giving vent to it in art? No. The heart's dross does not find its way onto paper: all you pour out there is ink.

Suzy wasn't interested in the details of her forthcoming treatment, what drugs she was to be given, what the blood counts might indicate, what to expect next. These were things to be endured, and it did no good to anticipate them fearfully. There'd be plenty of time for dread. She did, however, have one pressing question.

'My hair?'

'Yes.' Lawrence's voice was firm but – to my ear at least – wistful. Presumably he loved Suzy's hair as much as I did.

'Will it fall out?'

'Almost certainly.'

'All of it?'

'Yes, I'm sorry, it's – '

'How long do I have?'

Lawrence looked startled. They had agreed that this was not a helpful question. 'I don't really think – ' he began.

'Before my hair falls out, dummy!'

'Oh. Sorry. It might happen quite quickly when the chemo starts, or perhaps – '

'Then,' said Suzy firmly, 'I'd better make some plans.'

Lawrence had done his homework, and handed her a print-out from his computer tray, listing all of the top wig-makers in London, who proudly offered real human hair. It was not clear what unreal human hair might have consisted of. Perhaps it might have been plucked from sheepdogs? All of these ghoulishly estimable businesses guaranteed that their wigs would be indistinguishable from an authentic headful, even to the most experienced eye.

I immediately joined Lawrence in suggesting we make an appointment. At least it was something to do. Perhaps, even, there might be some fun in it? A Marilyn Monroe wig, or an Audrey Hepburn? Suzy had always loved playing with different hairstyles, long and flowy one year, gamine the next, let the grey out, get rid of it, add some blonde streaks, use a bit of henna.

'Nope. Not for me, thanks. I'd loathe wearing some impoverished Croatian's hair while she has to languish behind the curtains until her hair grows back, just to pay for the groceries for a few months.'

'But darling,' I said, perhaps a little plaintively, 'you can't intend just to go bald.'

'I don't have any choice in the matter,' she said tartly. 'It's only a question of what I am going to do about it!'

'And . . .'

'Hats! I've always adored hats. I am well known for the audacity of my hats. I'll have a look around, see what I might resurrect . . . Or perhaps I might try something new.'

'Good idea,' I agreed. 'Why not discuss it with Lucy, she might have some ideas?'

'Lucy! You've got to be kidding.'

She was quite right. Lucy! How idiotic! 'Yes. She'd have you dressed like Paddington bear.'

There was a long pause as Suzy straightened up from her slumped position, and a light shone in eyes that had been dimmed with exhaustion and fear. 'Oh you little angel, you! You are so clever!'

'What'd I do?'

Lawrence leaned over his desk. 'Yes, what did he do?'

'He's got it! It will be so chic. A Paddington hat. With just enough bald peeping out underneath to make it whimsical and absurd and tragic at the same time. So memorable! Red! I might get a brown one as well!'

I hadn't seen her so animated in weeks. It's no wonder Freud didn't know what a woman wants. A Paddington hat!

Suzy searched for a source, but most such hats were for children, and she eventually had some made. After her hair fell out, and she began to wear them around town – when she could face it, or at home when she couldn't – others began to copy her. How adorable it was, how chic, how audacious! For a time it was infra dig to be seen without one. But the fad passed almost as quickly as Suzy did.

Suzy hated the metaphor. 'I am not battling cancer, fighting the good fight, my body is not being attacked. I am just dying of a disease. How mundane is that?'

Hers was the fashionable position, but wrong. If she didn't feel like a soldier, I did. It was war: we marshalled our forces, found the best generals and military advisers, sought reinforcements, gathered an extensive arsenal of weapons, hunkered down and prayed for victory. It was as cruel as war, as arbitrary, as inevitable and exhausting.

She took to her bed, and belatedly began to do her homework. She read cancer memoirs and a variety of death stories. Brave ones, scared ones, morbid ones, mordant ones, sentimental ones, trying-not-to-be-sentimental-but-failing ones. Long goodbyes. Soon enough she wanted to hurl them across the room, but hadn't the strength. She took to flipping them, one by one, wearily onto the carpet by the side of the bed, a pile of death droppings.

'Throw these away, will you?'

'Had enough?'

'You'd swear they got ill just to have a hot topic to write about. Must get cancer! It sells! Who the hell took these cancer fuckwits seriously before they tumoured out? Well, fuck them. It's bad enough lying here decomposing without having to transmit the gory details.'

'You're not tempted to write something or other?'

'No! Never ever ever. Not that I have much time. But I am not going to write a fucking word, or read another C.S. bloody Lewis whingeing away for Joy. They want consolation, do they?'

'Everyone wants − '

She picked up a book from her bedside table. 'Listen to this arsehole!'

> For what is it to die, but to stand
> naked in the wind and to melt
> into the sun?
> And what is it to cease breathing,
> but to free the breath from its
> restless tides, that it may rise and
> expand and seek God unencum-
> bered?

'Maybe it consoles some people who read it?'

'It's shite. I'll guarantee he wasn't dying when he wrote it! There is no fucking consolation. I'm not some sort of deluded Christian or cod smiling Buddhist. I am a modern woman. There is me, alone, and soon there will be no me.'

What to do, when there is nothing to be done? Soon enough my principles, my taste, a lifetime of fine discrimination lay in ruins. Needs must. I purchased a jumbo flat-screen telly − a man delivered it and spent three and a half hours fiddling and making an intolerable racket. We

hid in my study until he knocked at the door and demon-
strated his handiwork: the TV suspended on the wall
opposite our bed in defiance of the laws of both gravity
and aesthetics.

'There she is. A real beauty. Sixty inches – I don't do
many that big. I'll show you how to use the controls.'

'Is it difficult?'

'Not at all. You have a Sky box, and only one remote.
Piece of cake.'

Sky! I had none of the usual objections. I knew nothing
of it, not even enough to know if I wanted it or not. Rupert
Murdoch was not one of my wee beasties, though we had
friends who spat out his name with a venom previously
preserved for the Antichrist. But he provided programmes
that were worth watching, in our extremity. Arts programmes,
documentaries about nature, a history channel. Fodder to
pass the time as the time passes.

Box sets? I thought they were for chess pieces. It turned
out they contained discs with multiple episodes of
programmes. There were a bundle of them by that super-
annuated sweetie David Attenborough, whom Suzy adored.
Life on Earth . . .

We lay side by side on the bed, holding hands, with cups
of tea on the bedside tables, watching Mr Attenborough
and his travelling circus.

I plumped up her pillows, and made sure she was comfortable.

'Isn't this fun, my love?'

'He would have made a good undertaker. A voice to die
for, so soothing. I liked that praying mantis, I wish vicars
were like that.'

Once you buy one of those monster tellies, and then
you add Sky, the floodgates of necessity open, and to hell

with your standards. I now purchased an electronic reading machine. Next thing I knew we would have a bungalow in Basingstoke with all mod cons, a satellite dish on the front of the house, and a paved garden. So easy to maintain!

A Kindle? Why would I do that? It was not, of course, allowed into my study, where my books would scream with derision and anguish, as they were exposed to the future of reading. Not the future of books. Books have no future. Screens, that's what people want. Soon we will all be implanted with inner screens at birth, and grow up reading inside our eyelids, bumping into what used to be our fellow men, as in the rush hour at Paddington station.

That I had capitulated to this was a gloomy thought, though unaccompanied by regret. I needed my Kindle. I could sit and read from it to Suzy, with its spidery little light sticking out of its cover, while she half dozed in the dark.

It was hard to find something to read that could still hold her attention. She was bored by the newspapers, couldn't tolerate magazine fodder, was heartily sick of literature, had scant interest in the biographies and memoirs of worthies who no longer mattered to her.

I tried to find something that might amuse her. When we were freshers at Oxford, we'd joined the P.G. Wodehouse Society, 'which exists to entertain its members' but didn't, though Plum himself continued to. We read him to each other on holidays in country cottages in the rain, in modest gîtes and paradors in the heat of the afternoon. He was an agreeable travelling companion, like going abroad with an attention-seeking but amusing elderly uncle.

I suggested that we make a brief foray, to see if he still amused us. Or her.

She was a bit doubtful at first. 'I couldn't bear to plough through a whole book. His plots are risible, like the worst sorts of bedroom farces. Just read me the funny bits. Can you find that one I used to like, the one about critics?'

'Which book was it from?'

'Either *The Clicking of Cuthbert* or *Summer Moonshine*, I think.'

'Let me look . . . I think there's some sort of anthology or omnibus . . .'

I looked up and down the pages, filled with whimsies and felicities of the most evanescent sort, before coming upon one of my old favourites. I do an admirable Bertie Wooster and a stonking Jeeves, and here was a chance to resurrect them in miniature.

First Bertie, reedy, querulous, filled with boundless, unfounded self-assurance, but distinctly lacking a bit of the old gorm:

'I mean to say, I know perfectly well that I've got, roughly speaking, half the amount of brain a normal bloke ought to possess. And when a girl comes along who has about twice the regular allowance, she too often makes a bee-line for me with the love-light in her eyes. I don't know how to account for it, but it is so.'

Followed by Jeeves, who always begins with a pause, and whose gravid tones are those of a genuine purveyor of information, leavened with a suitable degree of irony. I lowered the register of my voice, made it both airy and orotund, which, as Bertie himself might remark, is rather a fine trick:

'It may be Nature's provision for maintaining the balance of the species, sir.'

I waited expectantly for a guffaw, or a slow hand clap of approval as at an Oxford cricket match. None was forthcoming.

Suzy looked thoughtful, and a bit sad. 'You know what? It's not funny any more. Gussie Fink-Nottle, for fuck's sake! I'm sick of P.G. Wodehouse.'

'Honestly Suzy, that's a bit rich. After all, he's not a shit-slinger. He's an antidote to wisdom!'

'He's just as bad, he's a twitslinger! Fancy sitting next to Bertie Wooster at dinner! You'd want to hit him. Or that insufferable Jeeves. I'd stick a lamb cutlet up his nose.'

'He'd be below stairs.'

'Only the English think it's funny, all this class nonsense. What a sad lot we are. And we think Americans are dim and lacking in irony because they don't appreciate Wodehouse.'

I was rather shocked. He is such a useful reminder of the gorgeous foolishness of things, his wit a reliable antidote to life's hardships. There's nothing more soothing to the soul than a well-turned phrase.

'Put him away,' said Suzy, turning on her side. No amusement for the dying to be found there.

'I know what, love, I'll buy you some of those noise-cancelling earphones, for when that hound of the bastard-villes starts howling. They're good for music too, so when the yowling starts you can listen to some of your favourites.'

But music had lost its capacity to soothe. She found it irritating and insistent: Dylan and Leonard Cohen and Tom Waits, nasal whingeing in the wind. I felt similarly, not about her crooners and balladeers, but about my music – proper music. I once depended upon my beloved Beethoven and revered Bach to guide and to transport, but now they grated on me, feeling as insistent, calculating and manipulative as that dreadful Wagner cranking away on his Teutonic genius machine, bullying me to follow and to be moved.

'Something loud, you mean? Good idea, I'll have a fucking brass band. Why didn't we think of this before? You know, it's funny, I've rarely met a dog I didn't like. Even that ugly mutt next door, if it had a loving owner, might be affectionate and manageable.'

'Yeah, like having a pet lion. So cute until it eats you.'

'When I was a girl we had the dearest dog – Bobo. You know? He was a Golden Retriever – Daddy thought them appropriate to his position in the county – but he behaved like a lap dog. He loved me the most because I kept sneaking him bits of meat when he sat under the table. I used to get told off for it, but I did it anyway. He would curl up on my lap when I sat in a comfy chair, and he was as big as I was . . .' She stopped for a moment of recall, her eyes wet. 'He was so loyal, he followed me everywhere. I even taught him to pick up my toys when I left them in the garden, and bring them up to my room. I left the lid of my toy chest open for him, and he'd bring them up one by one, ever so gently, and pop them in.'

'That's amazing.'

'Not at all. He was a retriever. He liked picking things up, and stuffed toys are a piece of piss compared to half-dead pheasants. Daddy rather fancied shooting, but he was such a bad shot, and so neglectful of all niceties, that one day he winged a beater, and it was discreetly suggested that he might join the hunt instead. He was even worse at that, kept lagging behind or falling off. He finally dressed up in his red rags for the hunts, but never actually set off, just had a few whiskies until the hunters came back, and greeted them drunkenly.'

'Poor you. He must have been an embarrassment.'

'Not half. But he did actually love dogs, I'll say that for him. After Bobo died I was inconsolable, and took to my bed. And Daddy came up and lay beside me quietly. He hardly said a word – most unusual for him – just put his arm around me and kept still. It was so lovely, so lovely of him and so lovely to be with him, that I quite forgot, or maybe even forgave, what a bad father he often was. And six months later, when I came home from school for the summer, there was a puppy Golden Retriever, and Daddy didn't say a word about that either. Just introduced us, and left us to it.'

'Did it work?'

'Sure. Love is replaceable. But Bobo was my first love, you can't replicate that.'

I don't get it, this doggy stuff, these irrational attachments. When it came to pets, I put my foot down. Suzy was hard to say no to, but accepted that my aversion was so great that it would never have worked. She loved taking a dog for a walk, and was quite ready to scoop its shit into her plastic glove, bag it up and throw it in the appropriate bin in the park. But if she had been absent or ill, I could never have done so. As far as I was concerned, it could foul the garden like the mutt next door, and Suzy could clean it up. She gave in, with bad grace.

I never had a pet as a child, and cannot bear being importuned and slobbered on and followed about by an adoring and invasive member of an inferior species. I said this a couple of times, though I learned not to repeat it.

'If there is an inferior species,' Suzy protested, 'it is humans. Dogs are loving and loyal and beautiful. That's more than you can say of humankind!'

'Right, sure. You must introduce me to Sir Walter Scottie, or Labrador Leonardo.'

It was a view that I held firmly at the time, though less so now, when my opinion of my fellow man is so diminished that even a dog looks good by comparison. Or better yet, a horse. Horses are dignified and reasonable, they don't slobber and fawn.

Poor Bobo was run over by a speeding car in one of those narrow country lanes bordered by high hedges, and couldn't get out of the way. I'm not sure Suzy ever recovered from it. Her eyes didn't mist over when she remembered her parents, or various friends who had died prematurely. About those she ranged from indifferent to sad, about Bobo, she was, still, inconsolable.

'That fucking shitslinger Kübler-Ross promised me acceptance! That is so not happening. God, listen to me, my syntax is decaying too.'

'I think she was writing about grief.'

'Grief, dying. Same thing.'

'I was wondering, love – '

'What?'

'I don't know how to say this. If I should – '

'For fuck's sake, it's a bit late for circumlocutions. Out with it!'

'Well, do you still want to be buried in Oxfordshire? I'm surprised you don't want to be cremated. I do. I'm too claustrophobic for a grave.'

'Ashes to ashes? No, I like the idea of the fine and quiet place. But I'm frightened there might be a resurrection of the body, and on Judgement Day I would emerge from my grave like one of Stanley Spencer's doughy matrons in a hideous frock. As if the local Women's Institute had all died together. Maybe a poisoned apple crumble, like in a Dorothy Sayers mystery? *Death at the W.I.*'

'I'd read that.'

'Life eternal in Cookham? It would be enough to kill me. I'd rather be an angel on a fucking cloud, even that'd be less dreary.'

'I like your plot under the yew trees. Is it stupid, holding onto you like that? I can still visit you. Visit with you.'

'It won't be me, just some hired place for my carcass to rest in.'

'Don't, please don't.'

Lawrence was prepared to tell me in detail what was happening, and what was likely to happen and when. I dreaded and needed his visits, both resented and fawned on him like a victim with Stockholm Syndrome.

What he had to say was grim.

'It's palliative care. Frankly I sometimes wonder if it is worth it, all this chemotherapy business. She has a few months to live, and we can extend that marginally but at a cost . . .'

'Would you recommend merely letting nature take its course then?' I may have sounded a bit aggressive, because he bridled.

'I am a doctor. I will give my advice, and then do what you and she decide, and she says she wants the best available treatment.'

'Tell me about the side effects. She's getting more discomfort from the remedies than she is from the disease.'

He shrugged. 'That's chemotherapy for you. We hope to shrink the tumour by up to 25 per cent, but it's an unpleasant business, and some people experience the side effects more acutely than others. The Cisplatin causes nausea and vomiting, but there are drugs to counteract that. Haldol perhaps.'

I was unsure whether his specificity with regard to drugs, side effects, platelets, all the cancer stuff, was a form of respect, or an attempt to patronise me. But I made notes, and after his visit repaired to the internet for further information, in spite of his repeated injunctions not to do so. It infallibly made me feel worse.

'The burning feeling in her feet – we call it peripheral neuropathy – that is keeping her awake is associated with this. It won't go away. But that is the least of her problems.'

'She doesn't think so!'

'I can prescribe something for it. And she will need stronger sleeping pills. I am more concerned about her anaemia. Her fatigue and pallor are caused by low red cells, but the low white blood count is more dangerous, and you'll have to make some adjustments. Her immune system has been suppressed. She certainly cannot go out any more . . .'

'You might well say!' It had been weeks since she'd done so, and was clearly never going to again, until the final day.

'And you need to make sure that visitors haven't got colds or any sort of infection.'

That was good news. As the news spread that Suzy was terminally ill, a very large number of acquaintances, and a smaller number of friends, wished to come and have a final gander. I found this infuriating, and Suzy called them the rubberneckers. None lasted more than twenty minutes at her bedside, though few wished to.

'They put on these phoney quiet voices, all concerned and delicate, and I can't hear a fucking thing. I've got this hissing in my ears, it drives me crazy . . . I can't stand any more sensitive company. Not when I've got you.'

Each visitor came armed with special knowledge, and wise counsel. Of course chemotherapy and allopathic medicine wouldn't work. They made you worse! Poisoned the

126

system! It made no difference whether Suzy was listening – she closed her eyes and played dead: *Raw vegetables! Carrot juice! Vitamin D! Go to Bristol! No, go to India! Meditation! Laughter therapy!*

After one such visit I came into the bedroom to find her giggling. 'What's so funny?' I asked.

'Oh,' she said, 'that was Benjamin. You know, from the paper.'

I must have looked blank.

'The one who's married to Maid Marion.'

I didn't have any idea who she was talking about, being as interested in her professional colleagues as she was in my teaching ones.

'He had some advice. It took him time to get round to it, I could tell something funny was up. Sort of beseeching, and evasive and over-familiar, needy and creepy like so many men? You know.'

'I don't. Go on.'

'Anyway, he said he had a good woman friend and she'd discovered a miraculous way to deal with her cancer! I didn't encourage him. Every fucker is a purveyor of cancer miracle-cure stories, they're all like evangelical Baptists: everyone gets Saved! Praise the fucking Lord!'

Cut to the chase, I counselled. Another bore? So what?

'"You've never been a coffee-drinker, have you?" he asked. I was surprised he remembered.'

'So what?'

'"That," he said, "is because you're taking it at the wrong end . . ."'

I didn't follow this at all.

'Don't be stupid, it's obvious. If I'd encouraged him, he'd have put on a white smock, and got his rubber tube and bag out!'

'Forgive me, I'm not at all sure I'm following this.'

'Enemas! Coffee enemas!'

I was horrified. 'What did you say?'

'Say? Women deal with some version of this every day, some man perving. You just flick them off, tell them to be a good boy. That makes them even pervier . . . So I just told him to go home, and he slunk off.'

From then on, I could say that the doctor had prohibited visitors other than family. Henceforth, no one but Lucy, when she could manage to come. And her Sam too, I suppose.

There was no crisis yet, just small but perceptible gradations of loss and the drift towards death. I have all too little experience of dying or bereavement, my parents having shuffled off to, and then from, the dreary vastness of Australia, in some place with a crappy name, with lots of Oombas and Boombas and Boolas or Woolas. They didn't summon me, knowing that I wouldn't have come. Sir Henry had the grace to pop off quickly, and left no empty space in my heart, while Lady Sophia's slow retreat into death was a fine mirror of her long retreat from life, and she hardly left an aftertaste. I am largely *morto intacto,* which is odd for one of my advanced years.

During the first month of her chemotherapy, Suzy begged Lucy not to come, but as she began to recover from the trials of her treatment, she wanted more of her company. And less of mine, which was a disappointment − and a relief.

'And can we talk about food?'

Distracted, I got up quickly. Lawrence was in constant need of feeding. At his own home he made regular visits to the fridge, gazing longingly in search of a pickled cucumber.

'I'm so sorry, I should have offered something. It's almost suppertime, isn't it? Can I at least offer you some tea and toast? We make an excellent Seville orange marmalade.'

'No, I'd be quite happy if I could have a refill of this excellent red.'

He knew a little about wine, but not enough to risk it with me.

'Ah yes. It's a New Zealand Pinot. Central Otago, you know, they're making – '

He handed me his glass.

'Yes, of course. But what I meant was that Suzy's diet has to be managed carefully now. Simple food, but nothing raw. Is she eating properly?'

'Less and less. She likes porridge in the morning, and I've introduced her to Manuka honey. It's said to have many beneficial qualities, you know.'

He wasn't interested.

'Sometimes she'll eat a small piece of grilled fish, and a few vegetables.'

'That's OK. But I'm worried about you too. You look rather peaky yourself. I think you should see your own doctor.'

'No, I'm feeling fine.'

'Perhaps you are now. But you need to keep your strength up, it's going to get harder and harder. Suzy is going to need nursing care.'

'You know what she thinks about hospitals. And she would never consider a hospice. She says it would be the end of her!'

He had the grace to smile. 'I presume you can afford private nursing. I can recommend a good firm.'

'So far I'm managing.'

He put his hand up. 'She talks to me, you know. And the

diarrhoea and vomiting are going to get worse once I put her on something to help the anaemia. Pemetrexed might help that, but the side effects can be a little unsettling . . .'

'That is already happening.'

'Different scale. You won't be able to cope on your own. The nurses can come in and manage her medication, feed and wash and change her, give you some relief. Just for a few hours, maybe twice a day to start?'

Suzy's recurrent bouts of fluid expulsion from top and bottom were often accompanied by an incapacity to get to the bathroom on time. The vomiting was contagious: once I was exposed to it, I had it too. Suzy had lost the will, or, to be fair, the capacity to clean up after herself. I had to do it, and I sensed in her a grim satisfaction that, having shirked such duties as a young father, I now had the penance of performing them for her as an old mother.

Most of the time her room smelled beyond any chemical's capacity to freshen it. A lot of the time, she did too. And so did I. I'd wash the sheets, clean the carpets, clean her, clean myself – but we were still a cauldron of filth. Lawrence was right, we needed more troops.

'I'll see you next week, and thanks for the drink.' He got up, adjusted his jacket and straightened his tie in front of the looking-glass, as if displaying it to me. It was a sedate red and blue striped silk, perfectly adequately matched with his grey wool jacket, a bit sedate to be sure, ostentatiously un-vulgar.

He'd seen me examining his tie in his office! I wasn't dressing for him, but he was for me! How terrific is that?

'I'll show myself out. You get some rest.' He closed the door gently.

I hurried upstairs to see Suzy, who was slumped in half-slumber, exhausted by Lawrence's inquisitions and examination.

'Honestly, love, did you see his tie?'

Her eyes opened.

'He's trying to live up to your standards. He wants your approval ever so, poor lamb.'

Every now and again a crowd of witless Catholics are visited by a special kind of miracle. A statue of the Virgin Mary begins to cry, tears pour down its face – sometimes of saltwater, sometimes (in Italy) of olive oil. People wring their hands and hankies. But the only weeping statue actually sanctioned by the Pope – It's a fuckin' miracle, that is! – was in Japan, and everyone believed in it because it was broadcast on telly! Tears regularly flowed down its cheeks and dripped onto the floor below, dutifully recorded by the cameras. The Japanese swooped and gawped and celebrated.

One morning Suzy began to cry, lying absolutely still on her back, her eyes closed. Without a shudder or a sob, the tears poured from her eyes, down her cheeks and chin, her face gleaming like a stone in a lake. I held her unresponsive hand, and the tears welled and dripped and made their slow descent from their mysterious underground source. For the rest of the day she neither talked nor drank, did not move in any manner, nor do I think she slept. She simply flowed, overflowed, dispensed her waters liberally onto the sodden sheets, which I mopped and laid towels on. And then, sometime in the early evening, the flow stopped, she turned gently and painfully onto her side, and slept for fifteen hours. They were to be her last tears.

When she woke, her waters broken, it was with an odd sentiment, sufficiently powerful to make her sit up, with my help.

'I feel bad about Sheila.'

'What do you mean? Who's Sheila?'

'Shitslinger. I wish I could write to her.'

'Why poor? Write what?'

'She was only trying to do good. So were they all, all the shitslingers – Kahlil Gibran, Mr Tolstoy, the dreaded Eliot – all of them. Just wandering in the dark with flashlights.'

'But I thought we – '

'So did I. I thought I was allowed to patronise them – required to. Me!'

I was alarmed by this volte-face: Suzy, my dear cynical, unrelenting embodiment of the spirit of doubt, was about to have some deathbed revelation?

'I thought we hated wisdom? The universal tonic, the revivifier! One spoonful cures all maladies for all people! What we need is an antidote to wisdom.'

I did not tell her about my own, similar realisation. I'm not sure why, I think I felt shy about it. We teachers are shitslingers too, of a very minor and inferior kind. We ought to look up to Mr Eliot – he's a high priest of our degraded order.

She made a sound somewhere between a sigh and a groan. 'Boring! Enough now. And anyway, I have had a terrible epiphany.'

'Pay it no mind, love, it may be because you're heavily medicated. I find epiphanies always upset me dreadfully. I took laxatives for a week after my last one, before I could get it out of my system.'

'It was about my father . . .'

'I rest my case.'

'What I realise now is how much like my father I am.'

'Your father!'

'Sad, insecure, effortfully superior, full of himself because not full of much else. I got it all from him. He was my role model.'

'Darling, I think you need to drink some water, maybe have a nap. You're babbling.'

'I wish I were. I don't know. I don't know anything any more. I used to know, I think. But I can't remember where it all went.'

'My poor darling, I don't know how you can bear it. How we can – ?'

'I'm not me any more.'

'Because of how people are treating you?'

'I don't care about that, not any longer. Because I'm gone, inside, hollowed out . . . like the rind of a melon.'

She held my hand weakly. I had an irresistible desire to flee.

'Let me get you some ice chips, I'll be right back.'

She was doing her best to make it easier for me: to eat, to sleep a little, to make my recurrent necessary escapes. She'd ask me to do errands, or make her cups of tea from which she took a single sip. Then she would ask me to take the cup downstairs as she couldn't stand clutter.

'What is the sense of it? It's all gone. I can hardly talk. Can't eat or drink or go to the lav. No quality. I want to be dead now.'

'Soon, love, soon.' I put a few of the ice chips into her mouth. Her tongue was dry and cracked, and there were weeping sores in the corners of her mouth. I wiped them gently with a wet tissue. She winced.

'Sorry.'

'If God – '

'What, if God what?'

'If he gave a damn, he'd take me. Turn off the light.'

I reached towards the lamp.

'No! Put it back on. I get frightened in the dark. Stay with me. I didn't mean the lamp. I meant me. Mine.'

'So God could turn you off?'

'Yes, please. Be merciful, for once in his life.'

I took her hand. 'Soon, love, soon,' I said gently with tears in my voice.

She gave it a little squeeze. 'It takes too long. I'm ready. But the cells want to live.'

'I'd like to take her in for another scan. The acute situation in her back can be caused by immobility and referred pain, but it may well be a secondary. I suspect she may have it in her spine now . . .'

'How bad would that be?'

'How bad? She won't die any more quickly, or of a different cause. But she'll be in increasing discomfort.'

'Is that a euphemism?'

'Yes.'

He took a more substantial than usual sip from his wine glass and sloshed it around his mouth, which I found surprisingly offensive. He took yet another mouthful, swilling it again. It was his third glass.

'I can help with that, we're good at dealing with pain these days.'

'So why do another scan? I presume you can't do anything to help, whatever it is. Why put her through a trip to the hospital, and all that dreadful palaver?'

'It's my job to offer whatever can be done, and in any case palliative care is best provided in a hospital environment. But she won't agree to that.'

Suzy resisted the increase in painkilling medication, because it made her sleepy or unconscious most of the time.

'I want to hold on just a little longer,' she said, until the pain in her back overwhelmed her, and she begged for relief.

EXCRUCIATING

agonising, extremely painful, severe, acute, intense, extreme, savage, violent, racking, searing, piercing, stabbing, raging, harrowing, tormenting, grievous, dreadful, awful, terrible, unbearable.
ALL OF THE ABOVE. NONE OF THE ABOVE.
CROSS THEM ALL OUT.

'Will you give her something to end it?'
'I'm sorry, I can't do that. Not any more. None of us can.'
'Why not? Doctors do it all the time. We all know that.'
'They used to.'
'And they've stopped? Nobody told me. Why would that happen?'
'It's caused by the internet.'
'What? I don't understand.'
'Well, social media too. You know what I mean.'
'I most certainly do not!'
'Well,' he said. 'It happens like this. You help someone along with an extra dose of whatever, and the next thing you know someone writes a round robin email or tweets about the very kind doctor, or posts it on Facebook, whatever. And the next thing you know the person in imminent danger is you.'
'Me? Fine, I'll risk that happily.'
'No. I meant me. I've even seen people who posted grateful responses to the assisted death of their loved one on that dreadful *Rate Your Doctor* website.'
'And you won't help us?'

'I can't! Unlike you, I can not only be prosecuted, I can be struck off.'

'Look at me. Do I look like a tweeter? Does Lucy?'

'No, of course not. But secrets are contagious, they get around.'

'Are you saying you don't trust us?'

'No, not at all. I'm sorry to give that impression. I'm saying I don't trust anyone, including myself. I'm terribly sorry, but that is the world we live in. There's no privacy any more, and I simply cannot act with the kind of freedom I used to have.'

He shifted in his seat uncomfortably. He was by nature compliant, desperate to be liked, and recalcitrance didn't suit him. I renewed my attack, certain that he would weaken. For God's sake, why shouldn't he?

'Have you no heart? I thought you cared for her once. Help her! Help us! I won't be there. I won't look!'

'I'm so sorry. Of course I care, caring is what – '

'I am begging you.'

'And I am telling you no. I can help her, I will give her increasing doses of painkillers and sedatives. She'll sleep most of the time. Most people are unconscious when they die: it's the effect of letting go, and the appropriate amount of medication.'

'Which wears off! Between doses she's in agony, begging to be released! And you tell me you haven't got the fucking nerve to – '

'I can help her. But I cannot myself be the cause of her death.'

I was furious and desperate, qualities that go badly together. Lawrence was the only person who could solve our problem, but it was he who was, as it were, causing it. If I cajoled, he would find me easy to resist, if I attacked, easier yet. For the moment I hated him with a vehemence that was startling.

'This is hardly the time for such niceties of feeling. I'm surprised to find – '

He put his hand up abruptly. 'I am not saying that it would be unethical. It's not, in my view, not at the very end. But it is now worse than that. It's foolish, and indiscreet. Be patient. You know Freud has a wise remark in his book about jokes . . .'

I was horrified. 'You've picked the wrong audience. Suzy detests Freud almost as much as I loathe Jew—'

'Stop right now, James! I won't tolerate this!'

'—ish jokes.'

He gawped at me. 'It's time for me to leave, I think.'

'Spare me! I don't want fucking jokes. All I want is a fatal dose of morphine!'

'That is not my job,' he said.

'Promise me.'

'What, love?' Her voice was very faint now, and she could only talk one sentence at a time, short sentences. Pause, breathe, struggle against the empty spaces to inhale, locate some stray air. Try a little more, for a little more.

'You won't make me go to hospital?'

'I promise.'

'I hate hospitals, I'd rather die.'

'I know what you mean.'

She squeezed my hand. 'One more thing . . . please . . .'

I leant over to listen, stroking her shoulder. 'I can hear you. What is it?'

She paused to gather strength and breath. 'Lucy . . .'

'Yes, what about her?'

'Try to, to keep her away now.'

'Why, love? She wants to be with you, she loves you.'

Suzy closed her eyes, as if the effort to be understood was too much. 'I wanted to teach her – ' She paused. 'You know? How to do it?'

'Do what, my love?'

'How to die. That would be a gift.'

'And you've been giving it. When she comes, you are always so brave, and I listen to you two giggling as if you are having fun.'

She coughed, tried to sit up, fixed me with a terrible stare. 'Not any more. I'm too frightened, and it hurts terribly. Keep her away!'

'I'm not sure I can, love, not sure at all. You know Lucy . . .'

'Just tell her I'm too weak, sleeping all the time, and you will call her if there is any . . . you know . . . any reason.'

'I know. I'll try.'

She closed her eyes, and her head seemed to disappear into the pillow, which closed around her like a shroud.

Those fucking paedophiles, the Irish clergy, would frighten teenage boys, away on retreat from the world, to yank them back to the ways of righteousness. By way of prayer: sacred ejaculations to erase profane ones. I used to think the passage hyperbolic . . .

The horror of this strait and dark prison is increased by its awful stench. All the filth of the world, all the offal and scum of the world, we are told, shall run there as to a vast reeking sewer when the terrible conflagration of the last day has purged the world . . .

I would open the windows, and discreetly spray the room when Suzy was asleep, but the smells lingered, penetrating the fabric of our being. The nurses washed her, put ointment on the bedsores, wiped and soothed, but the room was pestilential.

'Christ,' she said weakly, sniffing. 'That's me.'

'No, it's just stuffy in here.'

'Me. Oh my God.'

'Don't you worry.'

'I'm so sorry . . . sorry.'

One afternoon there was a noisy scuffling in her bedroom, and the sound of the nurse's footsteps stomping around. Suzy was haemorrhaging violently – blood spewing over her, the sheets, onto the carpets. She was gasping for breath, clutching her throat, her eyes rolling back as the blood continued to flow. The nurse turned her onto her side, reaching for her mobile phone as she finished.

'I am going to call an ambulance,' she said.

Suzy shook her head violently.

'No,' I said, 'you're not!'

As she lay in the pool of her own gushing blood, her pyjamas sodden, like a starving bird with oil-coated feathers, I was rendered mute by a horror at once physical and linguistic, stunned into silence by fear and pity, words frozen within me, a reaction so purely visceral as to rescind my humanity, render me a weasel or a ferret, shrinking in repulsion and fear. None of the available terms applied: Horror? Fear? Shock? Distress? If they had to be used at all, it was only in the knowledge that they were inadequate, that nothing better was available. Like Love.

Nothing to say. I'm not used to this. I have spent my poor wasted land of a life being paid to say things, until they ran out, and then I did.

Our everyday emotional lives are so ludicrously over-valued, our feelings so intensely interrogated and inflated, that it is no longer possible to be mildly unhappy, a bit chagrined, sad rather than devastated. Everything is hyperbolic, stretched out and de-natured, and when the time comes, appropriately charged language is no longer available: 'The weather was miserable', 'The in-laws' visit was a catastrophe', 'I was so distressed when England lost the Test Match', 'She was inconsolable when she tore her new frock'. So what am I to say as I watch my wife bleeding and dying? That it is horrible, and I am devastated?

Better to say nothing and to write nothing. If I cannot speak, therefore I must be silent. The observation was made by a rather clever soldier in the First War. After that he became a schoolmaster and interfered with boys, which I suppose is what schoolmasters do. After that he became a philosopher.

Other writers returning from the war should have obeyed the injunction, and kept their counsel. What we think of as the great poetry of the Great War is largely tosh.

> If I should die, think only this of me:
> That there's some corner of a foreign field
> That is for ever England.

Dreadful. Or the sloppy, weak irony of Wilfred Owen's '*Dulce et Decorum Est*'. He was dead before it was published, and people were too kind to remark how poor it was. Either because they didn't know better or (worse) because they thought this the best that could be said.

Better they'd shut up. When soldiers come home from war, they do not speak of it, or if they do, only in muttered phrases indicating that what they have within them is inexpressible. Impossible to convey. What are they to say? The only words that convey the burden and depth of the horror are the names of the places: the Somme, Gallipoli, Auschwitz.

Suzy is dying, and asleep. I sit and write by her bedside. The rest is silence, even these words are silence, they emanate from the silence, and are silenced by it.

Leaning forwards, I could hardly make her out. Her throat gurgled, and she tried desperately to clear it, spitting out gobs of what was not quite sputum. She was drowning, her lungs inexorably filling. The nurses were able to extract some of the fluid, but her lungs refilled. I sat next to her, listening, cringing, past any remedy of hope or consolation. If I could have worn our earphones, I would have done so. Instead, I tried to find things to do, elsewhere.

She was a parcel of decomposing tripe. What remained was a sound issuing from her vocal cords like a final ghostly exhalation. As if she had passed and had only this final phrase to transmit.

'I'm sorry . . . I couldn't do better . . .'

Some sort of regret? Perhaps many sorts of many regrets? But not that old classical judgement of the adventures of her soul upon this earth? No. No words of wisdom? Not likely. Never. Not Suzy or even Suzy's ghost.

She could hardly sleep any more, save when the medication kicked in and the pain abated and she closed her eyes. Her face in repose took on a mask-like gessoed beauty, spare-boned, denuded of flesh and hope, fixed in a terrible serenity, still, her, just.

She was almost gone. If she recognised me, or even Lucy, it rarely registered in her features. She didn't respond, or appear to hear. The light had gone out of her eyes, which stared outwards but did not see. Everything that had mattered, Bobo and Lucy, our long years together, her writing and attempts at writing, the moments of bliss and sorrow, all had passed, and were as nothing, lost as a dream is lost, momentarily vivid, quickly faded.

She was somewhere, to be sure, but somewhere other, from which she would not return. She had set herself facing the dark, and whether her isolation was willed or imposed made no difference. She could rouse herself momentarily to get some liquid into her, but relapsed immediately. Still, there, and gone.

I dreaded her death, longed to sit next to her warm abandoned carapace, if only for a few more moments. Wished her dead too. And I felt a similar — is it appropriate to say so? — a similar disconnect from the world. I did not respond when the nurses talked to me, hardly summoned a word for Lucy, who came for a couple of days at a time. She said that 'when the time comes' she would take a leave of absence from work, and move in with me 'to see it through'. But Lawrence assured us that there was still time to pass, too much time, not too little.

As Suzy's ghost gurgled and hacked, striving for just that tiny sustaining moment of inhalation, I fancied that we were both suffering, clogging, filling up, past all intervention or hope of love. I did whatever I could to help her, when I was able. Little things: cold washcloths, more slivers of ice, plumped pillows, changing her position on the bed, though only when she was sufficiently drugged up. Closed curtains to keep it dark, with only a night light in the corner of the room, like Lucy used to have when she had nightmares.

One evening, after a particularly stressed and distressing afternoon, I propped her up and gave her some warm tea with Manuka honey to drink through a straw – I'd got her used to the sweetness gradually, said it was good for her and had great medicinal qualities. She managed to get it all down, a tiny bit at a time, and soon fell into a deep sleep. Her features relaxed, and the absent flesh seemed to expand and fill itself, so that I could see, for those moments, her Suzy face, the young, the beautiful . . . untroubled at last.

Goodnight, my darling, sleep well.

I sat and held her hand as she descended, and then I did too.

We are lumps of meat that live and then die. Material. The soul doesn't leave the body at the point of death. What does is gas and air and, if there is anything left in kidney or bowel, some of that too.

There's your soul for you.

I sat with her, with her body, and wished to remember, summoned images but they were grey and desiccated, and nothing came alive any more than she did. Moments ago she'd been a person, however wasted, a person who liked Dorset crab and cottages in Wales and her darling daughter, who laughed till she cried for hardly any reason at all – and a flicker later, carrion, the fearful rush of blood stilled. Gone? Not entirely. She lingered in the air not fully swooshed away yet into the unimaginable distances. I tried to hold onto her, but one look at her poor dear body made it clear: it was not her, not any more.

May God have mercy on her soul?

Lucy arrived in a few hours, and rang Lawrence, who came immediately, standing by the bedside for a moment, holding

Suzy's poor limp hand, still and warm, in his, and nodded as if to himself.

'Yes,' he said, and sat down on the bedside chair, putting his head into his hands, and wept loudly and unselfconsciously, wiping his eyes and blowing his nose. I stood in the corner watching him, envious of his generosity, his bountifulness. I had the desire but not the capacity to weep. My life has been a vale of unshed tears.

We sat together for a time, unspeaking. Minutes passed in the silence, perhaps many of them. Time seemed suspended, we were embedded in the amber silence. There was nothing to be done, nor anything to say.

Lawrence was more than professionally sympathetic. He had loved Suzy. But he was puzzled by her quick passing.

'It is so difficult for us to predict,' he said. 'As I told you. But I thought she had a few weeks to live. It takes time for the systems to close down.'

Lucy was sitting on the other side of her mother's bed, as we kept a vigil over her body. 'But you told us,' she said, with a wan smile, 'it might be anytime . . .'

'Yes, but I am still curious . . .'

'. . . and you have been quite wonderful to all of us. I know Mummy cared for you, she felt she was in the best possible hands.' Lucy knew that he had fancied Suzy, fancied her daughter too, the disgusting old goat.

'A post-mortem would clear things up, and put our minds at rest.'

Lucy began to cry, and rose to stand by him and to take his hand. 'Oh, dear Lawrence, please no. She has suffered enough. I can't bear thinking of her being cut up on a slab. It's so horrible! And what for? She was dying anyway, so she was lucky enough to go sooner than scheduled. That's good, isn't it?'

He did not, I noticed, let go of her hand.

Lucy gave him another squeeze. He purred with condolent delight.

'We don't want our minds at rest,' she said. 'We wish to put her to rest!'

He considered for a moment. 'I understand. Perhaps you should now call the funeral home and arrange for her body to be picked up. Do you have anyone in mind?'

'Yes,' said Lucy. 'I will ring them. The funeral will be in Oxfordshire. I hope you'll be able to come.'

'Don't you worry, sir,' said the burly man from the undertaker's. He was dressed in a shiny black suit with frayed cuffs, which might have fitted him ten years ago, but was now stretched too tightly around his ample gut. He was presumably required to keep his jacket buttoned up, which was not only unflattering but, given his present chore, genuinely unsafe. He could barely move his arms away from his body.

I stood in front of him on the stairs, ready to steady him as he fell, or to catch Suzy's body as it slid off the stretcher and plummeted into the hallway.

He was wheezing as he backed down the stairs, his equally challenged colleague above us, bending low to keep his end of the stretcher at step-level, thus achieving something almost flat. Suzy's body, recently and gently strapped to the surface, did not move a bit.

At the top of the stairs, Lucy was helping the top man by steadying the stretcher, bent double, huffing and crying and gasping.

Every two steps we paused, muttering 'easy now' to each other, 'no hurry'. We eventually arrived in the hallway thoroughly winded, and they unrolled the wheels and uprights from the bottom of the stretcher, so that the body – *the body* – was now resting at bed level.

'There, that wasn't so bad, was it?' Bottom man was bent over with his hands on his knees. The two of them paused for a few moments, catching their breath, or perhaps they were waiting for a tip. Lucy stood quietly by her mother's body, her hand resting gently on Suzy's shrouded shoulder.

A few moments later – I can hardly recall the passing of that time, the opening of the door, the wheeling out of the stretcher with its cargo of sticks and parchment, the placing in the back of the undertaker's vehicle, the closing of the doors, the meaningless thanks and pleasantries – the van drew away from the kerbside and joined the sparse line of traffic as she set out on her final journey westward, where we would join her in a few days' time.

We stood in the doorway, holding each other gently, watching the car draw away, becoming smaller and smaller as it proceeded down the road, until it was lost to us when a lorry drew up and covered the tail-lights. We craned our necks for a few moments, peering into the flickering darkness, but the lights were gone.

Part III

I hate this. I know everything involves compromise, and I am fully aware that the range of my loathing is panoptic. I have always rather prided myself on this, which I regard as a form of discrimination. Dr Johnson loved a good hater.

But this is surprisingly grating. Perhaps I started out on the wrong telephonic foot, enquiring from the gormless boy on the Europcar Rentals line why they had banished their 'e'?

He did not understand. Why should he? Perhaps no one had enquired before. Perhaps no one cares except me, who am hyper-sensitive to the comings and goings of the letter 'e'. In my first year at school, my fellows christened me Darky, which soon morphed into Sambo, by which cursed moniker I was plagued until the age of thirteen, when I made my transition to Winchester, and became once again, and finally, James. Darke, James Darke.

'Europe' has an 'e' at the end. There is no reason to drop it when conjoined with car. Why do you inflict this illiteracy on your customers?'

'I'm so sorry . . . Can I help you, sir?'

'Hardly.'

'Do you want to rent a vehicle?'

'Not any more.'

I hung up. I had only rung the damned missing-e company because they deliver cars direct to your door, pick them up again when you say, and offer a choice of 'Prestige' BMWs and Mercedes which, I hoped, might have tinted windows. But I never got far enough to enquire.

Perhaps I was not ready – quite – to go out? I thought I wanted to. I needed to. But if missing letters in absurd corporate names were putting me off, it was clear that some resistance was manifesting itself.

I had not once left the house in the last eight months. This morning, opening the back door into the garden, bravely, and putting a foot out into that formerly congenial space, caused me to blink at the direct sunlight, and to gasp at the feeling of openness. Not that I was very exposed, in a walled garden overlooked by a few flats. But I felt vulnerable, as if one of their windows contained a sniper whose sole desire, for all these months, had been to wait for me patiently, and then to assassinate me.

Looking about, there were signs of new life. It was – I had hardly been aware of it – sometime in the spring, May perhaps, and the daffodils were up amongst the weeds, and a carpet of bright pink and orange primulas aired themselves in the shade beneath the tree. Lilacs too, bless them. Ample symbols of regeneration, if you were looking for them, but all I saw was a cruelty so acute that it seemed designed to mock me, my own aridity and despair.

Suzy's garden was out there, just. What would it have been like if I'd exited through my fortress door, stood revealed on my doorstep, with pedestrians meandering by, cars swooping and honking like cross geese? I have always been sensitive to noise, but a sudden movement alarms me as well. A lorry trundling by, so one could feel the air move as it passed. A child rising from its stroller, demanding an ice lolly.

I fear that a neighbour – not that I know any of them – might be curious to see, at last, some sign of life from the empty house. One who might, even, come by to say hello? It's an intolerable thought. What if it were Spikeman, whom I had not seen since the curious incident of the dog in the daytime, gone to take his pooch for a constitutional? He wouldn't recognise me, but the brute would begin to cry at the very sight of his water-boarder. Or perhaps he'd attack, froth-jawed, bespiked, murderous for revenge?

I might have created the very conditions under which I *have* to stay inside. This irony was not wasted on me, but my major feeling, shamefully, was relief, as if an agoraphobic had been spared a bracing day at the seaside. I did not wish to go out. I wouldn't.

I will. I was not sure what the residue of my moral courage now consisted of, but I had never intended a life-time sentence in solitary confinement. A period of retreat and contrition, some time to recover, yes. To write, of course. To avoid unpleasantness, that too.

Well, I was not recovered. But I had written much of what needed to be recorded. Not purged, you cannot do that. And unpleasantness was what I could not go on avoiding. I would seek it out, in my tinted-window Prestige vehicle, because, unsought, it would morph into some unforeseeable awfulness that I am unable to contemplate – tumorous.

I had to get into the bloody car and direct it for an hour and a half through noise and movement, sunlight and people. Whether my – more than fastidious – my lunatic aversion to my fellow man abided, I could not quite say. I had made my peace with Bronya, and established a non-noisome relationship with the workmen, delivery boys, doctor and dentist and hairdresser and computer programmer who occasionally entered my house, and the sight and smell of them no longer nauseated me. Touch of queasiness perhaps, but tolerable in ones. How would I do in a crowd? I knew the answer to that. Avoid crowds.

Each morning, I might venture out cautiously, and gradually increase both the distance that I travelled and the amount of time that I spent in the street. Perhaps a week of that would enable me to reconnect with my gormless interlocutor at the car rental firm. (I tried various other intact-e firms – Hertz, Budget and Enterprise, for instance – but they did not have what I needed, save for an 'e'.)

I was diminished. I had lost weight, perhaps quite a lot of weight. My clothes hung on me, but it had been a long time since I saw myself in a looking-glass. Thank God for that. In the mornings, though, I couldn't make do without a small shaving glass, else I would have cut myself badly. I could not abide the thought of growing a beard as hermits do, and had always disliked men who hid behind them, and pitied their wives who got all bushied up. My face does not appear in the glass until I have applied the soap with my brush, nor do I pause to examine myself once the straight razor has done its chore. But in that brief moment, when the last of the soap is cleared, my skeletal face mocked me, as if ready to shed the remnants of the tight residual flesh, to emerge cleansed to the bone.

My personality, such as it is, had become equally skeletal. I agreed with Suzy that self-esteem is for idiots, but self-respect is something other, the very basis of the moral life, and I had none of that either. I could not act because I could hardly find a reason to prefer one action to another. Or, when I was able to, I could not summon the will or strength.

My temper, had I had someone against whom to direct it — I wish I had — is fierce, unprompted, inhuman and improbably silly. I derived no pleasure from this. Indeed, I got as little pleasure as I could. It's surprising how it falls away. I didn't listen to music, I didn't read much any more, in the absence of Bronya I hardly ate, and though I drank, I did so for the effect not the pleasure of the grape. I wrote, but you could hardly call that enjoyment (or even writing).

This inventory of my shortcomings might go on and on. My lacks, my emptiness, my fatuity. I used to have a life, though, I remember it — I miss it. Though diminished in appearance, temper and appetite, I am not some sort of monk. Just a penitent. And I'd had enough of it. I would start out slowly. Slop peach juice down the front of my dressing gown, uncaring, head out in the direction of the world.

Maybe I simply wasn't ready to drive again? I knew better than to drive to Suzy's funeral. Could hardly have got there, much less back home again. The car's been in the garage ever since. The battery will be dead, the bodywork filthy. Mice chewing the wiring. I could hardly imagine using it again, however much I love it: it is rusted with memory.

I once loved Paddington station, that lovely edifice of Victorian optimism and creative genius. Like all of the supposed great ages of English history, though, the nineteenth century was marked — defined, really — by the most appalling callousness. I have maintained this to George for decades, but he will not learn. Like Mrs Thatcher — whom he resembles in a variety of ways — he thinks Victorian values were both admirable and transferable.

But if you consult the great writers and artists of the Victorian period, what they have in common is a profound distaste for the culture in which they found themselves — its cruelty, philistinism and swollen self-regard, its Herculean capacity for turning a blind eye, and for blaming the victims of its own neglect. Its profound hypocrisy. This made it a great period in which to be a novelist, for the immortal Dickens and the slightly less agreeable George Eliot and Trollope and Thackeray to have something to get their teeth into. Novelists should feel ill at ease in their culture. Better yet, they ought to oppose it.

I was aware, squashed and harried and irritable underneath Brunel's beautiful arches, that I was thinking these turgid and unoriginal thoughts about the Victorians because I didn't want to think others, to remember where I was going, and why. To my dear one's graveside, to lower her in, to throw sod upon her dear dead body. Ironically, when I was young I used Brunel prophylactically while making love to Suzy. Nothing like the reiterated phrase, *Isambard-Kingdom-and-the-power-and-the-glory-Brunel* to delay an orgasm. Say it often enough, and you won't have one at all.

I was unaware, as I waited for the train to Oxford, that it was to be a catalysing moment for my retreat from the world. I was, of course, in a state of heightened susceptibility, exacerbated by having to employ public transport. Not being used to train stations, I was unprepared for the ways in which my fellow travellers would impinge on me. I don't mean the rush or the noise, the smells or the congestion, frightful though all of them were. No, what had happened, without anyone informing me, was that human beings had morphed into something loathsomely atomistic, unaware of and indifferent to others.

A young woman with pancake make-up so liberally and ineptly applied that she might have been a Virgin Airlines stewardess, hurried across the concourse, talking loudly into the air, some sort of mobile device in front of her face. She bumped into me abruptly, without missing a step, and when I shouted at her she did not hear, because she had some other device sticking in her ear, more aware of her ethereal interlocutor than someone two feet in front of her. I stumbled, righted myself, but soon tripped over a suitcase that was being tugged along behind some Oriental tourist, like the caboose of a train.

Taking refuge in W.H. Smith, I bought a copy of the *Daily Telegraph* – you got a free bottle of water with it, otherwise no one would buy it – so that I could do the crossword on the train, and was just queuing to pay when I was bashed by a large backpack attached to a young man who had turned abruptly to look at a checkout tray containing chocolates. I reeled backwards. He didn't notice.

I made my way back to the concourse as gingerly as a soldier in a field of land mines. The train boarded ten minutes later, crowded as all Oxford trains apparently are. I found a first-class carriage with a designated quiet zone, which wasn't. When I upbraided a florid gentleman who insisted on talking on his mobile, pointing to the clear symbol on the window forbidding such practice, he told me to fuck off. I had an impulse to explain to him that I was on my way to my wife's funeral – my attire may well have suggested some such sombre occasion – but it would have been humiliating, not for him, but for me. Casting the pearls that were her eyes before the swine that he was.

Of the events at the church, and afterwards at the interment, there is nothing that I can say or write. Nothing comes of nothingness.

Worried by my state, and unconvinced that I could manage to get home on my own, Lucy insisted on accompanying me on my return journey.

'That's kind, love,' I said. 'I will be OK.'

'You won't, Daddy. You're pale as a sheet. I'm sure you're having your palpitations – did you bring your pills?'

'No, I – '

'You never look after yourself!'

On the train we sat in silence. She held my hand, until finally I wrested it free. There was too little worth saying, and too much unsaid.

She accompanied me to the taxi rank at Paddington, and as I stooped to enter the cab, she pulled me to her and gave me a fierce hug. 'Well,' she said, 'we got through it. Let's let a couple of days go by, then we need to have a long talk.'

'I'm sorry, darling, I'm not up to that.'

'I understand.'

'I'm not sure that you do. Not that I do either, but I need to be alone for a time . . .'

'Of course you do. I'll keep in good touch.'

'Wait for me to call you. Please. I will, when I am up to it.'

I entered the cab and closed the black door firmly, without looking back or out.

That would buy me some time, but not a lot. Lucy needed to talk as much as I dreaded it, and she was unlikely to understand just how serious I was about needing to be left alone. And how much time I had in mind before I relented. If I was lucky, she might wait a week, and then the phone would ring, if I still had a phone. And when that didn't work, and the email bounced, she would get alarmed, and then angry, and storm the gates. It gave me just about enough time to construct my defences.

I made it just in time, thanks to the estimable Cooper. But my battlements couldn't stop Lucy's correspondence, or her entreaties, or her fury, though they could deflect them into George's wastebasket.

I'd thought I could count on him, and he had betrayed me. Our reckoning, following his impertinent email, was likely to be quick and fierce. In short, I allowed him in. In the spirit of the Light Brigade, he had threatened to break down my door, though I doubt that he would have tried, it was mere Tennysonian posturing. But it was preferable to yield, if only to counter-attack. He had announced that he would arrive on the 11th, which was (studiedly, I thought) the six-month anniversary (can that be the right term?) of Suzy's death. Knowing how sentimental he is, he will have reckoned that this would drive an arrow through my emotional armour and into my heart. Which is an odd metaphor for reawakening feeling.

At 10 a.m. the doorbell gave its single plaintive chime, and I answered it immediately. I'd been waiting in the hallway. George is never late. Or early. He looked anxious, and had an old-fashioned thick leather briefcase dangling from his hand like some vestigial appendage on a possum.

'I suppose you'd better come in,' I said.

'Thank you.'

'Can we get this over with quickly? Neither of us can be enjoying it, I must say. I will explain, and then perhaps you can go.'

Normally the soul of politeness, deferential to man and schoolboy alike, courtly to women of all sizes, kindly to small furry creatures except when killing or eating them, George none the less bristled. 'I do not wish to hear what you have to say! You have behaved in a dishonourable and cruel manner.'

'Oh, do shut up, George.'

He recoiled as if I had struck him, and made his way shakily into the drawing room, which I'd hardly entered since Suzy died. It hadn't been cleaned since Bronya left, was fusty and begloomed, bereft of the bright morning sun. George looked about him curiously. He rarely noticed his surroundings, which had been supplied for him by schools and colleges for his entire life, but even he was aware of something more than usually insalubrious in the air.

He opened the shabby briefcase, which had wide brass buckles which made a clanking sound when released, and brought out a parcel of letters, held together – a typical touch – with a black ribbon, as Queen Victoria might have done with Albert's epistles.

'I could not throw these away. It would have been sinful. They are yours.' He handed them across to me. 'You must promise me something . . .'

'Yes, yes, I know.'

'. . . that you will not destroy them without reading them. I beg you not to do that.'

'All right, George,' I said, to his obvious surprise. 'You have my word.'

I rose from the sofa, the parcel of letters in my hand. 'And now I would be grateful if you would leave. Thank you for coming, I know you mean well.'

He didn't get up from his chair. 'No,' he said, 'I cannot do that. You are my dearest friend.' He reached into a small pocket on the side of his waistcoat, and removed a paisley silk handkerchief, which he folded gently and began to apply to his streaming eyes.

'For pity's sake, George, please don't. I beg of you!'

I had forgotten how tearful Victorians are, how they wallow like happy hippos in displays of grief – Dickens. His audience. George loved a good weep, it was a traditional sign of refined sensibility. He leaked, he honked, he began to sob, he mopped his beard.

'If you have an ounce of love left in you . . . read Lucy's letters . . . whatever they say. They will bring you back into life, and remind you of who you really are.'

'Used to be!'

He rose from the chair and approached me. I cowered back into the sofa, fearful that he was going to embrace me, baptise me in those salt, estranging tears. 'No! Don't! Pull yourself together!'

Making the kind of effort he would have associated with one of Tennyson's heroes, he stopped, wiped his eyes, blew his nose, and deposited the besodden handkerchief back into his pocket. 'Sorry, sorry. My dear, you have no idea how this upsets me.'

'I'll make tea. Calm yourself. Strong Darjeeling, no milk or sugar?'

'Of course, thank you . . . And there is something else . . . some other things.'

'What do you mean?'

'Well, first of all, I have another little contribution. Some more "Indignations". I've typed them out for you.' He rummaged in a side compartment of his briefcase and handed me two folded sheets of paper. 'There's rather a lot – some new ones. But the most wonderful is from a letter to Miss Coutts, which has the phrase "perpetual scald and boil". Isn't that wonderful? And so perfect for you!'

'It is rather good, it describes exactly how I feel. Like an out-of-control kettle. I'm glad to know about it.'

'It's not about you, you silly old bugger. It's for your title! I never quite warmed to the working one.'

'What's wrong with it?'

'It's bland, and academic. It's basically a sub-title. Titles are to pique interest, sub-titles to focus it. And so what about this? *Scald and Boil: Charles Dickens and the Rhetoric of*

Indignation. What is so peachy about it is that they could be characters in *Bleak House*. Scald and Boil, Attorneys at Law.'

'Brilliant, you're right. It is now my title. All I need now is some text . . .'

'It'll come, it'll come. Are you still referring to it as a monograph?'

'Goodness me, yes. I could never write a book on Dickens, I'd be too intimidated by the proper scholars. Monograph sounds modest and studious.'

'Perhaps this is a good period to be getting on with it?'

'Bury my grief in work? How Dickensian. He loved death, he found it animating. He always wrote best when somebody was dying, either in real life or in fiction.'

But in truth, though I had a surfeit of grief, there was almost none of work. I'd been musing on Dickens's 'Indignation' on and off for years, in a desultory public schoolmasterish manner, and had little to show for it. The idea seemed plausible, initially. I admired how angry he was, and the ways in which he expressed it. 'Charles Dickens and the Rhetoric of Indignation'? Or perhaps *Outrage*? Maybe *Disgust*? I am in favour of all of the above.

Who gives a damn? I'd really abandoned the project years ago, like a PhD that had gone sour. I did not tell poor George this. He thought me, foolish chap, a fellow Victorian, and had encouraged me accordingly. If I could have done so decently, I would have handed the project on to him, but he was a Tennysonian through and through. Dickens was too sloppy, too fascinated by filth, too worldly for George. He was happier in Lotos-land, soothed by sonorous melodies.

'So. Thanks for that. Most helpful. But did you say there was something else?'

'Yes, well, after Suzy died there were floods of letters of

condolence. I presume that's what they are. I kept them too.' He started to rummage in the briefcase.

'No! Please, no.'

'But surely James, you need to acknowledge them?'

'Do I? I suppose I could have a card printed, and send it to all those who have written.'

'It's a bit impersonal, but better than nothing. I'd be happy to look after that. What wording do you want?'

I pretended to think for a moment. 'I think the following would be appropriate, don't you? *Thank you for your recent communication, expressing sorrow about the death of Suzy Moulton. I'm sorry about it too.*'

'Honestly, James!'

'Indeed. All most of them are doing is being polite, following form, making sure they feel they have behaved properly. Hardly an ounce of true feeling in most of them. I've written such rubbish myself.'

'Let's leave it then.'

A few minutes later I saw him to the door, and pulled him to my chest, briefly.

'Thank you, my very dear old friend.'

His eyes misted again, and he turned to go. 'Of course.'

I'd left the letters on the kitchen table. Pouring myself another cup of tea – I hate it lukewarm, but this was not the time for a fresh pot, better a stewed one, makes a better metaphor – I opened the first letter, which George had placed at the top. It was written a few days after the funeral, in her bold, dear hand – she'd taught herself some sort of ersatz italic script when at school, and used a fountain pen with a midsized nib and dark blue ink. I wondered if black would have been more appropriate.

Dear Daddy,

What a day! I guess we got through it, but when I got home I went to bed and howled enough to bring Sam running with a glass of red, and frightened poor little Rudy. He wanted to know about the funeral, and was sad and cross that he wasn't allowed to come. He says he misses Granny, though in ten minutes he will be watching TV happily enough. Lucky him, I won't. I think I will never feel normal again, or do simple things with simple pleasure. An anchor is tugging at my chest, and I feel if I don't resist I will be pulled under, and my heart will drown.

I am desolate that there was nothing I could do to console you, save to hold you up and get on the train with you.

I understand you need some time. Perhaps you might go away? There's that lovely hotel in the New Forest you used to go to? Couldn't you get a room there, stay inside, have yummy treats from room service, maybe a swim once you're feeling better?

Just a thought.

I do love you so. I feel as if – my own dear family notwithstanding – it's just you and me now. We can look after each other, can't we? We owe that to Mummy, bless her. I'll come down to see you in a week or two – perhaps a week on Saturday? Just by myself. It'll be good to have a talk.

Your loving daughter,

Lucy xxxxxxx

The second letter was slim, just a single sheet, hardly bulging the envelope, which looked like it might be empty, and bore (like the others) the stamped Post Office instruction to redirect it to George.

Dear Daddy,
What's going on? I don't understand. It is a week now since I wrote to you, and no answer. I get that, perhaps it is too hard for you, just now? (It's hard for me too!)

But I rang you, and the voice said the number had been disconnected. Your mobile number doesn't work. Emails to you get bounced.

Perhaps you have gone away, as I suggested? That would be a relief. I rang that hotel in the New Forest, but they said they had no record of any reservation in your name.

I feel frantic with worry, it's as if you had disappeared into thin air! Please, please, I beg you to be in touch!

Your worried Lucy, who loves you so much! Xxxxxx
P.S. Rudy says he SO misses Gampy! He does dote on you, you know. And you on him! Don't leave us like this! Don't leave us!

Well, what did I expect? What else would she say? Had the letter arrived on its proper schedule, it would have been intolerable to even see it, and I could not have opened it had I wished to do so. I can now, and I remember why I couldn't. I wish I hadn't.

I do wish Lucy had learned to write properly. I spent years trying to teach her the rules of grammar and punctuation, but she is still addicted to those exclamation marks. It's awful. If the Spartan boy didn't use them when the fox was chewing on his vitals, I don't see what right anyone else has to. At least her letter is handwritten, and she cannot use those typographical figures – they have a name – that make smiling faces. Or frowning ones. Thank heaven for that.

I loathe being called Gampy. I'd settle for Grandfather, it's a biological fact and hence a requirement, I suppose, though I have no sense of being such a person. I have begged them to give me this minimal gravitas, to which I think myself entitled, but *Gampy* has got stuck in Rudy's little brain. It's not that he thinks it's cute. He thinks it's my name. I gather Sam called his grandfathers similarly, so he is – once again – responsible for a risible bit of idiocy. My son-in-law, the social worker.

Anyway Rudy, poor little tyke, won't remember any of this, he's too young and it's too painful. Children are wonderfully self-preserving. They filter memory, cleanse and sanitise it, unless it's too awful to renounce. And this isn't.

Or is it? These gummy spots of time that inexplicably adhere when so much more is erased, how do we account for their tenacity? Why do I remember holding little Lucy's hand, but not bathing her, or combing her hair? Why do I have such a meagre store of memories about her?

Or indeed of myself? My childhood prior to the age of five has largely been erased, leaving only smudgy traces, generated largely, I suspect, by old family photographs. There I am, aged three, feeding the ducks in Regent's Park with Granny and Grandpa. They are dressed in the stuffy adult garb of the 1940s, he in a wide-lapelled suit and trilby, which he wears at a surprisingly jaunty angle, she in stiff undergarments that make her look like a dummy in the window of Selfridges. Grandpa has a funny short moustache, black in the middle, but grey at the sides. Grandma's is sparser, with one long wispy hair.

They pose before the camera – who is taking the picture?

– uneasy and formal, summoning a smile that will not emerge, required by the form to look happy. Which, if you only took the damn camera away, they were.

They loved taking me to the park on Saturday mornings. The fat white ducks would come out of the water and waddle up to us as we opened our bag of stale bread. Close to my feet, quacking. The cement path was slippery in the rain, covered with yucky duck poo. Granny held my hand, and I fed them with my other. It was exciting and frightening. I had to hold my hand up high or the greedy duckies would grab the bread with their beaks, right out of my fingers. Maybe they'd try to eat my finger too. I can see this, I can remember it. I have constructed it out of the raw material of the photo and something buried in me, undead.

My schoolboy and undergraduate years, largely undocumented in the family album, are available to me as through a mist. I was self-conscious about being photographed and intellectually opposed to it. I refused to own a camera, or to appear before one. Recording, rather than living, I would sniff. I wish I had known better, but why would I? Later on, Suzy and I travelled a bit, as little as I could negotiate. I am of Larkin's party with regard to 'abroad'. I disapprove of it. Even dear Lucy's childhood reappears only in vignettes that I rather suspect I have invented, or at least elaborated considerably.

Opening her third letter, I knew things were about to get a lot more memorable. Anyway, I don't have enough time left to me to forget painful things, though I let a lot of the non-essential stuff slip away happily enough.

My short term memory is shot, shocking in its absence. Sometimes I don't even remember what it is I am trying to remember. I have invented a set of rituals that help get me through my daily chores, to evade the casual eclipses of my mind:

Teeth brushed? Feel the toothbrush. Is it wet? Surprisingly hard to tell sometimes. Never mind, doesn't hurt to brush again.

Flies zipped? Wait for another wee, it'll be coming soon. Remember to zip. Forget.

Had my coffee? Don't empty the plunger, and see if the grounds are wet.

Drunk enough water? Suzy says I get very dehydrated and it makes me grumpy and low on energy. I never remember to keep myself topped up. Do not know how to remedy this. Nor do I remember if and when I have. Keep a bottle of water on various tables, see how full it is (if I have indeed remembered to fill it).

Eaten lunch? Who cares?

Taken my pills? Need to make a note each time. Pad in bathroom next to pills on the shelf, with list. *Remembered to note taken pills on list?* Sometimes. Most of them are prophylactic, which may mean I am a hypochondriac. Statins to warn off cholesterol, beta blockers for fibrillations, tranquillizers for life.

I resent having gout, but the medication has unpleasant side effects so I won't take it. Better to suffer (a lot!) very occasionally. It migrates from toe to ankle to knee, and once it has set in I hobble and swear for a week. It's unfair. I am the wrong demographic: I eat abstemiously, though perhaps I drink a bit too much, and I hardly carry an excess pound, even at my advanced, unexercised age.

Gout is a somatic metaphor, as that irritating American woman with big black hair used to say. I am overheated, swollen, aching, need to take to my bed and get off my feet. My first attack came a month after Suzy was diagnosed, though I had no idea what it was. I thought I must have bumped my ankle. I'm always bumping into things. But after three days, when it was swollen and red and throbbing and felt like a knife was stuck in it, it occurred to me that it must be the old Semitic blight.

Dad!

I came by the house yesterday, to find it virtually boarded up. The door has been changed, and my key will not work. There is no letter box! How did you do that? And why? No door knocker. The bell hardly rings.

And there's a spyhole? Who are you so afraid to see? It has to be me, doesn't it? You're hardly a target for the Mafia. No, it's Me!! Your daughter!!! Whose mother has just died!!!!

For God's sake, what is wrong with you? I rang the bells of the neighbours, but no one even knows who you are. Ah, the friendly joys of London life, the mutual concern, the sense of community! That nasty fellow next door said he thought he'd seen you peering out the back window into his garden, and wanted to know more about you. There was something creepy about him, as if he could do horrid things. Nice neighbour that one is!

This means you are in there, hiding, like some neurotic Victorian spinster. I banged on the door, and came back later and did it again. I left a note on it, so perhaps you will know what I was feeling. (The note was not half as angry as I am now!)

For pity's sake – for your own sake, for mine – for all of us, come out. It cannot be as bad out here as it must be in there.

I'm furious with you, but we need to be together. I can get over the anger if you will only meet me halfway. Any way. Just meet me. This cannot be allowed to go on, I fear for what it is doing to you, and to me, and to us. Mummy would be appalled.

There's nothing the matter with you! She's the dead one – so you have to be the live one!

Lucy

The only good news is that the next letter was shorter. The contents were predictable.

If you cannot see me – yet – I hope you might meet with someone – maybe that funny George from school? He seems harmless. But you have to let someone in or that outer door is going to become an inner one. A symbol. It already is. Is everyone locked out? I hope not! Even prisoners are allowed visitors. If they will allow them.

Which was tolerable enough, and hardly hurt a bit. But then, this next missive:

You bastard! How could you? Even after these months I cannot believe that you could sink so low. First you abandon your loved ones. You lock yourself up like a lunatic. OK my therapist says I have to understand the extremities of grief. To understand, to forgive you. If I ever see you again.

But this takes the biscuit: you fired Bronya! How dare you! She wanted to help! I told her everything. About you and Mum and how terrible it all was. She has been trying to get you out of yourself, make sure you eat, tried to rekindle some warmth in you, get you interested in books and talk again.

And you get frightened, poor little you. Somebody getting a touch too close? Fired her by email! Without the guts even to do it to her face, you just slink away. Coward! There she is, living on nothing, sharing a room in Uxbridge, sending a few pounds a month home. Being kind to you. Oh no! Thanks anyway.

And the funny thing is, she says she forgives you.

I don't.

Go to Hell. Stay there.

Bronya? Lucy? What? How? I have never used the term – it's a cliché beloved of second-rate novelists and makers of worthy documentaries – but here it comes: *dumbfounded*. Even that is thin and inadequate . . . The hell with the little Spartan boy, I feel some exclamations coming on: Bronya! Lucy!

What the fuck?

Lucy never swears, this is totally out of character for her, whose girlhood reaction to Suzy's foul mouth was to offer to wash her own out with soap. I would feel proud of the vulgar new her if I wasn't numb with astonishment.

Of course the letter was written two months ago, before Bronya's night-time visitation. My God! Lucy would now know about that too. Which means, does it not, she might have let herself in, instead of Bronya? Too frightened, I suppose.

Could she have put Bronya up to it? It's outrageous! *Darling Bronya, maybe you could sneak in, and throw the old man, you know, how we say in English, a pity fuck?*

And she accuses me of abusing Bronya, of treating her instrumentally!

For the first time I feel inclined to answer. To fight

back. I'm sick of cowering and being abused. A rent girl. Hot Sex from Sofia! That'll get the old codger up and about!

Bitch.

This is the last letter I will write.

I no longer have a mother but I am close to her. She is dead but not to me.

I have a father? No. No father. He is alive, but not for me.

I hope you are scalded by shame, but I doubt it.

Goodbye.

And then, postmarked a month later, an overstuffed envelope, the last of the series.

Dear Daddy,

I'm sorry, I'm so sorry.

I don't want to lose you, but you're lost. Wherever I look you're not there. I don't know what to do. I know I can't leave you marooned or hiding like a hermit in a cave, or whatever it is you now are.

Sam says I am being a wimp (he means, as usual!) and that I ought to let him come down to London with me and a hammer and a screwdriver and an axe if needs be, and simply roust you out, drag you blinking into the light. That's not like him. He hates fights and confrontations, but he's so angry with you, and so frustrated.

I'm not, not any more. I am sort of, I don't know what to call it, I always get so anxious even talking to you, much less writing, you're so pernickety and precise. When I was little – and not so little! – I was shy and tongue-tied, not because I am basically like that, but because you made me feel bashful and inadequate, as if whatever I said or did was never going to be right, not quite up to your high standard. Standards. I was such a compliant little girl, so easily hurt, so anxious not to cause that unpleasant wince you make when something isn't quite good enough, when your eyebrows raise a little, and your mouth purses: an opinion, an action, a way of saying. A sentence.

But, who cares? I am sort of post-angry. Not resigned, I'm certainly not that. I know I need to reclaim you, get you back to yourself, and to me. And to your family, which, however much you shrug, is basically all you have, all that matters. You don't know this, but it's true.

I also know that Sam's way won't work, it'd make things much worse. You can drag a hermit out of his cave, but all he'll do is blink and shrink and slink back.

For God's sake, people lose their partners, people die, it happens rather a lot. We suffer from it, we are knocked sideways, we grieve. But we don't run away, don't hide like a mole in a hole – I hope that offends you, I'm sick of having to interrogate my metaphors.

We knew Mummy was dying, she was ready to go, it was a relief and a release for all of us when she finally passed away. So why are you so determined to follow her, to pass away from us all, from yourself?

This is the closest I've ever got – God isn't this sad? – to talking to you frankly, and fully, with proper feeling and in my own stumbling way, my own voice, do you call it? Ever since I was a girl you've loomed in my imagination like a mythical figure, not God exactly, but someone strong and silent and towering, who needs to be placated, and whose judgements will be severe. Not wrath. No. I can hardly recall you raising your voice to me. Just some sort of remote being that one ought never to displease, but often does.

One? I know whenever I call myself that there's something gone wrong. One? Who's that? Posh talk, crap. I'm just trying to say I have always been in awe of you, and wished there could be some real communication between us. Or do I mean some communion? Like there was between Mummy and me. Yes, I know we fought, and I know she was always trying to remake me in her image, but she was there, she cared.

And you know what? Is this pathetic? I took her for granted. Mummy was always there, on the phone, in my house, in my face. And you never were. I'd ring, and you'd pass as little time as you could asking the obvious questions – How've you been? How's little Rudy? – never anything about my work or friends, because you have no idea what I do, or who I love – and grudgingly at last do give my regards to Sam. Hold on, I'll get Mummy.

Mummy I could take for granted. I had her. It is you I have . . . what? I don't know the word. I wanted to say yearned for, but that sounds icky. Maybe you'll know what I mean, you're so good with words, and I'm so halting and lame.

Rudy keeps asking me where you are, and where you went. At first I said you were very sad after Gramma's death and needed to be alone. Rudy said that was OK, but the next day he asked, 'Does Gampy have to be alone still?' Then I said you were ill, but not very, not like in a hospital. And now what am I to say? That for some reason, some unfathomable reason, you do not care to see him, or me, or Sam? He's a child, he thinks everything is about him. And he knows that his grandfather has abandoned him.

And to me, ever and always, if a ghost a very dear ghost. Undead, just frozen. Tell me what I can do to warm you up, anything, whatever, anytime. Tell me and I will come. Ever since I left you at Paddington, so long ago it seems now, so very long, I have been desperate to talk to you. There's still issues we need to talk about, aren't there? I'm not sure if they can be resolved, but for goodness' sake can we find a way to talk? For once? And at last?

You can rely on me. Can I rely on you?

Lucy xxxx

What is one to say to that?

The Mercedes – the windows mildly tinted, insufficient for an endangered Colombian drug lord, but better than nothing – arrived precisely at 9 a.m. A courteous young woman knocked at the door, dressed in an unnaturally crisp, unbecoming uniform of synthetic material, printed in bilious discordant tones, festooned with the corporate logo, as if to mock me. 'EUROPCAR! EUROPCAR!' She took me efficiently through the paperwork, copied my licence details onto the form, tried to sell me various unnecessary insurances, asked me to initial the document in a variety of places, handed over the keys, and made off. A colleague in another Europcar (a Ford) waited at the kerbside for her.

I was ready to go, because the rental car was parked illegally just outside the house. I could have put one of those fill-out forms for visitors in the windscreen, and kept it there for a few hours, but what's the point? The longer I delayed, the less likely I was to get myself going.

It was hardly a Prestige Mercedes, merely a basic – the Americans call them compact – E-class saloon, of the sort that rightly become taxis in Berlin, which impress everyone who rides in them except the Germans. I should have asked for a top-of-the-range Vauxhall, an altogether better (and cheaper) vehicle. What a sucker I am.

I felt happy in it nonetheless. I put my luggage in the boot, adjusted the seats and mirrors (not as easy as it sounds), found Radio 3 on the stereo, and placed my provisions on the seat next to me. Thermos of coffee, mobile phone, downloaded route instructions from the AA website, bottle of water, Valium, digoxin, paracetamol, ibuprofen, and a hip flask of brandy.

It should only take an hour and a half. I started the car and moved slowly away. Unused to the automatic transmission – a barbarous invention that takes the fun, and control, out of driving – I missed the clunky solidity of my beloved 3.8. Nothing like those old Jaguars (*not* Jags) to anchor you to the road. The Mercedes, in comparison, felt as if it were floating. But there was none of the anxiety that I had anticipated, cocooned from the world, with that curious and inappropriate sense of privacy and invulnerability that afflicts we drivers, until we run over a dog. It's so comfortable to be behind the wheel, I love driving, and the car, though underpowered and pedestrian, handled neatly and accurately as I took it through the first turns and roundabouts on the way to the M40.

It was so fine, it felt new – renewing – listening to a Bach Brandenburg Concerto, entering the Westway, humming along, waving a finger conducting the orchestra. I hadn't felt so alive – indeed, I had hardly felt alive at all – since Suzy died. Because of a car? Not quite . . . but it helped. Perhaps I should get the Jaguar out of the garage when I got back, smarten it up.

At the ramp on the entry to the A40 there was a sign announcing Road Works, and we came to a halt, inching ahead for the next twenty minutes. Next to me was a filthy nondescript van with a youth playing his stereo so loudly that I could feel my steering wheel vibrate. The music – if it could be called that – was harrowingly invasive. Rapping? Heavy metals? It rasped like a file against my nerves, and of a sudden I was enraged that I should be so thoughtlessly subjected to it.

I wound down my window and gesticulated towards the driver. He neither saw nor heard me, nodding his head to the thump! thump! thump! of the bass, lost in his hideous, empty, meaningless little world. I was filled with a loathing so intense that it quite took my breath away. I wished I'd had some Spikedog-repellent to throw in his eyes. I looked at the seat next to me, hoping to locate something else – if not better – to throw out of the window to attract his attention.

A bottle of Valium tablets! Not for throwing, for relief! Cap off, wash 10 mg down with a glug of water. It tastes of plastic. Could I throw the bottle itself? That'd work, but then there is no water. It'd be worth it, after all I still had my thermos. I lowered my electric window, grasped the water bottle firmly in my right hand, and took aim. It wasn't as easy as it sounds, strapped into a seat, unable to turn sideways. I might use a side-arm backhand motion, remembering Suzy's tips when she'd tried fruitlessly to teach me tennis (rather like teaching a canary to ride a bicycle). No wrist action. Single, taut sweeping motion. Steady backswing, wide shoulder turn, eye focused, follow through. I can do this, I counselled myself, thinking of my aim when I'd lobbed Spikedog his retributions.

The van's window was partially open, the sound issuing from it like a sub-nuclear blast. I could feel it on my face, my cheeks wobbled. A good shot might actually hit him between the eyes. Even a poor one would make a thump against his window. But even as I contemplated this revenge, I knew I couldn't pull it off physically. Emotionally I was ready for a fight, yearning for one, but there was too little space, too small a target. The damn bottle would bounce off the door frame and bop me on the nose. Life begins as tragedy and ends as farce.

The traffic moved on, and the offending vehicle and its offensive occupant moved ahead of me, to be replaced by a sedate Jaguar with a gentleman in it. I took the cap off my thermos and poured a cup of lovingly made coffee. It tasted slightly off, though I always use a glass-lined flask. Never mind. Wait for the Valium to kick in, only not too strongly or I'd end up, shudder, in Beaconsfield, marooned in the fibrillating heartland of England.

On the motorway at last, there was a curious sensation, as my speed reached 80 and the extraordinary engineering of a modern car − and of 10 milligrams of Valium − kicked in. There was virtually no sound from wind or road, and even more oddly, no sense of movement itself, as if I were stationary in the car and the road was unrolling itself under me, like those machines Lucy once played at seaside arcades.

I was rather enjoying the sensation, instead of driving, I was just sitting in the comfort of my leather chair while the unfurling asphalt did all the work. Listening to the music, I had a desire to recline the seat and close my eyes.

If he hadn't honked furiously as I drifted into the fast lane, we would have collided. The driver shook his fist as he overtook me.

Shaken, I pulled over to the left. There was a hard shoulder that I might have availed myself of, but suddenly the rush of passing vehicles frightened me, and I felt I would rather be in it than perched defencelessly at its side. I slowed to 45 miles an hour, in itself unsafe, in order to get some sense of the road in which I was in control, rather than it. It worked slowly. Cars honked as they passed. Elderly gentleman, hapless tootler.

I turned off the music, which jangled my nerves. Nothing would have calmed them, for the Valium, oddly, made me feel both drowsy and anxious, adding to my problems rather than solving them.

Eyes on the road, calm and steady, I reached the turning to Oxford and made my way along the endless approach road into the suburban wastes of Risinghurst, around the ring road until the Woodstock Road exit, then slowly towards the centre. The Old Parsonage Hotel – the best available in a city which should have good hotels but does not – was on my right. Whatever its deficiencies proved to be, it was within easy reach of both Merton and St Anne's, neither of which I had visited for many years.

I eased into the small car park, found the last available space, turned off the car, remembering to put it into 'Park', and slumped over the wheel. Time passed. I may have fallen asleep, because there was a sharp knock on my window, startling, and a young man peered in, concerned that some old duffer was using the only available parking place for his afternoon nap.

I tried the window, but it would not work. Turned on the engine, pushed the button.

'Can I help you in some way, sir?' he asked in a manner studiedly neutral, but incipiently confrontational.

'Yes. Of course. I wish to check in. Your desk will be expecting me. Darke, James Darke. *Doctor*.'

'Welcome to the Old Parsonage, doctor. I'll see to it that your bags are delivered to your room. The registration desk is on your left as you enter the hotel.'

I'd booked a Junior Suite – a term that irritated me, only Americans call themselves Junior – for a week, and after the formalities of checking in, was escorted to it. On acquaintance, the emphasis was certainly on the 'Junior'. But it was tucked away on the ground floor, with windows opening onto a small summerhouse in a courtyard garden. The sitting area was as small as the bathroom, but there was a small desk on the outer wall of the bedroom, adequate for my writing materials and computer. I'd even brought my mobile phone. I have a horror of making personal calls on a hotel phone, with some nosey receptionist listening in, while simultaneously charging you enough to buy a decent lunch.

I had requested an extremely quiet room, and it was, at least at that time of day. It had a minimal ersatz country-house charm – not offensive – impersonal, but not alienating. Perhaps too much grey for my taste. But there was the desk and a hard chair, with internet access if I needed it. I wouldn't. I plonked myself onto the sofa, feeling more alone than I had in my many months in the house. But it was good, at the same time, to emerge at the mercy of the world. And of my daughter. My dear Lucy.

After a nap that failed to refresh, leaving me groggy and irritable, I ordered a pot of Assam with shortbread from room service. The waiter paused imperceptibly after leaving the tray, as if he expected a tip for accomplishing the Herculean task of bringing it to my room.

After my trials on the outward journey – like Stanley, having conquered the dark spaces – I was hardly up to a further expedition into the street. Best to settle in for a while. I'd brought some minimal reading sustenance, in the form of the *New Yorker*, *The Economist*, *The Spectator*, even a copy of the *LRB*, with its dread typeface. Po-face, I should call it. I considered throwing it out immediately, but sometimes there's something instructive in it.

Magazines stink of death, whatever temporary moment they celebrate soon past, unremembered. They are lightweight, disposable, generally ill printed and badly designed. Inadequate containers, even, for an order of fish and chips.

I hadn't brought any books, there was something physically repellent about them just then, not sure why. The dust, the mouldering paper, the smell of dissolution . . . The death of the book? I could no longer read one without a struggle. I kept falling asleep, drifting into unrelated reverie, uncompelled by the arbitrary fantasy that the author had put before me, some fiction that was supposed to make me excited but didn't – like trying to penetrate a long-abandoned lover, grown old, baggy and strange, desirable as a stewed cabbage.

Anyway reading would have distracted me. I needed to keep writing. To tell some final bits of a story partially mine, partially that of others, essential in that fruitless way that all intensely felt human projects are. The proximity to our old Oxford addresses, the colleges, the flat in Park Town, would be a spur to memory, and the painful warmth of nostalgia.

In the morning I took a walk to clear my head and to revisit some old haunts. *Old. Haunts.* Rather than walk to Merton – though I could feel a magnetic pull towards my old college – I walked north towards St Anne's, making my way past the porter while his back was turned, and entering the grounds for the first time in almost fifty years. Though Suzy had invited me to accompany her to the occasional Gaudy – she liked keeping up with the girls, now women – I couldn't imagine why I should. I didn't go to them at Merton – I loathed the very thought of it, the creepy recidivism – so why go to hers to meet the aged incarnations of youngsters whom I'd never met?

Suzy's former room was on the left, up staircase B, overlooking the quadrangle. Sometime after we met she had invited me for tea – a hopeful sign, I thought – and when she showed me in, she immediately apologised for the clothes strewn about, stained coffee cups on the top of her desk, saucers of smelly cigarette butts with lipstick rings – the louche fusty air of the garret. I suspected that she cultivated the look, and the manner, but I was wrong. It was as natural to her as the wave in her dirty blonde hair, or the odd tuck of her chin.

She noticed me looking about. I couldn't help it, my face is made for judging and is incapable – volition has nothing to do with it – of dissembling. My stray thoughts deploy themselves across my features, be they disapproval or doubt, lust or disgust. My nose twitches, my eyes fix, my jaw clenches. I must have sniffed or recoiled, however inadvertently. She had already described me as 'fastidious' during our first sustained conversation after a seminar on Chaucer. I was rather hurt by the accuracy of this. As I looked around her room, she shrugged with a touch of bravado: 'You'll have to forgive me, I'm a bit of a slut.'

Such provocation, this charming archaism! What an opportunity! I had an immediate impulse to act. I looked around the room for a duster, perhaps even a Hoover. In twenty minutes I could have made a serious difference here: I loved cleaning and straightening. Even my scout wasn't good enough at it – the rooms looked worse after he'd finished with them, and he was forbidden from doing anything other than cleaning the windows, which he did adequately. On being so instructed he looked at me intently, searching his vocabulary for the absent term *anal*.

'Bit particular, sir?'

'I am. It'll save you trouble.'

'It's no trouble, sir. It's my job.'

Wash up Suzy's filthy cups, empty those reeking saucers, fold the clothes and put the others on hangers into the wardrobe, dust, straighten, make up the bed. She must have had a scout more sluttish, even, than she. Or did St Anne's not rise to scouts?

She saw me looking at the rumpled sheets and wayward counterpane of her bed, and mistook my intentions as much as I had mistaken hers. But I wouldn't have entered it in such a state. Or her. Start as you mean to go on.

Some weeks later, when we were semi-officially a couple, she asked to visit my rooms. The prospect was alarming: if she was a bit of a slut, I was a lot of a fusspot. I made sure, painful as it was, to de-Jamesify my premises as far as I was able. I allowed two unsharpened pencils in my pen and pencil holder, kept my typewriter slightly offline on my desk, allowed a few novels to drift out of alphabetical order, neglected to plump up my pillows and cushions, let the Persian carpet drift off-centre. When the time came, her hand went to her face, as if to adjust a mask to keep her germs from entering the atmosphere. I wanted to shout: 'But look, it's messy!'

God knows what she saw in me. People must have wondered, though I was reckoned, at the time, to look something like Peter O'Toole, which was presumably intended as a compliment, but was inaccurate. I was taller than he, and slimmer, and my eye lacked any semblance of a come-hither twinkle. I was like one of the grave-diggers in *Hamlet*, only funnier and better dressed. Anyway, I detested actors and the theatre, taking Miss Austen's view of them: all that feigning and dissembling overheats the imagination and the blood. Give me a great poem any time.

We'd go for a coffee after tutorials – not a modern make-it-while-you-wait-for-a-long-time concoction assembled by a so-called barista – but for some builder's coffee at George's in the Covered Market. She was interested in me, though I was too naive to recognise a sexual motive, which would have frightened me. In her asexual presence I was natural, opinionated and argumentative. She liked that, she was a competitor through and through. 'Sporty' we called it then. I'd met the type, of course, at school, and never bonded with any of them.

I reluctantly allowed her to initiate me, sometimes going to the Parks to watch the University play cricket. I rather liked that. I would make up a luncheon hamper, Suzy would bring a bottle of wine and thermos of coffee, and I could sit in a deckchair and read *The Times*. Now and again a weak case of the claps would issue from the assembled watchers – never more than about sixty of us – and I would belatedly join in and say 'Well played!' in what I thought of as a hearty tone.

'Oh, do shut up, James. What are you applauding for anyway? You were reading.'

'I am joining in the spirit of the game. Jolly good stuff!'

She glared at me. The next term she conceived a plan – by way of punishment for my cricketing inattention – to go up to the Manor Ground in Headington to watch Oxford United. Instead of a hamper – 'totally wrong, love!' – we arrived a few minutes early and queued to buy meat patties in baps with stewed onions and red sauce, and bought a beer inside the ground.

I munched and quaffed stoically, settled into my uncomfortable seat, observing only that I would prefer a deckchair.

'You're lucky to be sitting at all! I would prefer standing myself, but you're such a wimp!'

'I rather object to that. We're called sybarites. And you won't find many of us here.' United employed two brothers, one in the middle of the field, called The Tank, who later became a manager and smoked cigars, though palpably a Woodbines man. The other, smaller and redheaded, was called George, and could – even to my eye – play a bit, unlike most of his fellows. They were a hapless lot, but unobjectionable. Those days, players went to the ground on public transport, drank at the local with the locals, made a living wage. Kept their working-class roots. You couldn't have picked them out in the street, and most of them would have been embarrassed if you had.

Now, top-division teenagers make more money in a week than a University Vice Chancellor does in a year, drive fleets of supercars, fuck whoever and whenever, wherever and however. Spoiled brats, deracinated, unattached to any community other than their own. Their game a hateful, ubiquitous spectacle. I gather it is now largely peopled by itinerant EU mercenaries, and by Africans, whom they sweep off their native veldt, hang up in a tree to mature for a year or two, and then unleash upon their slower and less gifted white contemporaries. Within a few years they are making more in a week than ten thousand of their poor compatriots make in a year. I'll bet none of those starving millions catch any trickle-down.

In the new spirit of enforced sportiness, during summer term I would occasionally meet Suzy at the college tennis courts – she played number one for St Anne's, and was hoping for an invitation to join the University squad. She would have preferred a blue to a First, though eventually, to her disappointment, she got the latter and not the former.

'That bitch Hilda,' she said, 'I can beat her three out of four times, but she's fucking the Secretary and I haven't got a chance, unless I go down on that frightful dyke, like the rest of them. No way!'

One afternoon I arrived to find her in the midst of a strenuous session with – to my surprise – not one of the lissom college girls, but a blocky, ginger-haired, red-faced lad, hardly taller than she was, who gave the ball a ferocious wallop. When he announced the score, it was obvious – from his accent – who he must be. He'd been pestering her for a knock-up, and she'd finally capitulated, though she hadn't told me. Or perhaps they'd been knocking away all term? She'd been airily dismissive of him – 'a real Lancashire hotpot, that one' – and had apparently decided to teach him a lesson. Or, two lessons.

The first was on the court, where it was clear, even to my untutored eye, that though her suitor could smash a first serve and bash a forehand, the rest of his game was rudimentary. His backhand faltered, he moved about the court like a bear, his game had neither variety nor delicacy. She ran him around, hit drop shots, acute angles, under- and over-spin, conducting the rallies with contemptuous grace. After one supreme example, in which she'd drawn him to the net with a drop shot, flicked a lob over his head which he manfully retrieved, only to be drawn in and passed, he sat on the baseline gasping for breath. She hardly gave him a look, or time to recover, before taking her place to serve.

She moved with wonderful ease, and if I closed my eyes, I could hear no more than the swishing of her skirt – can one really hear a skirt swish? – as she glided about the court, with satisfying thwacks every now and again. This was in that prelapsarian age before a certain Miss Seles began to emit a hideous grunt whenever she hit a shot. Everyone was so appalled that no one thought it seemly to ask her to desist, as if she had begun farting and couldn't stop. She not only looked like a piglet, she sounded like one.

I was delighted when I read that she had been attacked, taking it as an appropriate protest against her acoustic crimes: designed to shut her up, and all those who followed her example, like smacking the fat lady if she sings out of tune. I assumed that the insertion of a modest kitchen knife into her back, as she sat at the side of the court, was intended to be threatening but not life-threatening, an aide-memoire: *Shut up or you will be even sorrier!*

But it turned out – how often one is disappointed by one's fellow man – that her attacker was merely a stalker, without an aesthetic or critical bone in his body. What a shame. I am opposed to gratuitous stabbing. You never know what it will lead to. Poor Miss Seles recovered slowly, which was good, and eventually returned to the courts, which was not. Generations of grunters and screamers followed, most of them Eastern European piglets swilling and squealing at the money trough, and the tennis authorities were too intimidated and witless to ban them. I have hardly watched a match since that time, nor do I care who wins the now degraded Wimbledon, where silence is demanded only of the spectators.

In her own elegant way, Suzy was knifing her opponent, humiliating him, making him cringe with frustration as he ran about manfully and fruitlessly. She wanted both to wind him, and to wind him up. She mimicked his accent when she announced the score. She had an aversion to Northerners that amounted to a phobia, though she was ignorant about geography – the North started in Birmingham and ended in Scotland – and could not distinguish Yorkshire from Lancashire, she adamantly maintained that the whole area – and its people – stank of the mill and the pit: grimy, ugly, blackened by toil.

'After all,' she'd say, with mock reasonableness, 'look at what they name their towns! Bury, Blackpool, Burnley, Grimsby, Hull (though they spell it wrong). That's probably how they say it: "What the hull, luv." Blackburn, for fuck's sake! And that awful place where they play cricket and chant at those lovely West Indians, and wave bananas. Tell me who the monkeys are, really! Thank God they change their accents quick enough once they come down south, else they'd be laughed back home again.' (Hearing this, I decided to suppress any reference to my own Northern antecedents, shallow though those roots were.)

The English are masters at making foreigners – and better yet their fellow countrymen – feel insecure. The French? Pah, you can flick their arrogance off like a bogey, and be untouched by it. It's merely gestural, nothing to do with you. But a nicely educated English public school product can make you feel undermined, and ashamed. Suzy could do it effortlessly, but often chose to try. She treated her Lancashire suitor with an amused contempt that, had he not been a stolid Northerner, would have shrivelled his ego and made him slink home. Even so, as she kept announcing the score in her cod-Lancashire accent – 'Aye, that'd be forty love, luv!' – he became increasingly uncomfortable, even though her accent was risible. All she did was add a lot of 'ayes' and 'lads' and 'luvs' and overlay a generic, ill-observed 'Northern' inflection.

When I challenged her about this afterwards, she laughed. 'Northerners,' she said, 'are not only crass and ugly, they're as insensitive as Germans. You can say anything to them – they do it to each other all the time, as long as you add "lass" or "lad", any old insult will do – they hardly even notice.'

'I thought he was rather hurt.'

'Was he? Good. Maybe he'll leave me alone now.'

He never asked for another further knock-up. I, on the other hand, found her callous aggression surprisingly exciting.

I was still a virgin. Luckily. A number of my fellow school-boys had lost their cherries, both active and passive – the former rather admired, the latter scorned – pursuing in-house activities that frightened and rather disgusted me. There was something of a vogue, amongst these boys, for reading novels with lashings of buggery. Apparently these were serious literature: the Edmund White sort of books. I looked into one or two of them to see what the fuss was about, but the more Vaseline there is in a novel, the less gripping it is.

I'd have my furtive wanks, hurried and embarrassed, as a way of letting off steam, but I'd never developed that frenzied enthusiasm for orgasms that defines the average schoolboy. No, my sexual life was solitary, silent in the lavatory stall, clandestine, flushed.

I knew that Suzy's slut remark referred to her untidiness, but perhaps not only that? She was cheerful, free, physically luxuriant, and wore her body with an ease and grace that rather astonished me, straight-backed and stiff-shouldered as I was.

I've always found running an uncomfortably conscious act, and appear – I have, alas, seen a videotape of myself at a trot – as if I had learned to do it from a manual. Lift foot, bend knee, lean forwards, plant foot at same time as raising following foot, establish momentum, repeat until perfected. It never was. I ran as if comprised of metallic bits. Whereas Suzy had nothing self-conscious in her carriage, she loped, as great a pleasure to watch as a leopard.

Not that I'd ever seen a leopard. Or a girl, either. I knew – even I, unconscious though I was, untutored, diffident, gawky and constrained – that it was only a matter of time until that body and mine were entwined on or under that Indian bedspread, in the dinky single bed in her college room. It was a fearful prospect.

What bits of porn were available in the slink-to-Soho magazines and videos had hardly entered my field of vision. Of course some of the boys had bits and pieces of portable naughtiness, which were passed about until the pages fell out, and a few videos were said to be available around the school, though there was precious little time to watch them, with the constant fear of being found out, humiliated and rusticated, and exposed to one's parents as a pervert.

Nowadays, eight-year-olds with access to the internet might offer tutorials on deviant sexual practices to Stekel and Krafft-Ebing, and are presumably overheated in some unthinkable pre-pubescent way, rubbing their immature stiffening willies, lubricating and throbbing in their front bottoms.

Vaginas. I was – I still am – unclear what the best word is. Suzy used 'pussy', which was a bit cute, as if in conscious denial of the perils that lie below. Anyhow, it is hard to make a relationship with a cat. I don't like them. At school Boylston called their nethers – and girls in general – 'gash', with a leering flourish that suggested he knew and loved how archaic and improper the term was.

'For fuck's sake, Boylston,' I said, 'you make it sound like a wound.'

'It is. Why's it bleeding all the fucking time?'

Cunts. I settled upon the Old English term, as having some historical and linguistic gravitas: Chaucer used it, and it is still fresh, racy and modern. I'd seen the occasional picture of one, but knew it would be inadequate preparation for the real thing. I was full of awe and fear and longing at the prospect.

I knew the general idea. It was like a car. It wouldn't run properly if it was cold. But if you warmed it up slowly – no zoom-zoom pedal to the metal, just a thoughtful and unhurried transition from first to fourth with a smooth forward motion – then the internal oils would warm up, lubrication would spread through the system, and you would get a satisfying ride. If it was a Ferrari, you might hope for more than that, but I could never afford one of those.

Once I got over my initial apprehension, and learned to delay the onset of orgasm by the repetition of a few judicious internal mantras, our love-making became increasingly active and satisfying. Suzy took me through the rudiments, introducing me to this, demonstrating that. Nipples got erections too! Even mine. This was a clitoris. Bit like a dick. But for the first few weeks it was a simple enough missionary matter, and it was up to her – she admitted to four previous lovers, though she may have been swanking it – to lead the way.

What really alarmed me, even after the loss of my virginity, was how different cunts were to what I was used to, how much more dangerous and complex. A multi-tasking sort of organ. When it wasn't peeing, it was bleeding, dicks went in – careful! – or babies came out. Like the sea, it was deep and dangerous, unfathomable.

One evening, back in her room after our afternoon seminar, we finished off a bottle of Spanish red wine – £1.99

at our local, better suited to vinaigrette dressing than drinking – and Suzy said 'let's fuck!' She was libidinous. Girls were. Autonomously. They did not have to fall in love, or have a reason, or be drunk. They were not sluts, they just liked – some of them anyway – to have lots of sex. It was news to me, and like most men of my generation I never entirely took it in. Lust was something that men felt and women responded to, that was the natural course of things.

Once we had our clothes off and were in the bed, it appeared that she had something geographically new in mind. First she turned herself round, and started nibbling at my cock. And as soon as I had registered the unexpected delight of this, she had flipped about and there was her cunt in my face. A second before there'd been a ceiling, the top half of a window, some faded damask curtains. Then – a cunt. It was baptismally wet, and I was obviously expected to immerse myself in its waters and be saved. Oh Jesus God, oh God Jesus.

I was shocked, about to drown in a marine world of tiny pink crustaceans newly escaped from their shells, swim-mingly alive, briny, edible. I took a deep breath. You can do it, I thought. Sink or swim. Sink and swim. I stuck out my tongue. 'Higher up,' she urged, adjusting her body. I found just the right sea creature and licked it as instructed. It worked a treat. I slurped away blissfully, as she reciprocated below, and my cock was engulfed. I was sucked in, enfolded by her arms, her legs rounded my head, she had improbably multiple limbs, suction valves, watery depths: chaos, an octopus, a biological process.

When I opened my eyes once more, I was staring directly at – virtually into – her arsehole. I closed my eyes. I opened them again. It was still there, it was not going to go away. To my surprise it was less alarming, once I managed to isolate form from function, than the roiling seascape below: simpler, and less alien. Ineluctable, moving and beautiful, with its concentric folds of lightly pleated shell pink, what one might later have described as a silken organic garment by Issey Miyake.

Following this rite *de* back passage, my dick now slick and plump as an oyster, full of the most profound satisfaction and gratitude, I pushed myself up on my elbow and dared to kiss her nose, gently.

'What are you thinking about?' she asked.

'I think I adore you.'

'Oh. Don't.'

'Why not?'

'Adoration is for the gods and the magi. I'm not having it. I'm no angel.'

'Thank God for that!' I said.

'I'd be quite happy just to be loved,' she said quietly.

I didn't answer.

A shocking image of the devastated landscape of her dying body interceded. Like coal fields seen from above, that green and pleasant land transformed into slag heaps, dark and burning encrustations, the smell of the undergrowth, the nostril-clogging stench of decay. Her poor breasts, the ruined seascape of her genitals – depleted, scabrous, stinking, encrusted, riddled with bedsores, weeping.

O Dark dark dark. Irrecoverably dark.

For a time the image obliterated the light and I reeled at the insistence of it – the memory. An effort of will pushed it forcibly aside, still potently on the margins of consciousness, lurking and threatening to reappear, and recovered for a few moments my poor dear young Suzy, my girl, my wife, my first and only love.

For, after all, what do I have now but a heap of mutually informing and obliterating images? Time, now, is neither forwards nor back, it swirls and eddies and carries in its occasional tumultuous currents all that I have been, and intimations of what is to come. I see Suzy young and old, vibrantly alive and incontrovertibly, memorably, indelibly dead. I see myself as well. My devoted, hopeful, ignorant young self, my soon-to-be discarded body, my remains.

Starting a novel is the hardest part of the process, Suzy said, except for finding the right voice, honing the language, establishing a point of view, getting to know the characters, developing the narrative, and finding the right ending. Though she plucked her First in English with the facility of a gamekeeper, when she took to fiction her ease deserted her. 'As well it should,' she claimed. Being an undergraduate was easy, and fun, being a novelist wasn't: Joyce and Nabokov weren't fooling around. Or, actually they were, but they were playing in earnest: they were Professors of Fooling Around.

She drafted *The Gristmill* in her last year at Oxford, and rewrote and revised it obsessively over the next two, before it was published to considerable but not universal praise when she was twenty-four. Most critics – she got five reviews, two of them in the broadsheets – looked forward to her next work, suggesting that this one was promising, but not quite satisfying.

Suzy agreed. Indeed, she thought it less good than that. 'But it is the best I can do,' she said. 'Alas.'

She was as serious as a novelist as she had been airily clever as an undergraduate. If you wish to do justice to the comic awfulness of life, she maintained, you have to *concentrate*, which was her favourite word at the time. To concentrate is both to focus and to distil, and that is – isn't it? – what a novelist is supposed to do. She'd never done so before, things having come too easily for her, but she found she rather liked it. It was to be her undoing.

The Gristmill was a densely written but modestly readable *roman-à-clef*, as is predictable and allowable with first novels, and her father found it an uncomfortable experience. He wasn't used to discomfort. He disapproved of it. He was moved, Sir Henry, by the praise his daughter was garnering, for it redounded to his credit, having fathered such a clever – and pretty! – girl. But her portrait of a pompous mock-country squire, too bloated to know that he is a figure of fun, rather discomfited him.

'Not based on me, of course!' he maintained at dinner parties, when someone brought up the subject. Which they did. It became, for a few months, a Dorset dinner-party game, to provoke him in this way.

'Well, dear Henry, you must admit he looks like you, and he sounds like you, and he has many of your attributes.'

'Attributes? Nonsense! He has none of my drive and integrity, nor my sense of fun,' he boomed. 'No, what my clever little one has done is use my shell and filled it with someone else's sand.'

The metaphor rather confirmed the description his little one had made of him: that he had both a loud voice and a tin ear, as if the forcefulness of his delivery had impaired his capacity to hear what he was actually saying. That was all right, though, as no one listened to him anyhow.

Suzy never worried that her old man would be more than temporarily slighted by the portrait: 'he's way too self-absorbed for that. What he will remember is that he is in my novel, not what it says about him.' This was prescient, and *The Gristmill* was rarely mentioned again between them.

Instead, her father hoped that she was at work on another novel? Perhaps one set in India? What a splendid idea!

Unlike her parents, I was unambiguously proud of my brilliant – and pretty! – girl, and pleased to be able to support her. To become a novelist at such an early age, you needed either an indomitable capacity to write while you were also making a living, or a reliable source of external funding to allow you guilt-free days in your study, struggling to make something out of nothing.

Following the death of my grandparents when I was a child – I had few memories of them, just those old photos from which to construct some meagre, moving but inert stories – I'd inherited some money. It was rather a lot, though I never told Suzy how much, nor did she ask. The sum was put in a trust fund, conservatively invested by Coutts for both income and capital growth, and it ensured that neither of us would have to make life-choices based on the need to make a living wage. We would never be wealthy, but we'd have a cushion against any fall.

But we wanted to work: I to teach, she to write. To embark on lives – it seemed rather noble to us – of reading and writing, transported by what we found in the world of books. Literature was our passion and guide. In our careers, we congratulated ourselves, we wouldn't be able to distinguish between work and pleasure. Which is, surely, the desideratum of happiness?

Suzy set to work on a second novel, and found herself drawn, to her consternation, back to Oxford. She was cross about it.

'It's supposed to be up to me, isn't it? I don't want to write a fucking undergraduate novel! How boring is that? But they keep on at me, scenes and memories and characters – Mrs Bed's tutorials, afternoons trying to punt, worrying about Schools, all the boring old Oxford tropes – and when I try to turn them off, to stop up my ears and close my eyes, all I get is static.'

'Am I in it?' I knew myself a better man than her father, and though I had no doubt – or not too much doubt – that she loved me, Suzy had that chip of ice in her budding novelist's soul, a sharp eye and sharper tongue, and I had no desire to see my adolescent fumblings memorialised in print.

'Of course not, darling. Don't worry, you're quite safe . . .'

'That's a relief!'

'. . . I don't have anything to say about you. I don't want to write about you, or Oxford, or – how boring is that? – myself. I want to move on, only my subconscious won't let me.'

It was not the first time I had heard her say so, nor would it be the last. Novelists do go on and on. I'd found myself ceasing even to listen – she rarely spotted it when I went onto automatic pilot – when a wisp of memory drifted into consciousness. I pushed my chair back from the table and went to find the right book.

'Hey, am I boring you that much? Sorry! Where are you going?'

I returned with a biography of D.H. Lawrence and began to leaf through the index.

'How do you spell "*asinorum*"?'

'What?'

'As in *pons asinorum*.'

'How the fuck would I know? I presume *pons* is just p-o-n-s – '

'Never mind, I just found it! Listen to this! It's something Lawrence said to Jessie Chambers after he published *The*

White Peacock. "Publishers take no notice of a first novel. They know that nearly anybody can write a novel, if he can write at all, because it's about himself. A second novel's a step further. It's the third that counts though. That's the *pons asinorum* of the novelist. If he can get over that ass's bridge, he's a writer, he can go on.'"

'What a pompous arsehole,' said Suzy. 'Put him away.'

'Never mind that. What he's doing is giving you permission to write your Oxford novel.'

'Hooray! I have Lorenzo's permission. Now I can get it off my chest, if novelists are allowed to have tits.'

New Oxford Blues was published three years later, and like its predecessor was written in haste and re-penned at leisure. If Texas University were one day to acquire Suzy's archive, there would be boxes full of material relating to the book, from its initial incarnation – written in only eleven weeks – through the multiple drafts and stylistic revisions that made up the final product.

But even in its final iteration, *New Oxford Blues* betrayed – to some of its critics, but most of all to Suzy herself – the fact that her heart was not in it, that she had reverted to her old undergraduate facility, however much she strove to disguise it. She was meticulously, obsessionally observant, and would sit stand for hours in front of my college ('St Anne's has no soul compared to Merton,' she would say ruefully) or in its gardens, observing the changing colours of the stone, the effects of rain and light on the gargoyles on the Chapel, the gradual growth of the mulberries. She had a dozen different ways to distinguish gradations of sunlight. When you read her prose, you had the illusion that you were seeing real things, because she had looked so carefully.

I found this acuity obsessional, though I did not say

so, for ours was a marriage based on the necessity, and virtue, of withholding. Or perhaps I mean learning when to shut up? The business of living together was, in most respects, easily accommodated: the bathroom smells and morning breath, the different ways in which we went to sleep, woke up, breathed, snored, farted, all the organic stuff that drives many young couples into disarray. No worries. I had more money, and shared it, she more libido, freely dispensed.

But there was one area that took years, if not to resolve, then at least to accommodate. She was, by her first wry admission, a slut. She spread herself heedlessly across every available surface and floor, did not straighten up, clean up, even look up as she created a swathe of devastation in the flat. I found this intolerable, and said so repeatedly, and she was happy to reciprocate by labelling me as an obsessional control freak, and worse. The problem – which took years to resolve – was that we were both right, but incompatible.

In those early years we negotiated a truce, creating what we called the demilitarised zone: parts of the flat – the kitchen, sitting room and (particularly) loo were designated a no-woman's land of tidiness and right order, patrolled by me – others (her study and latterly her bedroom) could be as promiscuously messy as she wished. I winced when I went into her spaces, which I did as infrequently as possible.

The fiction was that we had agreed on this mode of peaceful coexistence, but actually I imposed it on Suzy gently, subtly and by degrees. In a marriage someone has to set the boundaries and – this sounds worse than it actually was – *the rules*. Suzy was largely unaware of it, but that is what I did, and we were happier for it. She never got any neater, but confined herself to barracks. She even became a tolerable cook, though rather inclined to muck about with perfectly good recipes, in the interest of some creative personal input. She had recurrent love affairs with various spices and sauces – galangal, harissa, pesto, garam masala, the list went on and on – which she dispensed with a profligate and undiscriminating generosity. She enjoyed her experiments with flavour more than I did. Worse was her capacity, which had to be experienced to be credited, to use every single pot, pan and utensil in the kitchen in the preparation of even the simplest of meals.

But while I allowed, indeed encouraged, her to learn to cook, she was under no conditions allowed to do the washing up. At first I thought her incapacity to tell a clean dish or utensil from a dirty one was purposive – *if you're so fuckin' fussy, why don't you do it yourself?* – but she was quite happy to eat off her self-washed filthy plates, so I accepted that she either didn't notice or didn't care, and insisted on doing the washing up myself. She was delighted to accede to yet another example of my fussy ways.

Nor was she allowed to put things away, or the items would never be found again. I took firm control of all our necessary papers, and filed them accordingly. In the kitchen I had an equally admirable system: clear, consistent and reliable, so long as Suzy never put anything, *anything,* away. I did the shopping, put the food and goods in the right places, cleared up after meals, checked that everything was in its right place. She didn't mind, indeed hardly noticed, because she never learned – even after repeated instruction – where things were. She didn't care.

She saved her attention for 'things that matter', and her writing had nothing slapdash about it. Suzy wrote as if she were sometimes a painter, at others a meteorologist. Reading a draft of her work, I tended to skip these passages. If I want clouds and trees, I can go for a bloody walk. I want novels bright with observed life, with ideas and narrative drive, compelling characters, both passionate and ironic. And such a fiction has no need of thunderstorms, or noses with sinuous varicosities, or gradations of cerise. None of the *business* that English novelists are addicted to. Get to the human content: all this compulsion to describe things merely indicates a lack of faith in the form, makes it some sort of activity that transforms things unto words, in order to make you see an imperfect version of the thing in itself. Boring.

Her new novel also had a fault – if one counted it as such, perhaps it was merely a characteristic? – that drove me crazy. Suzy's characters, when they were in a state of heightened feeling, angry, argumentative, or emotionally moved, were inclined to speak in paragraphs. In one instance, a whole page was given up to some speech or other, while the character's interlocutor presumably had a short nap.

'He does go on, doesn't he?' I said.

'So what?'

'It isn't accurate. People don't talk like that. Listen to them anywhere. They interrupt each other, make short declarative statements, assert this, react to that. They don't speechify.' This was perhaps stronger than I intended. Or perhaps, after exercising a wide-ranging critical restraint with the various drafts of the novel, I was getting frustrated. Or hostile, perhaps. Suzy reacted as if I were.

'It's not a documentary, for fuck's sake! It's literature. And I'm not Harold bloody Pinter. It doesn't have to be terse. It can be expansive. Characters in a novel – exactly because they are *not* real people – are more articulate, more able to organise and to adumbrate their thoughts. Smarter, clearer, than real people. That is part of why we like characters in a novel more than we like people on the Clapham omnibus.'

'If you are not careful,' I said, carefully, 'you will end up writing like fucking Philip Roth.'

'What about him?'

'Paragraphs, nah, not just. I read a bit of one the other week – I have no idea why I keep trying – that had characters talking pages' worth. First one, then the other. They all sounded just like Philip Roth. Big surprise! It was absurd.'

'Which novel are you talking about?'

'I can never remember, hard to tell them apart. Something about the Sabbath? I couldn't finish it, horrible protagonist, I couldn't bear him.'

She looked shocked. 'Mickey Sabbath? I adore him, he's so exciting.'

'Whatever do you mean? Exciting? You mean like titillating? You *fancy* him?'

'Don't be provocative. He's better than fanciable, he's well written.'

'Rubbish! And Roth'll never win the Nobel. Can you imagine a bunch of po-faced Swedes wading through all that sex and verbiage? Too many Jews, too much talk – '

'Pinter is one of them!'

'That's why he doesn't write about Jews. If he did, he couldn't be terse. Only Gentiles are Pinteresque.'

In spite of all her attentiveness, *NOB* (as Suzy called it, pleased by both the class and sexual connotations) was essentially an easy novel, so she'd made it as difficult as she could, both for herself and for her reader. The prose was over-managed, the plot seemed to suggest that she was trying to find the hardest way to tell what was essentially a simple story: a girl goes up to Oxford from the shires, has the usual intellectual and social *rites de passage*, and emerges neither stronger nor wiser, though feeling herself to be both. A coming-of-age book, spirited, hopeful, naive.

I read each revision with an increasing sense that I ought to say as little as possible by way of criticism. Suzy could tolerate a discussion of a stylistic point, or one of plot development, was open to questioning about the clarity of her observations – all this and more, but I was silently clear that this was not a good novel. Had I foolishly said so, it would have confirmed what she knew and she wouldn't have thanked me for it.

NOB sold better than *The Gristmill*, though it was widely regarded as something of a disappointment. But Suzy's name was already out there, and a considerable number of readers – the book sold over 5,000 copies in hardback, which was respectable for an up-and-coming young novelist in those days – had anticipated something more achieved than her first novel. They were disappointed, but they didn't much mind because they got a lot of sex, protracted and raunchy. At the time, English women did not write explicitly about sex, and the fact that Suzy was both young and pretty – the author photo on the rear cover was vamped up, at the publisher's insistence – guaranteed that the book would be widely noticed. Suzy did interviews for the Sunday supplements, appeared on Radio 4 and at the Hay Festival, which she adored and where she got a good audience, with a great many men in it.

Sir Henry never mentioned the novel to Suzy: this one was worse and more shaming than her previous bald parody of bald him. I imagine he read it in the privacy of his study. He would have found it titillating, and managed, by a sleight of whatever passed for his imagination, to abstract the blow jobs and quickie shags from their incestuous context, and regarded the heroine simply as a damn sexy girl, of indeterminate provenance.

I was more deeply implicated in the goings on – though

how specifically it was impossible to say, even after repeated study of the relevant men, and passages. I knew Suzy had had previous lovers, though details had never been forthcoming, thank God, but here they were. The men were no doubt composite figures, but in the various goings and comings I could recognise significant moments in our own sexual history. I was furious.

'You promised,' I shouted, 'you said I would not be in it!'

'I have no idea what you are talking about. You're not in it. I'm not either. The characters are all made up: they are words on a page. It's a fucking work of fucking fiction!'

'But people are tittering when they see me . . .'

'You're just jealous of my old boyfriends. How pathetic!'

'I thought they were just words on a page! All of a sudden they have dicks? How typographically pornographic of them. And I met Mandy in the Covered Market yesterday, and she positively blushed and simpered when she saw me. I could swear she was checking me out . . .'

'Your problem. Get over it.'

I did, it didn't matter, none of it. I had my PhD to finish, having abandoned Oxford and begun commuting to Cambridge, where I had rooms in Clare, though I rarely used them, to apprentice myself to an invigoratingly fanatical acolyte of Dr Leavis's.

For Suzy it was time to write a big book, a worthy enactment of the high seriousness that she brought to her craft, as she modestly called it. It is one thing to be promising at twenty-four: at thirty it is a sign of arrested development, or no development at all.

D.H. Lawrence had reassured her that *NOB* would be an insignificant step in her progress as a writer. After all, hadn't he followed up *The White Peacock* with the (even worse) *The Trespasser*? Both sunk in autobiography, both with as much sex as you could get away with in 1911 and 1912. And then? *Sons and Lovers*! The third novel, the one that testifies to whether a writer really has anything in him (or her) other than adolescent reconfigurations of adolescence. Time to cross that *pons asinorum*.

It is rarely useful to have studied Latin. I'd spent too many of my childish years conjugating away, pleased at my capacity to master the material and please my masters, but without the slightest sense that this dead language might ever come alive. When it occasionally did, I was delighted. *Pons asinorum* is an ass's or, perhaps better, donkey's bridge. When I added this simple bit of translation to my rudimentary knowledge of Classics and mathematics, I remembered that the term was applied to Euclid's fifth proposition in Book I of his *Elements of Geometry*: 'the angles opposite the equal sides of an isosceles triangle are equal'. Since this is the first of Euclid's propositions to require an effort of understanding, it became known as the bridge to the others.

But I was surprised to find, after a little judicious research, that there was another medieval term to describe the theorem: Elefuga, a sort of portmanteau word combining the Greek for 'misery' with the Latin for 'flight'. I did not tell Suzy about this bit of arcana, for she was discovering its truth for herself. Every morning she would retreat to the study, coffee in hand, sit at her desk, pen and notebook to the side – and sit, and sit. Sometimes she cried as well, though she was careful to do so quietly and to remove the traces.

'Misery' is both too strong a term to describe this state of mind, and too weak. Starving people, victims of disasters, the bereft, the dying, the grief-stricken, are miserable. Suzy knew this, and was suitably ashamed at the intensity of her unhappiness. She was blocked, as she called it, a state that admitted amelioration in a way that genuine wretchedness does not. All she had to do, she admitted, was to write the fucking book.

As she failed to do so, her desperation was real, and intense, and protracted, and seemed to admit of no cure. Someone can feed a starving person, or give succour to the dying. But for Suzy, sunk in gloom, there was no comfort. Nobody else could solve her problem.

But if misery was unabating, there was always flight. After six months, she abandoned her scratchy and inadequate attempts at a first draft. The hell with it, she wasn't good or tough or confident enough, and the idea of writing a novel set in India (!) was proving both intractable and uncongenial. She busied herself with other and lesser projects, helped me with my research, got a job in a second-hand bookshop, and resolved never to write another word of fiction, a resolution that merely confirmed her inability to do so, as if a paraplegic had resolved to give up mountaineering.

But a cripple may dream of mountains and yearn for the freedom of the snowy wastes, to climb, to breathe thin air, to endure. And Suzy, in her bookshop for those next couple of years – she liked the shelving of books, the occasional treasure that they purchased, the enthusiasm of their customers, the search for rare or merely out-of-print books – even there she was unhappy, and dreamt of the dangerous slopes of her abandoned literary ambitions. She wasn't aiming high enough. She wasn't aiming at all. She was avoiding.

Her depression did not deepen, neither did it go away. She got through the days, pretended to me and to herself that she was satisfied with her choices, and privately mourned the self that she could not become: the writer, the proper writer.

Various friends recommended psychotherapy, and I, though I knew nothing of it, would have supported any action that might lessen her gloom. But how does one find such a person, the right one? There are institutes, and lists of accredited therapists. Friends suggest the well-regarded Mr X or the ever-so-insightful Mrs Y. But it is a protracted and intimate and costly process, and you cannot do much in the way of product testing.

At the supermarket you can pick up the grapefruits, feel them, look them over, smell them, pick the best of the bunch. You exercise more discrimination in that choice than you do in choosing therapists, who rather object if you sniff them. Suzy had only two requirements. She would prefer to work with a woman ('they are less untrustworthy') and she would under no conditions consult a Freudian: 'if I feel the need of a penis,' she maintained firmly, 'I want it inside me, not outside.'

She sampled a couple of sessions with one or two candidates, but left their rooms feeling demoralised and unconvinced. And then she was introduced to Dr Julia Frommer, who had trained with Alice Miller. After a couple of exploratory sessions, in which Suzy probed and fingered as much as was seemly, the two agreed to work together and see how things progressed.

She loved the idea of such a project, came home after her sessions and made a transcript of what had been said, adding her own comments and interpretations. She kept these in the top drawer of her desk, rather hoping, I suspected, that I might have a peek.

I did. Or rather, I didn't. Perhaps it is the same thing? I'm now required to write in detail – to remember? – scenes at which I wasn't present. I can pretend that I had a genuine source in her desk drawer – novelists are required to do this all the time – and perhaps I did. I can't honestly remember. The only way for me *honestly* to remember is to make it up, and in so doing make it true.

The satisfaction of writing in this journal is that I compose myself in it. I am unworried by recounting, with apparent exactitude, events, feelings, sentences even, that happened many decades ago. How do I know that these renderings are accurate? They're not.

Or they are. Most of what happened in the long distant past is irretrievably lost, which is why it feels much more creative and agreeable – and real – to write about it. In the present you are mired in clarity, however mitigated; the past is so misty that you can be true not to what happened – who knows? – but what might have happened, should have. Aristotle says something similar, only not so crisply.

If I were to show Suzy this account of her sessions, she wouldn't be so prolix as to disagree. I hope she'd have been proud of me, of the spirit of what I'd done. That, after all, is partly why I am writing. For her.

The initial signs were promising. Suzy had no desire to rabbit on about how unhappy she was, nor did Dr Frommer care to know the details. It became their joint goal to remember and to reanimate the forgotten and repressed child that Suzy had been, who was certain – according to this mode of thought – to have been unhappy, unloved and lacking a voice of her own. Unhappy children make unhappy adults. Happy ones, happy ones. It was a simple enough formula: all you had to do was to recover the 'inner child', the little Suzy who had been so thoroughly repressed both then and now, and make her feel validated and freshly alive.

'It's like the Everly Brothers, isn't it?' she said, from the comfy depths of her armchair.

'I beg your pardon?' Was it possible that Dr Frommer had never heard of Phil and Don? And if so, what the hell was she doing with such a stodgy therapist, sunk in Bach and Thomas Mann, no fun at all? And – this was a bad sign – Dr F had no taste for puns, a thickening of the ear, no relish for wordplay. She had not responded when Suzy had described her second Indian governess as 'a breath of fresh Ayah'. She probably didn't get it. Suzy felt a new wave of gloom.

'The Everly Brothers! "Wake Up Little Susie"!'

'Oh. I see.'

Ever the good student, and anxious to please, Suzy worked at her new project assiduously, discussed every moment of it with me (though enjoined not to by Dr F). She dreamt copiously, fantasised and free associated, indulged herself in acts of active imagination, and otherwise began, bit by bit, to foreground that impoverished and angry little girl whom she had so long shunted into the hinterland of her unconscious, and who – Dr Frommer maintained – had been struggling to be heard ever since. Unregarded, little Suzy felt stifled and angry and unloved. Allowed to re-emerge, listened to and psychically cuddled – all that unhappiness was not her fault after all, why should she cling onto it any more? – the adult Suzy would begin to feel the benefits.

The procedure was not, Dr Frommer insisted, in any way analogous to Freudian purgation: little Suzy was neither a malignancy to be removed, nor a pustule to be squeezed. Perhaps, Dr Frommer suggested, it was something like having a baby? 'It is, after all, bringing a child into the world. And she is your child!'

Suzy had no problems with the theory, and read her way

through Dr Miller's works enthusiastically and with only minimal criticism. She wrote out the key thought on a piece of paper, and taped it to the wall above her desk:

> Learning is a result of listening, which in turn leads to even better listening and attentiveness to the other person. In other words, to learn from the child, we must have empathy, and empathy grows as we learn.

The ideas were just dandy. The problem was that, having located her inner child, Suzy didn't like her.

'Snivelling little bitch,' she said, having recovered a memory of a particularly nasty scene in which, having been denied some treat or other, she had howled for an hour, vomited on her mother's lap and then told her ayah to fuck off. She was four at the time, and given to such scenes, and language, on a regular basis. For a time, the neighbours' children had to be protected from her, lest she infect their vocabulary permanently.

'I was a ghastly little girl – no wonder nobody liked me.'

This was not, her therapist explained, an uncommon first response to the emergence of one's former incarnation. Of course she didn't like little Suzy, because she had introjected her parents' attitude to their little girl: Sir Henry and Lady Sophia (Dr Frommer, irritatingly, gave them their titles) didn't like her either, had shunted her off to her ayahs without compunction, and devoted themselves to furry pursuits.

And so little Suzy felt she was a burden, who did not deserve her parents' attention. She was too needy, too tearful, too insistent: her many childish tantrums expressed her unhappiness and caused her parents to withdraw even more.

'Perhaps,' said Dr Frommer, 'your desire to achieve fame

through the writing of your books is an attempt to gain their attention and approval? And perhaps you are now blocked because your unconscious doesn't approve of this project? The unconscious can be very wise, when you learn to listen to it.'

This irritated Suzy more than usual. 'I don't want to fucking achieve fucking fame. I want to write a good book. And far from courting my parents – my father, by this effort – I am alienating him with every fresh paragraph. He's a buffoon. I hate the bastard.'

'Ah, yes, why do you suppose – '

'Will you tell me something?' asked Suzy. 'I have been wondering . . . What sort of accent you have? Your English is too careful, your mouth cuddles your words, as if you were protecting something.'

'I am not sure what you mean.'

'I mean what Henry Higgins meant. You're fucking Eliza Doolittle. Where do you come from originally?'

This discomfited Dr Frommer, as was intended, and there was a longer than usual silence.

'Vienna. I came to England to do my analytic training, and have been here ever since.'

'I knew it! Mittel-European! I keep expecting you to say your w's as v's. *Ve have vays of making you talk!*'

'Well,' said Dr Frommer, carefully avoiding any hint of a 'v', 'that has answered your question, I hope? Perhaps we can continue now?'

'Continue? I'll give you continue! This is exactly what I have been repressing, and now it's out, isn't it? Shall we call it negative transference? The fact is, after all these months, I have come both to rely on you and to dislike you intensely.'

'Yes.'

'That's it. Your Mittel-ness! Mittel-class, Mittel of the

road, Mittel-brow, fair to Mitteling . . . Boring and earnest, and joyless and relentless. I want to get out of this chair and shake you!'

Dr Frommer was pleased to hear this, the most direct and deepest feeling that Suzy had yet released into the room. She looked at her watch. The outburst had been timed to end the session.

'We have a lot of material to work on next week,' she said. 'I will see you then.'

'You sure vill,' said Suzy, rising abruptly and departing without a further word or look.

Next session, Dr Frommer began where they'd left off. 'I believe,' she said, 'that we made good progress last time. You were having a tantrum – shouting, wanting to hit me. That was the voice of little Suzy.'

'Don't fucking patronise me. That was big Suzy!'

'I want you to know that, however horrid you are, I will never reject you.'

'You mean, until the money runs out?'

'I mean as long as you don't run out. You will be tempted – clients often are at this point – to give up therapy, to turn against the parent-surrogate with whom they are so angry. But we can work through this anger. It is a good sign.'

'You're quite right. I do want to give up. I don't want what you are offering. It isn't going to be good for me.'

'What do you take me to be offering?'

'I dunno. Reconciliation with my inner brat, I suppose.'

'The judgement you are making is not in your own voice. You are repeating the judgement of your father, and making it your own.'

'My father is loveless, and narcissistic. But his take on my childhood self was spot on.'

'I do not see why you need to hold onto this.'

'I *was* spoiled, petulant and self-referring. Daddy and Mummy were ashamed of me, Ayah indulged me entirely. For her I could do no wrong. Anything I wanted, I got. She doted on me as much as my parents ignored me. It was the wrong combination of elements, and it made me what I was. And still am: angry and foul-mouthed. And I still need to be doted on.'

There was silence at the other end.

'And you know what? Last night I had – everyone should have one, they're great – I had an epiphany. *I have no psychological problems . . .*'

'Why do you conclude this?'

'. . . *I have moral problems*! I am not unhappy because I am a victim of others, but because I *am* petulant and self-referring. I need help, but I need – God forgive me for the term – spiritual help, not psychological. I am depressed because I think I deserve things.'

'I think,' said Dr Frommer, for the first time with something of an edge to her voice, 'I think we may have self-esteem issues to resolve.'

'Fuck self-esteem. Self-esteem is for losers who go to workshops with other losers. Does no one believe in badness any more? Or humility?'

'Can you not forgive yourself?'

'Why should I? I am spoiled. I've always been spoiled. I do have low self-esteem, it is one of the few things that I admire in myself.'

Suzy got up. The session was only half over. 'I'll send you a cheque for this month's sessions. I'm starting to feel better already. Thanks for nothing.'

By Suzy's reckoning, Dr Frommer looked relieved.

★

At exactly 10 a.m. the next Thursday, when her session would have been starting, Suzy went into the study, gathered the few pages of the new novel, and threw them in the bin. She had very little idea what to replace them with, except that it was not going to be set in India.

It didn't go well, but Suzy rather expected that, was reconciled to it. Her depression had been transformed, as Freud had recommended, into ordinary unhappiness. That was fine with Suzy: makers of things are necessarily unhappy, it goes with the job description.

'After all, what are the best novels? They're records of human misery. *Madame Bovary. Portrait of a Lady. Crime and Punishment . . .*'

I should have known not to argue, but couldn't resist. I love counter-examples.

'Oh yes? Perhaps you're forgetting *Ulysses*? Or *Huckleberry Finn*, or – '

She didn't take the bait, she snapped it off at my wrist. 'Shut up, James! That doesn't matter. Writers do something at which they are bound to fail. We're Platonists. We struggle every day to make something perfect, to assemble the very best words in the very best order. And every day, in almost every image, and sentence, and paragraph, we fail. All we can do is fail better.'

'And feel better?'

'Nope, it still hurts.'

I was resistant to this, which I thought romantic and inflated. As long as Suzy held onto this exalted set of notions, she was never going to get her book written. This was the result of her having adopted the highest models. If you have Sam Beckett peering over your shoulder, interrogating every phrase, then you will be unable to write with any freedom or authority.

Aspiring writers would do better to have read Physics. Anything, really, rather than English. 'Isn't it better to regard what "artists" do as a form of craft? Potters make beautiful objects, don't they? And they don't make such a damn fuss about it!'

'It's not making a fuss. It's just trying to get it right. That's all I want to do.'

I was unable, at such times, as she stared at her keyboard and hit so few keys, to conceal my irritation. She'd given up her therapy when it started to hurt, taken the easy route. Pretended to take a moral high ground, rather than the psychological low, and in so doing occupied neither. And wasted a lot of money.

'What is the "it" you are working on, then?'

'Not sure. I'll let you know when I do.'

Writing was most assuredly art, not craft, but it did not depend on inspiration, though that occasional visitor was welcome when it came. Mostly it was work, and Suzy respected it as if she were employed in an office. She broke for a second coffee at eleven, and worked through until lunch. It was a short working day, but a novelist can do a considerable amount in four hours, if they actually write.

What Suzy did was sit and fantasise, make notes on yellow Post-its and in notebooks, and occasionally on the screen. Other than this – I later gathered – she thought about sex, then thought about it some more, and then masturbated.

'This is what writers do,' she thought, as she lay on the couch facing the window, pants around her ankles. 'We are wankers, we need to keep ourselves excited.' She had attended several workshops and had a regular writers' group, and when she broached the subject, she got a rowdy acknowledgement that her fellow writers felt, and did, much the same.

'It's the anxiety!' said one of the men, who was working on yet another dreary book about walking in the Lake District, admiring rocks and sheep.

'I can't bear it. A wank gets me through a couple of hours.'

'And then you do it again?'

'Yup. My record is four in eight hours.'

'How many words did you write that day?'

He didn't remember. That wasn't the point, was it?

One morning, disobeying the injunction never to enter the study when she was writing, I walked in, in search of a new typewriter ribbon, to find her sprawled on the sofa.

'Oh my God! I'm so sorry. I just needed to – '

'OK,' said Suzy, 'we have a choice. You can either join me, or we can be embarrassed about this forever. Seems simple to me!' She shunted over to the side of the couch, and beckoned, continuing to play with her nipple. I came.

The scene was followed by many others of much the same kind, in which I would walk in – at more or less 1 p.m., after she had finished her writing – to find her naked and ready on the couch. It was like a set of undreamt dreams come true. We made love more often, and with more pleasure, than ever before.

And then Suzy was pregnant. I had always left matters of contraception up to her, aware that she was forgetful about taking her pill. We had agreed that the consequences of such laxity could be accommodated, though Suzy was not entirely sure that they would be welcomed. For me, too, bringing children into the world – this godawful madhouse – seemed a rash and cruel thing to do. Better to leave them unborn, swimming in the celestial soup of the spermatic discharge, than to create a little Emma or Conrad, gasping for air, ready to demand a lot, and likely to receive too little.

It was a cavalier and irresponsible attitude, and we were rather proud of it. Our married friends charted menstrual cycles, took temperatures, calculated ovulating days, stopped wanking to keep up the old sperm count, and frequently managed to produce their children in the summer, when there was nicer weather, and more holiday time to welcome them. No thanks, all this self-conscious family planning. If a child was to happen, it would. If not, not. But once Suzy found herself enlarging, rather bemused by her bump, but pleased at the growth of her breasts, and thrilled not to have her bouts of PMT every month, she had to acknowledge that some planning might be a useful thing. We were going to have a baby. By all accounts the actually process of giving birth was horrid. Could something not be done about it?

Ourselves children of our time, we decided to have a child of our time. For the last four months of what we were encouraged to think of as 'our' pregnancy, we went to natural childbirth classes, a zeitgeisty Oxford movement started by a proselytising, good-natured matron called Sheila Kitzinger, for whom the term 'earth mother' might have been invented. It was her counter-intuitive belief that, as childbirth is a 'natural' activity, it ought to be relatively straightforward, if only approached in the right manner and spirit. She could teach this. She'd had a bunch of kids herself, and apparently pushed them out in a jiffy, having hips as wide as a Hottentot, and presumably a birth canal to match.

There were six couples in our class, plus several women on their own. None of us had children, because those who did presumably knew the ropes, or had been strangled by them. We did breathing exercises – both men and women – learned the rhythm of contractions and about the gradual entry of the baby's head into the world as the cervix dilated. There would be pressure, to be sure, and no doubt there was discomfort too, but the group was relentlessly positive with regard to pain. Quite the opposite, said our mentor. Like the act that caused the baby, giving birth to it could be an ecstatic, endorphin-drenched process. A form of delight! African women did it standing up while tilling the fields, ululating over the maize. Think: *African woman*! Breathe: *Like sex*! Remember: *A BABY is coming*! We're having a baby! We can do it on our own. No gas, no air, no epidurals, no Caesareans. It's natural: *Let's do it, together!*

We were uterine fundamentalists. One evening, a woman in her early thirties, who had been participating reluctantly, presumably at the request of her rather keen vagina-less partner, got up off the mat and started to put on her shoes.

'What's the matter?' asked Our Leader.

'I'm sorry. This is just not for me. I cannot believe that the fact that childbirth is natural means I should look forward to it, much less celebrate it.'

There were murmurs of disapproval in the room.

'Why is that?'

'I hate the whole process. The big belly, the swollen tits. It makes me feel like a cow. And all this push-push business, like we were sitting on the loo . . . I don't feel "positive and creative" or whatever the recommended phrase is. It's humiliating. I can't wait to get it over with, and I will take whatever drug helps me to get through it . . . Why are we all denying this? Why all this bullshit? It's going to be agonising! Everyone knows that!'

She put her shoes on, and left, not angrily, but with a resigned, steady tread. You might have called it bovine, had you been hostile. I certainly wasn't: my sympathy was entirely with the cow. We'd been suborned into this misleading gloop – deluded middle-class youngsters pretending that we could deny and subvert the laws of nature. Childbirth is natural, our cult chanted. It's positive and creative! It won't hurt, not much.

On the day, it did. Lucy was not exactly reluctant to enter the world, which would suggest an inappropriate knowingness on her side of the uterine walls, but she was in no hurry, or perhaps just unable to hurry. After all, it wasn't up to her. On our side of the process, Suzy and I breathed and panted, hoped and prayed, and very little dilation accompanied our efforts. This wasn't in the script, or if it was, we had practised the wrong scenes and hardly knew the lines for this one, until Suzy found just the right words.

'Give me the fucking gas and air, now!' she shouted.

I had never been so proud of her. From then onwards, she practised her breathing exercises with useful intakes of Entonox, and I was released from the fatuous collegiality of mock pregnancy. It was a considerable relief. After all, it was she who was pushing the damn thing out – or failing to push it out – not me. 'We're having a baby!' *No, we were not.* She was doing it, and it wasn't a baby. It was a recalcitrant lump of impassable stuff. She had constipation of the uterus.

'Fucking Sheila Shitslinger!' Suzy muttered. 'Call a lawyer! We're prosecuting under the Trades Description Act!' She pushed mightily, and her cervix dilated minimally further. 'So this is natural childbirth? Never again! I want more drugs! Unnatural childbirth for me!' She pushed again, and again. 'It's the greatest fucking con in the history of fucking women!' Push. Again. Push. 'Fucking Shitslinger!'

Lucy was born an hour later. Her exhausted mother could barely hold her in her arms, and I soon took her over. I'd been told that new-born babies have no capacity to focus their eyes, having just popped into the world, and presumably unable to tell what is worth focusing on. But brand new Lucy met my eyes with her cloudy new ones. I moved my head a tiny bit to the right. Her eyes followed. We looked at each other for a few moments, until my eyes clouded too.

Lucy was put into a crib beside her mother's bed, and both of them settled down. Suzy was still high on gas and air, which the hostile nurse – who hated natural childbirth – had rather over-administered.

'I'm rather pleased with myself,' she said.

'And so you should be, love. So am I!'

'You don't know what I mean.'

'Well, of course it is you who actually had the baby,' said I, irrationally hurt at her claiming primacy in the process, assigning me a menial's role.

'But we did it together, right? Remember: *We're having a BABY*!'

'No, no.'

'What?'

'Not the classes, all that rubbish. Any damn fool woman can have a baby, millions of the little fuckers born every year. Actually, it hurts and it's rather lowering to the spirit. Bit gross really . . .'

She wiped her forehead. I was distressed to find both that she felt that way, and that I shared the feeling. Even with our new little person lying at our side, it was a crunching anti-climax. How could that be? Why'd nobody warned us? We'd been fed on the pabulum of New Parenthood, and none of the received wisdom applied.

'But no one until me has invented the word "Shitslinger". It's like a new category, isn't it? You can divide the world into Shitslingers and non-Shitslingers. Much more useful than Good and Bad, or Beautiful and Ugly. It's what the poor cow lady was trying to say. And all this fatuous encouraging and enhancing is caused – which is what is ironic, and funny and sad – by goodwill and the desire to help others. To transmit something that will be useful.'

'You mean wisdom, don't you?'

'I do. The whole shebang. Special insight into the big issues. An answer to the meaning of life. Rules to learn, maxims to apply. I hate all the fuckers. The one-answer-fits-all hucksters. Priests, politicians, therapists, sages, and all the other charlatans. And especially natural childbirth teachers.' She winced. 'Can you tell that bitch nurse to get me some painkillers?'

At the side of the bed, little Lucy slept deeply, subliminally aware of the happiness surrounding her, presuming that it was she who had caused it. She woke every few hours to guzzle the bounty of her mother's breasts, and looked into Suzy's face as she was fed, a thoroughly content parcel of original sin.

Our linguistic euphoria was a drug-induced displacement activity, which wore off in due course and left Suzy free to attach herself to the new baby. Lucy, we agreed. I love Lucy. And Suzy, somewhat to my surprise and to her astonishment, rather liked being a mother, braved the wakeful nights and screaming colic, the coming of teeth and exiting of surprisingly large and regular turds. I was expected, in that new world of new men who were supposed to do their bit, all their bits, to pitch in, do the midnight feed with a bottle, carry Lucy on my front in a pouch, strain the baby food.

Change nappies? I tried. Even Suzy could see that. I may have been unwilling, and somatically repelled, but I knew my duty when I smelled it. The only problem, once I had unfastened the tabs of the disposable nappy and pulled it down to review its contents, was that I gagged, stepped back, did my breathing exercise, re-encountered the noxious mass, gagged again. And then vomited.

'For fuck's sake, you do carry on so!'

'I'm not,' I said, wiping my mouth yet again, while poor Lucy squirmed on the changing mat covered in shit from bottom to thighs. 'I'm not carrying on. I am trying. The spirit is willing.'

'And now I have two babies to clean up,' she said. 'Let me do it.'

'I'm so sorry. I don't think men are cut out for this sort of thing.'

'You're certainly not.'

Women are more physical than men, more in and of their bodies, inured to being poked and prodded, to pap smears and breast examinations and speculums. They are shaved, given enemas, produce babies, feed and change and look after them. It's men who are shy and squeamish. I faint at the sight of blood, turn my head away when a telly programme shows an operation – or, to be honest, even an injection, as I cannot watch the hypodermic pierce the skin. When I encounter the needle, I pinch myself so hard that it distracts me, and close my eyes, while pretending to the nurse that I am merely breathing quietly and restfully.

Suzy took over the mucky duties resentfully, feeling that if I were sufficiently a man and a father and a helpmeet – most of her friends' husbands did their fair whack at the changing table – I would suppress my nausea and get on with it. After all, she enquired icily, did I think she enjoyed wiping a bottom?

'It doesn't make you sick, though, does it? There's something fundamental about nausea. You don't control it, it controls you. It's Sartre, isn't it?'

'No, it's not. Do shut the fuck up. If you're going to be useless, there's no need to be pompous as well.'

The elementary school was plonked glumly a mile from the city centre, on a corner of two streets of which it was impossible to say which was the more unprepossessing. That the not entirely unattractive town of Abingdon should have this ghastly appendage beggared belief. That my grandson Rudy should go to such a school was a humiliation that attached equally to him, to his family, and to me. I had offered to pay fees for a decent prep school and then, hopefully, Winchester, but his parents were adamant in their hostility to private education.

'Elitism pure and simple, based on class and money.' Sam was not short of opinions on the subject, though he had no arguments to back them up, only assertions and class prejudices of his own. He was a product of a Northern secondary school – 'didn't do me any harm!' – and had done sufficiently well at A levels – two Bs and a C sort of thing – to get into Sheffield University, where he read Sociology before training as a social worker.

I knew enough not to argue with him. Private schooling would offer Rudy a better education, a more likely entry to Oxbridge, a pool of friends and contacts who would serve him well in later life: I knew that. So did Sam. Only I thought it was desirable and he thought it abhorrent. Nothing to argue about there, as if we were debating whether sprouts are delicious.

I pulled the Mercedes to the kerbside opposite the school, sufficiently early to find a place, suddenly aware that it stood out amongst the humble vehicles that were filling the spaces. School let out in twenty minutes, and the road would soon be filled with mums picking up nippers indistinguishable as to sex, their hair of similar lengths, most with a backpack, sloppy trousers and a puffy parka to keep out the spring chill. Who looked and behaved and talked like clones. So would the children at the local prep schools, only they would dress better and talk more intelligibly. And with better accents.

Spotting Rudy was thus impossible, for my eye is untrained in the subtle differences that would enable me to tell him from a Bertie or a Betty. No, what I had to do was look for Lucy's battered Volkswagen Beetle, and Rudy would head her way.

I had ensured that I would not be noticed. I had my two sets of tints – windows and sunglasses – as well as a rather flattering homburg that was once my father's. I pulled it low over my eyes, like Humphrey Bogart playing Philip Marlowe, and staked the place out, waiting patiently, smoking my cigar. Europcar would hate me, unless I could air the car sufficiently in a week. But I suspect they have sniffer dogs who yowl and issue fines at the veriest hint of smoke. Whopping great bill for detoxifying the car. Nice little earner for them.

Opposite the school was a small row of shops, with its own service road and parking, which harried mums used at pick-up time, to the annoyance of the local shopkeepers. There was a Coral bookies, a Spar market, a couple of charity shops, and a newsagent eking out a living a penny at a time selling sweeties to the children and cheap magazines to their mums. I wondered if they sold sour lemons, and if Rudy liked them. If Lucy still did. Two of the shops were boarded up. Even at this peak time, there were only a couple of potential shoppers, killing time before the children were released. If it had been more cheerful, you might have described it as desolate.

Lucy drove up at 3.25 and, as her car approached, I had a moment of anxiety that she would park close to me, though I'd tried to wedge the Merc into a tight spot. But she tootled right by, her engine wheezing, and parked four cars down on the opposite side, sat behind the wheel for a few moments, before emerging to meet Rudy as he came out.

Wreathed in smoke, darkened by tint, disguised by hat, I peered at my daughter, suppressing the desire to rush out and take her into my arms. She'd changed. It was nothing as perceptible as a haggard or wasted visage, indeed, she seemed to have gained weight, comfort eating I suppose, but something had slipped from her. She'd inherited very little from Suzy – neither gay assurance, nor social ease, not even the capacity to dress well. She had nothing of her mother's beauty, but they shared an unconscious physical grace, a way of walking that made people in the street turn and notice. Suzy and she, walking in the park, were like animals on an African veldt, proud and unconscious, beautifully pelted, unpredictably skittish, and dangerous. Other children and their mums eyed them, wanting to make an advance, but rarely did. There was something self-contained about them, powerful, physiologically aristocratic.

Suzy revelled in her physicality, but Lucy was embarrassed by hers. She had excelled at hockey and netball at school, was invited to join the county junior sides, but took no pleasure in it and eventually quit, saying she disapproved of competition. 'I don't want to make other girls into losers! It makes them cry. And then they both resent me and idolise me. I hate it.'

She not only abjured sport entirely, she renounced her ease, adopted a slouch, was no longer an object of admiration in the park, or anywhere else for that matter. She took to frumpy as if it were fashionable, though she disapproved of fashion as well.

It was worse now, nothing so obvious as a slump of the shoulders, or a shortening of stride, though there was something of both. She moved ponderously, burdened by weight, as exhausted and defeated as a runner who has dropped out of a marathon and wants to cry, but is too proud. She brightened as Rudy ran towards her and hoisted him up into her arms, backpack and all. She winced at his weight, less strong than she had been, though it looked like he'd grown. Hard to tell in that hideous puffball parka. Purple.

I was afraid even to let down the window, my view obscured by smoke and my various disguises. Through my glasses, darkly. I could not know them yet, lest I should be known in return. But what I saw was bowel-searing, and I gripped the armrests as if to steady myself from a faint, still, unreleased by love. They crossed the street hand in hand, some fifteen feet from my windscreen as I hunched in self-protection, knotted with stomach cramps. I tried to remember how to breathe. Oxford. Shitslinger. In. Out.

They returned from the newsagent's with Rudy clutching a Magnum, picking away the chocolate slices from its surface, willing to face the drear vanilla underpinning for those few moments of delight. Lucy looked at him, and a smile – her smile – appeared briefly and it was as if the light had re-appeared in her eyes.

I drove off, without looking back.

I could email, or ring. The former was cowardly and impersonal, the latter guaranteed a salvo that would resink the

Bismarck. I sat on the sofa, the remains of afternoon tea on the table before me, quite unable to do either. No hurry, after all. She didn't know I was near, thought me still lost.

I am.

No hurry. The next morning, I braved breakfast in the dining area, which was only a quarter full and as quiet as a room should be at 8 a.m. I interrogated the colour of my three-and-a-half-minute boiled eggs, which was sufficiently orange, dunked my wholegrain soldiers into their centres, sipped a double-strength latte, which of course was not good enough – it's impossible to make coffee adequately for multiple cups. Starbucks is wretched, of course, but even fancy hotels, as this aspires to be, cannot quite get it right. I pursed my lips, braved a second cup for the sake of the caffeine, but couldn't finish it and pushed it away.

'Finished with that, sir? Everything all right?'

You're not supposed to answer, because it isn't a question, it's a gesture. Meaningless as 'have a good day' from someone who doesn't care if you're dying of cancer.

'The coffee is insipid. I can't finish it.'

She looked as startled as if I'd burped in her face. 'I'm so sorry. Shall I get you another?' She looked at me rather strictly from under her eyebrows, like Princess Diana in a strop, suppressing the rejoinder 'Presumably the first one was just dandy? You glugged it down fast enough, you irritating ponce.'

I didn't look up from *The Times*. 'No. Just take it away. And I'll sign for the bill now.'

I suspect I was so cross because of the decor, not the coffee. The walls of the bar and dining room were liberally hung with the sort of modern English paintings that, had an amateur daubed them, might be accounted charming. But they were weak, vapidly pretty, lacking power or conviction, the painterly equivalent of 'have a good day'. Sitting in the dining room amidst dozens of them, I felt ashamed of the pictures of my countrymen, comparing them to what was being produced in France at the same time. I have my reservations about Matisse and (particularly) Picasso, but they have quality and conviction. Whereas here the bucket-shop Bloomsbury pictures were merely depressing. The blessed Vanessa and horn-dog Duncan studied in Paris for a couple of years, and when they returned before the war they could actually paint, but rutting and daubing away in Sussex quickly forgot how to do it, and churned out inane rubbish for the rest of their lives, most of which was eventually purchased by gullible Americans, who thought all those Bloomsberries the ultimate swells.

It was impossible to succour one's soul in such an atmosphere, to be anything other than cramped and irritable, impinged upon by the pretentious and second-rate. And that's just the painting. Think of the people. Or better yet, don't. I had become a room-service addict, however cramped my very Junior Suite might be. At least the company is better, and I set a very low standard. I resolved to take my meals in my room, or elsewhere. There must be somewhere decent to eat in Oxford, in which you are not assaulted by the decor?

The walk down St Giles, across the Broad, the cut-through past Bodley and the Radcliffe Camera, the quiet lane that led down to Merton Street, would have been replete with memory, had I allowed it. Instead I walked in a fug, though my steps quickened as I walked the long-ago familiar paths, became less doddery, my legs suddenly recalling days less soaked with pain.

Former happiness, I suppose you might call it, if you remembered what it felt like. I'd loved being at Merton, schoolboyish and innocent. I made brass rubbings in the Chapel, went to Evensong, studied in the library in Mob Quad rather than one of the less intimate University venues, preened in my scholar's gown for meals in Hall, relished the combative exigencies of weekly tutorials.

I'd been lucky, and scored a rather grand set of rooms on the second floor in the front quad, with a generous study and slightly less capacious but perfectly adequate bedroom attached. On the outer oak door my name was displayed in a brass holder – JAMES DARKE – and I felt, for the first time in my life, adequately provisioned, even celebrated. The rooms proclaimed me, and I was proud.

And cold. The stone walls attracted freezing moisture, stored it, and redeployed it as if they were storage heaters designed to refrigerate. I slept in pyjamas, socks and a woolly sweater, and tried to tuck myself fully under the covers in case my ears iced over and fell off. When, in a moment of the most extreme discomfort, colder than Scott in the Antarctic, I left my electric heater on two bars overnight, which just about managed to take the chill off, I was roundly criticised by my scout in the morning. Profligate. Spoiled.

I suspected that the college authorities were delighted the rooms were so cold, for they were a perfect disincentive to sexual activity. Not that this was allowed – gentlemen were not to 'entertain' ladies in their rooms – but the rule was unenforced as long as one was sufficiently discreet. Anyway, no one in their right mind would have contemplated love-making in such an atmosphere, it was hard enough managing a brief bout of self-abuse, because you had to tent up the bedclothes and cold air would inevitably get in. But two bodies, no matter how carefully swathed by blankets and heated by lust, could not have relished a libidinous encounter. Even with the electric heater on. And so, for much of the winter, Merton became a sex-free zone.

I wandered in past the Porter's Lodge, hoping not to have to introduce myself as a (very) old Mertonian, free to wander at will, for tourists were carefully shepherded except at permitted hours. My feet recalled the cobblestones of the front quad, and the steps to the Hall drew me upwards. The portraits of antique College worthies above the dining tables looked down on me, familiar and not unwelcoming, now I was as old as they. I used to be rather afraid of them, as their long dead immortal eyes gazed down on us boys, knowing us for frauds and sensualists. As they had been too, no doubt, but the paint had banished memory, and now they were merely upright, blameless and disapproving, shellacked with virtue, monitoring us as we ate and gossiped and drank, and headed into the darkness.

In Michaelmas and Trinity terms, in the freshening spring and mellow autumn, when the gardens showed off their treasures and the college became a quiet little paradise, then we could entertain our girls in the warmth of our quarters, and luxuriate in their caresses without the slightest shiver or chilblain. Suzy, not unnaturally, but also not ungrudgingly, preferred to make love in my rooms, however pernickety she found my mode of living. When I wasn't looking, she would de-alphabetise my books, a gesture I never found in the least congenial.

Merton was a sensualist's paradise compared to St Anne's. Her crimped room overlooked a patch of grass with a few mature trees, surrounded by some immature buildings. We had to sneak up to it in the darkness, and a few hours later make our way out again, past the Porter's Lodge to the freedom of the Woodstock road, giggling, smelling of drink and sex, satisfied, triumphant.

★

Revisiting my Oxford gargoyles I am aware only of loss. There's nothing consoling in the 'memory' of those innocent times. Memory is not a form of resurrection. I would not recognise the young James and Suzy if they bumped into me on the High. They're gone. We're gone. She's gone, dead. We both are. Everybody is. That's what it is to be alive.

And here I am in this godawful hotel room, slopping about in that residual gloop, trying to recall, to resurrect, mocked by memory, unmanned. But really my strongest impulse is to forget, to make it all go away – our foolish youthful selves: James, Suzy. Suzy's form in that bed at Merton, the craggy nodules of her spine traced by my fingertips, the dear squishy pads of her toes, that piece of grit in the corner of her mouth like a minuscule pebble sucked from the bank of a stream. It happened, didn't it? Who knows? The images lack clarity: they are called not recalled, they're fictional now. I have to make them up. Memory makes novelists of us all, bad novelists.

Overcome by grief at the loss, the waste, the transience. We're not immortal souls even in this life, much less the next. I don't blame God. We are not created in His image, in any image other than that of a minute helix of DNA pursuing its inexorable ways. We are neither made nor crafted – just spermatic instances, penetrated eggs, larvae, spawn. No one can make sense of it, there's nothing there to work with.

No one can sleep with such thoughts ricocheting around his head. I got up too quickly and the room started to sway, sat down again to let the dizziness resolve itself, rose again more temperately, put on my dressing gown, walked to the window. It was an uncommonly clear night, the stars more visible than usual in haze-infested Oxford, thousands of pinpricks of light insistently recommending themselves as sources of contemplation, as multiple metaphors. It frightened Pascal, the silence of those infinite spaces. I don't know why. The gigantic scale might be dread-inducing, but what's wrong with silence? What did he want his heavens to do, talk? God presumably, with his commandments and proclamations and prohibitions – yack yack, what a bore. Give me a little peace and quiet any day.

Might those pinpricks of light in the darkness evoke the myriad souls who have passed, or perhaps the faint sparkle of memories we seek to console us? It's too much for me. I'd rather eat a chocolate Hobnob, brew a cup of tea. There is something obscene in the desire to make sense of what is too large, too inchoate, too lacking in meaning to comprehend. Fruitlessly seeking an appropriate image, to appropriate an image. It doesn't matter, exquisite or clichéd, words fail. The night draws to a close: the light obliterates the lights.

I preferred going to her modest little college for our trysts, slumming it rather than watching her cast envious eyes on my chambers, wistfully aware of her banishment to the utilitarian and the modern. In her room I tried very hard – and no doubt failed – to avoid denigrating judgements of tongue or eye. She was ashamed to be a member of St Anne's, which had only recently joined the University, having ascended from its status as a mere training institution of some sort.

It was a step down – more like a staircase down, Suzy acknowledged ruefully – from the heights of Somerville or LMH – but St Anne's had the great virtue of being willing to accept her, with her modest record at A level. Yes, she interviewed fluently, though her school reports, and worse, her ambiguous recommendation – 'she is a sprightly girl, fluent and self-confident, but rather inclined to trade on both charm and talent' – put off the grander colleges. Fortunately her mother was, if not a friend, at least a regular acquaintance of Mary Ogilvy, the Head of St Anne's, with whom she had been at school. A lunch à trois was arranged, and Suzy's offer of a place was wrapped up by coffee-time, months before any application was lodged. Miss Ogilvy was a shrewd judge, and her decision had nothing to do with her feelings for Lady Moulton, whom she had always disliked. No, she was intrigued by Suzy, who, she suspected, might blossom if transplanted from her drear Dorset habitat and family.

Suzy arrived at St Anne's feeling that she should have done better, and knowing that she hadn't. She settled in. Put up her Grateful Dead posters, bought throws and bedspreads and Moroccan pillows, burned incense, played the Stones on her portable turntable, and occasionally entertained me for a few happy hours.

We rarely spent the night together, and looked forward to having a place of our own. Living with one's girlfriend – they were not (blessedly) called partners then, which still has a business-like connotation to my ear – was rather risqué, and when Suzy's lamentable *père* heard of our later cohabitation, he worried – her mother confided with a giggle – that his daughter was now 'used goods'.

'I got used a long time ago,' Suzy laughed, and her mother, having sensed this as only mothers can – fathers try not to notice – was far from disapproving. She'd done the same, and not with boring Henry either, who still didn't know it, or chose not to.

My windows overlooked the front quad, and we would gaze out together into the night, naked and giggling, wondering if anyone would spot us. I'd stand behind her, hands cupping her breasts.

I looked up, and from that very window a girl was gazing pensively into the quad. For a moment her eyes trailed over me as I looked up at her, an elderly stranger, met mine of a moment, and moved on, indifferent, as the rooms were indifferent too – the quad, the Hall, carrying on as they had for centuries, inhabited by thousands like us, stony and remote.

I'd been to St Anne's. Done Merton. A few days had passed, and I felt no closer to – what? Picking up the phone? Writing an email? Writing a letter? Too distancing and formal. And I could hardly drop in, could I, ring the bell, stand there like a pathetic scarecrow from the past, importuning, red-faced and stuttering? I'm here, I'm near, but the distance has paradoxically enlarged with every advance I make in her direction.

Do as Suzy and I used to do? Neither of us had access to a phone, except to make outgoing calls. Home, that sort of thing. Or we could receive calls through the College, though this was understood to be for emergencies. No – one would write a note, go round and put it in the pigeonhole at the College lodge. *Meet me tonight at 8 at the KA for a pint?*

So: *Meet me tomorrow at midday to discuss my shameful, craven disappearance? I will come to you.* That sort of thing? Best of a bad job. I sat down. Took some headed hotel notepaper from my desk drawer. Got out my pen.

Darling Lucy,
I am so wretchedly sorry to have caused you such pain, and at such a terrible time. I can hardly explain how or why this happened. I found myself – how can I even say this? – incapable, lost, stricken, bereft – no, all and none of the above. Words fail me.

All I can say is that I did not want to hurt you. That I knew I was doing so. That I was harpooned by grief, and that every day for many months I was quite incapable of human discourse. Even with you, my very dear girl. Especially with you.

Can you forgive me this, a little, if only enough to allow me to come to you and to talk? I would give anything if, for a moment, I might embrace and recover you, and perhaps you, me.

I can be reached at The Old Parsonage Hotel in Oxford.

Your inadequate penitent, loving you, loving you always, still,

Dad

No. Never. Not that I can do very much better, but it won't do. Talking about the failure of language, what rot, how inappropriately appropriate. She'd be offended and laugh, or sneer, and she'd be right. What a wretched effect I am become, how lost to love.

WRETCHED

miserable, unhappy, sad, broken-hearted, heartbroken, grief-stricken, grieving, sorrowful, sorrowing, mourning, anguished, distressed, desolate, devastated, despairing, inconsolable, disconsolate, downcast, down, downhearted, dejected, crestfallen, cheerless, depressed, melancholy, morose, gloomy, glum, mournful, doleful, dismal, forlorn, woeful, woebegone, abject, low-spirited, fit for the rubbish, useless arsehole

And am I, envelope in hand, to creep up her drive, drop my contrition through the letter box, skedaddle back to my car, hoping she will not hear the sound and open the door, or come to the window? See me skulking away, as I have skulked away these long months. What better to confirm her opinion of me, to strengthen the regret and abhorrence that she must feel?

No. I will ring her. I have my phone, and her number.

The receptionist said yes, they could accommodate me for another week. Am I happy to keep the same accommodation?

'Delighted, thank you.'

'Thank you, Dr Darke.'

I walked in the Parks, strolled along the river, sat on a bench, ignored the daffodils, read *The Times,* prevaricated, lost in funk. In a fit of apparent free-spiritedness, if I were either free or had any spirit, I decided upon an antidote to the culinary adequacy of my hotel and sought out my old haunt in the Covered Market for a nostalgic bean feast.

The old working-class café was still there, filled with the same tradesmen and builders and undergraduates who'd been in it forever, as if in a modest circle of Hell. I ate a full English breakfast so proletarian it embarrassed me to be seen in its company. My stomach began to growl at the stench, anticipating the dire gastric effects to come. Processed fried white bread, tinned baked beans, mushrooms that had never encountered a field, stewed tomatoes lacking any taste other than a faint residue of acidity, eggs so battered that they assaulted you, fatty undercooked bacon, a sausage made up of the grisly scrapings and remnants of what was once, perhaps, a pig. Instant coffee with longlife milk.

I first ate here almost fifty years ago, in this very place, and the breakfast was as I remembered it. Maybe it was the same one, and they'd kept it warm for me? I wasn't always as fastidious as I'd now become, nor so superior. I read the *Daily Mail*. Burped. Went to Boots to buy some Eno's.

I made a point of getting straight back to the hotel, in case my bowels made immediate protest. Yesterday I was in the loo four times, on each of which I strained and produced a little, knowing there was more to come, almost ready to travel, but not yet. Repeat again, and a few hours later again. My anus felt like it had been injected with Botox, a baboon's would look pert and virginal in comparison. I knew that if I didn't keep trying to expel, my perverse, recalcitrant passage would slowly melt and disgorge its partially impacted contents into my pants.

Business idea! A line of underwear for the elderly in shades of brown! Perhaps they could be branded 'THE HUMAN STAIN', if Philip Roth hasn't copyrighted the phrase. Featuring pants with brown paisley designs of rugby balls, West Indian cricketers, leather boots, chocolate bars, bagels, coffee beans, redwood trunks, acorns or pine cones, bears or armadillos. Or turds, that'd be cute. You could do a whole line of them: Spiketurds would be too gross, but I rather fancy horse droppings with bits of yellow straw sticking out. You could mess those with impunity, it would be like filling in the blanks.

If you hang around the underwear department at Marks and Spencer's and watch the old folks, you can tell what they are looking for. Entirely preoccupied, without embarrassment, solipsistically bowel-defined, they are seeking pants in the darkest available colours, anxious not to expose their leaky frailty to spouses, nurses, cleaners or launderette attendants.

Brown pants! Problem solved! I could clean up on this idea: any Freudian knows that where there's shit, there's money.

I returned to my room, my stomach surprisingly settled down, and rang Lucy. My hand, to my surprise, was not trembling, though I was pretty sure my voice would be.

She picked up at the third ring. 'Hello, Lucy here.'

She first began to announce herself like this, answering our phone, when she was three. It delighted her to proclaim that it was she, not Mummy or Daddy, and whoever called was charmed by her directness and innocence, and would pause to have a few words. She loved talking on the phone, chattering away inconsequentially, and eventually had to be persuaded to fetch whichever of us was being called. 'Daddy,' she'd say, handing over the receiver, 'it's a man. It's for you.'

'Lucy, Dad here.'

There was a long silence, and it was hardly up to me to break it.

'Who?'

'Darling, it's Daddy. Won't you please talk to me?'

'All of a sudden you want to talk?'

'I've wanted to all along. I am so sorry. I feel dreadful to have hurt you so . . .'

There was another and longer silence.

'I'm not talking to you on the fucking phone.'

'I don't want to either, darling. May I come round, please? I'm in Oxford. I need to see you . . .'

'Wonderful! So you need to see me now, in your own good time? What about me needing to see you? And after Mummy died and I wrote to you and wrote to you, and you were hiding in that damn house, too frightened to answer the door, or a letter, or a phone call . . . So now you're ready?' Her voice was grinding, metallic, hardly recognisable.

'Please. Yes. Please. I am so wretchedly sorry. I'd like to explain if I can, but I'm not sure how. But I want to see you and be with you and be your father again. If you will allow me to.'

'Tomorrow at the house. Ten o'clock. And if you funk it, don't bother to try again.'

She put the phone down. I rang off and lay down on my bed, desolate yet buoyed by the sound of her voice, however hostile, my dear Lucy's voice that despised me.

I'd apologised, cringed, wet myself with contrition. It didn't make me feel any better. There was scant pleasure in the humiliating process. No relief, no satisfaction. It had to be done, but unlike those bumbling Catholics who exit the confessional grinning inanely, purged of their sins, there was neither cleansing nor forgiveness in secular contrition. God wouldn't forgive me. Lucy won't. I don't. My abject apology was a necessary step to get me from a state of misery to one of what? Less misery? Big fucking deal! Yes. It was.

I couldn't sleep, turned on the light, tried to read a magazine, but the print sauntered before my eyes. The telly showed a black and white movie, some sort of thriller, some cops and some robbers. I turned it off. Made tea from my supplied kettle, ate chocolate Hobnobs. Turned off the light, turned it on again.

I have a distressing recurring dream, but I am hesitant even to write it down, which gives it a sort of credibility and transfers it from my twilight world into the light. Harder to get rid of in that state. I hate accounts of people's dreams. Suzy used to record hers in the middle of the night when she was in therapy, transmit them to Dr Frommer, come home and write down the interpretations, and then wish to discuss them with me. They were all boring, or at least the recounting of them was, curious how it takes thirty seconds to have a dream and thirty minutes to tell it. After a few tries she ceased imposing them on me.

In a novel, when the hero has an Important Dream – and they never have less than whoppers – that goes on for two pages, I always skip it. Who gives a damn? Just a dream, imbued with phoney significance by an insistent writer, a cliché. Like Dostoevsky's horse being beaten.

I'll do it anyway, I only have myself to bore.

I had been kidnapped and forced into the boot of a car, screaming, terrified, clawing, urinating. The car drove for hours, then stopped. The doors opened and closed. I heard footsteps walking away . . .

I had it at least once a week, always the same. It terrified me, and I woke up sodden, screaming, palpitating. I waited for ten minutes to regain my breath and equilibrium, to still my heart, and then stood in the shower under hot water for ten minutes, then cold for one. Took a Valium, got back in bed – the dream never comes twice on the same night.

I know what it means. I take the point. So why won't it just go away? The hours passed as slowly as if I were entombed in that boot, and almost as fearfully. I lapsed into a series of short periods of sleep, apparently fleeting, though when I checked my watch, again, it seemed as if I had been asleep for an hour, or two. But my thinking was uninterrupted, and it was clogged with remorse, and fear, and arid regret. Of anticipation of seeing Lucy, hearing her voice, touching her fleetingly, I could locate none at all.

I got out of bed at 7.30 – the forthcoming hours lay like an endless desert before me, searing. I forced myself not to look at my watch, put it in my pocket to avoid temptation, as I walked round and round St Giles. Waited for an hour – at least an hour! – to pass, then checked my watch to find it had only been twenty minutes.

The Mercedes had a slight film of dust, squat and abandoned in its parking place. Unlike my 3.8, though, it starts every morning. I set out, heading more or less towards Abingdon, around a road system become so circuitous and complex that I gave up, and merely tried to head south-ish, perhaps to kill the remaining time in the country. Maybe go for a walk somewhere, anywhere.

I wanted to arrive at Lucy's toned by contrition, concil-iatory, yet – can this be credible? – hopeful. I missed her dreadfully, and I knew how much she has always loved me. Surely this could not get swept away so easily?

So easily? I take the point.

Lucy hated anyone being late. I suppose it is because she leads a provincial life – no traffic jams, Tube strikes, buses blown up by terrorists, nothing to slow progress unexpectedly – there's nothing to do in her Abingdon suburb except be on time. I rang the doorbell at 10 a.m., and it made a drear cacophonous, triple-chiming church bell sound that gave me the creeps. It was already installed in the house when they purchased it and, despite my frequent entreaties that it be changed – I offered to pay, to arrange it, to oversee the work, *anything* – Lucy and Sam kept it. They said that little Rudy liked it, but I suspect the reason, aside from inertia, was that it irritated me. Suzy, predictably, claimed to adore it. *Very* middle England, she'd say.

Lucy kept me waiting, then opened the door so quickly
– so harshly, if doors can be opened harshly – that it rather
startled me, as if by a slap. She didn't have her hands on
her hips, but she didn't have them round me either. She
stepped aside. 'I suppose you'd better come in.'

'Thank you.'

She looked at me closely. 'My God, you look terrible.
Don't you eat any more?'

She was dressed in faded jeans and a baggy orange sweater,
and some sort of rubbery shoes that would have looked
ugly even in a gymnasium.

Suzy would look at her and say, 'Darling, I despair. Can't
you make an effort, just sometimes?'

'I know it is a continual surprise and disappointment to
you, Mum, but I'm not you.'

Suzy never gave up, or gave in. She would arrive with
a smart new scarf, or a pair of well-cut linen trousers from
a shop on Regent Street, and Lucy would accept them with
mock grace, but never be seen in them in our presence.
Suzy liked to hope that she would use them for best when
she went out with Sam, but their outings were confined
to kiddies' activities, and the occasional Indian or film.
Nothing to get your glad rags on for. I suspected she gave
them to charity shops, brand new.

I followed her down the hallway, turned right into the
sitting room – Sam calls it the parlour – and waited for
instruction.

'Sit down. I'll make coffee.'

'No thanks, love, I've had a couple already.'

'Well, I need one.' She set off into the kitchen. In a few
minutes the kettle was whistling and I could hear the top
of a jar being unscrewed.

I was there, choosing to be at her mercy. It was up to

her how we began, and she was taking a long time to make her coffee. Keeping me waiting? Composing herself? Thinking what to say?

She sat down across from me, and put her mug on the coffee table. 'This is such a surprise. I thought I'd lost you. I hardly know where to begin.'

'I know, I'm sorry.'

'Will you stop saying you're sorry?'

'No! Never. I will always be sorry.'

'Who cares? It's not enough. What I want is an explanation.'

'I did warn you at Paddington. I said I needed to be alone, didn't I?'

'Alone? You call that alone? Why the barricades? Why no phone? No email? No response to my letters? That's not fucking *alone*, that is designed to escape completely, to reject me.'

'Not just you, everyone.'

'There *is* only me! Just me! Mummy died and you ran away when I needed you most! And when she needed you most, you ran away too, you couldn't bear it, you scarpered from her bedside, hid in your study . . .'

'I can only say I did my best, and it wasn't much good. Sometimes I was paralysed by the sheer awfulness of it, her impending death, all of it. I had no experience of – '

If I remember correctly, from our days in the sunlight in the Parks, sitting with Suzy in our deckchairs, eating cucumber sandwiches, there is such a thing as a losing wicket. It's when you get in for a moment, but can't stay there, the conditions being too dangerous and uncongenial. I gather a batsman can retire in such peril, for fear of being badly injured. Lucky him.

'For fuck's sake, neither did I. So what? If your heart is

full of love, you sit there, like I did when I came. Hold hands, wipe brows, get into bed and have a cuddle, offer anything and everything by way of reassurance.'

'I don't think that's very fair.'

She picked up her coffee, drank it down with a slurp and banged it back down on the table, wiping her lips with her sleeve, which she had been forbidden to do as a girl and which she knew irked me, though that was hardly her intention now.

'I don't understand,' I said deliberately, 'why you are so surprised by human frailty. So disapproving. Implacable. Of course I am sometimes weak and incapable and selfish. I don't think myself exceptional in this regard.'

'It's a matter of degree, isn't it?'

'I suppose I mean I am mid-spectrum, selfish-wise.'

There was a long pause, during which she maintained her eye contact with me, and I felt it impossible to break the connection. If that is what it was.

It wasn't.

'Oh. "Mid-spectrum"? So your average man murders his wife, does he?'

The receptionist greeted me as I stumbled into the lobby, having miraculously guided the trusty Merc safely back to the hotel. Presumably God wanted me alive, to keep tormenting me. He'd got a new Job, the bastard.

She wanted to offer me an upgrade, how marvellous. And there was me thinking all the joy had been drained from the world.

'You're one of our regulars now, Dr Darke. We can offer you a full suite, which we could have ready for you later this afternoon. It's much roomier, and still very quiet. It would be at the same price. Shall we move your things for you?'

'No, thanks.'

'It would be no trouble at all.'

'No, please . . . I may be leaving soon.'

'I'm sorry to hear it, doctor.'

'I need to get back to London.'

'Nothing serious, I hope. Are you quite all right?' She looked at me with some concern. They'd got used to me, grumpy old sod that I am. After all, I was probably their best customer at the moment, their oldest member.

'Will you be checking out tomorrow?'

I hesitated for a moment. Would I? At the moment the allure of my London fortress, with its blank black door and impenetrable defences, was almost irresistible. It was enough having to face Lucy's anger at having been abandoned – but this? Now this? How the fuck was I supposed to respond to such a charge? How could I return to her wrath and the inevitable interventions of plonker Sam?

'I don't know,' I said to the concerned receptionist. 'I'll let you know. I think I need to lie down.'

This nausea and dreadful dizziness were metaphors and instructions: rest, withdraw, keep yourself out of the world, stay inside. Go back into the dark. Be sick.

As the linguistically challenged Sam might have put it, there are grave issues at stake here, and I was unable to draw the necessary distinctions. I tried, and failed, to clarify the regress: *to murder, to kill, to assist, to release.* The kinds of discriminations that sent the lawyers and the priests running in their black gowns, anxious to legislate. But all the fucking wisdom in the fucking world couldn't help when what you had to do was what you were not allowed to do. When the obligation of love is paramount, if only one could be clear about it, and all the rest is just stuff: laws, injunctions, prohibitions.

Perhaps I sounded as if I was justifying myself and mounting a defence? That's what Lucy required of me, and what I would not do. Might I try, though, to explain? To see if her mind, as ideologically processed as a slice of Kraft cheese, would admit that, sometimes, you must do the thing that shall not be done? Didn't Isaac's father have a similar problem? But mine, crueller even than his, was not directed by the will of God. To murder a perfectly healthy and adored son? It's revolting. He should have revolted. Said NO.

I accept neither the charge nor the verdict.

I accept both.

How does one – how do *I* – say this to my dear grieving daughter and her dunderheaded mate? How to make them understand? Beg them to follow me, here in the darkness, in order to understand that I am . . . what? Say it. A man who loved his wife, and who acted righteously. In spite of all.

Righteously? I hate the term, I hate the concept. When you are pushed into a moral and psychological and legal corner, you use what language you have available. Cross it out. How fallen a creature I am.

What to do? Have a shower, lie down, eat something, write, get some rest. Stop gnawing the threads and knots of rights and wrongs, ifs and buts. Darke hath murdered thinking. There was only one thing left to do, and I shall do it. Face the music, however harsh, painful and ugly to the ear, however discordant. Go to Lucy's tomorrow.

I sent her an email to say I would be there at 2 p.m.

I was sufficiently recovered to eat a decent breakfast in the dining room, amidst the aesthetic tat and unprepossessing, though quiet, morning diners. Lovely eggs, really, and the coffee was perfectly tolerable. The waitress looked relieved.

I would have liked to have arrived at Lucy's with some decent scones, but they would be unobtainable in that insalubrious suburb. Empty-handed but dry-eyed, I knocked on the door. After all these months it was almost a relief. I never believed, quite, that I could get away with it. Lucy is like her mother. 'I want,' Suzy used to say, 'to be someone on whom nothing is lost.' She noticed things, it was what she did, if not for a living – she'd never quite made it pay – at least as a living. Lucy had inherited the capacity, without the obligation to write things down.

The door opened slowly this time, but the shock was even more acute, for it was not Lucy who was behind it, but Sam.

'Hello, Dad,' he said in the pseudo-sensitive tone of the social worker, 'it's good to see you. Do come in.'

It wasn't good to see him. I'm not his bloody Dad, no matter how many times I have pointed it out. Lucy says Rudy likes to hear him call me that. I felt ambushed and betrayed, and contemplated for a moment returning to my car. Skedaddling.

He took my arm and led me indoors like a recalcitrant horse. I looked about. When I am in their house I scan, inventorise and disapprove. I try not to, but I hate being in an ugly environment – it makes me ill. I look around and recoil, as ever. Three-hundred-and-sixty-degree tat. IKEA bookshelves, filled with elderly Penguins. Badly framed posters of rock bands and brown-hued left-wing heroes. Three-piece velour suite. Modern pine dining set, varnished. Carpets with swirling patterns. The parlour painted a noxious mushroom colour, with its rear wall in maroon.

I wish Lucy would yield in her resistance to the model her parents offered, consent to be better, more appropriately and tastefully housed. She knows that I – and her mother – have always loved her, but also that we could not rejoice in the unimproved faces she turned towards the world. Comprehensive school, Sheffield University, the Oxfordshire housing authority . . . dressed like a militant lesbian, for God's sake.

'Lu's making coffee. Or maybe you'll want tea? Come and sit down.'

It would have been undignified to bolt, and I allowed myself to be corralled in the sitting room. Lucy joined us, carrying a tray with three mugs, a bowl of sugar lumps, and a Battenberg cake with three blue-and-white faux Chinese side plates. She pushed aside a jug with a few partially opened daffodils in it, which hadn't been there yesterday, and set the things down.

'I thought that Sam should be here, so he's taken the afternoon off.'

'Good of you,' I said, nodding to him. 'Of both of you.'

Lucy looked puzzled. 'What do you – oh, I see, you don't know. Of course. I'm not working now, I took leave of absence when Mum was dying, and then I found I couldn't go back – '

'I see . . . and you need Sam to be here now?'

'This is a family matter,' she said firmly, aware that I would have banished Sam if I could. 'And frankly I'm not sure I can handle this on my own.'

'And I'm not sure I can handle it – or even want to handle it – with Sam here . . .' I nodded to him, 'No offence but – '

He nodded back. 'None taken.'

There were a few moments of silence as the coffee was

poured, the cake sliced and distributed. Sam stirred two lumps of sugar into his cup, an infallible indicator of his working-class roots.

'So,' he said, taking a hearty gulp, 'let's try at least. Lu's told me about your talk yesterday. I thought it might be helpful if we could triangulate – '

'Excuse me? Could what?'

He laughed uneasily. 'Sorry, bit of jargon. I just mean talk, the three of us, share points of view sort of thing?'

'I see.'

'Why don't you start?'

'I think Lucy should. She's the one who is accusing me.'

'It's not an accusation. It's a fact!'

'Darling,' I said, 'I did not murder Mummy. I only – '

'Don't you dare! Don't you deny – '

Sam raised his hand, and gestured towards her. 'Why not let Dad finish, Lulu? We want to know what he has to say, don't we?'

I cannot recall ever feeling grateful to him before, but I was determined to put my case. No, nothing as formal or as clear as that. We were not – were we? – in a judicial proceeding, though I felt as if I were in the dock and was about to be handed a Bible to swear at.

'You saw what was happening. She was in a pitiable state. She couldn't sleep without morphine, wasn't eating, barely drank anything. She was like a living skeleton and she wanted to die. She kept moaning. You remember? *No more, no more, I can't take any more, please God, please . . .*'

Lucy had begun to sob. 'Of course I remember. She was ready to die. She wanted to die.'

'Of course she did.'

'But she didn't need your assistance, she was going to see it through!'

I didn't know what to say? Of course I did. But I didn't want to say it, not all of it, not the tangle, the contradictions, the wretched skewed feelings, no, not all of that, no thank you. What I wanted to say was too hard, too complex, too – I don't know how to say this without sounding patronising – too complex for minds like theirs, both of them fed on the pablum of crisp and clear definitions, procedures and conclusions. This was good, that bad. This – if it came to argument – was preferable to that, if you had to choose. And you do: you have to choose.

It was a disaster, a fucking train wreck. I'd seen it coming – indeed, I'd solicited it – but the sheer horror of it was dizzying. I was in the dock. I had to plead. Not guilty or not guilty. Just for understanding.

'I'm fully aware of that. What I did may be regarded as both immoral and illegal – '

'You're guilty! You should at least feel guilty!'

'I am and I do. But I also feel proud of myself. I cannot see why we must be defined and trapped by maxims and laws. Do this! Don't do that! Aren't we told to do unto others? Or to act such that our actions become a universal law?'

'Oh please!'

'I didn't know what to do, or how to do it. I was trying to think with my heart . . .'

Sam looked at me steadily. 'I don't know what that means,' he said.

'Neither do I. It's the best I can manage. It means something – '

He waited for me to continue, but I'd told him the complete truth, and was left with nothing else to say, but a lot of feeling. I had promised myself not to raise my voice. Hah. He may have made me defensive, but he'd also made me angry. The two go together after all.

'For Christ's sake, Sam, Lucy,' I said. 'Think of what you are saying! Don't you think we ought to treat our loved ones as well as our pets? Not allow them to suffer gratuitously? Help them to die when they can no longer live! I would want you to do that for me. I beg you to.'

Her head jerked up. 'What? Even if you don't want me to at the time? I get to decide?'

'Yes.'

'You cannot ask that of me! I forbid you to. So everyone gets to consult their own little conscience? That is fucking moral chaos. It's not up to you, or me, or anybody! You're *not allowed* to kill my mother!'

There was a long pause. 'I did. I'm sorry. I regret it.'

'Oh?'

'But I would do it again. It was the kindest thing I have ever done.'

There was what felt like a long pause. Probably measured in seconds, though. Minutes are not a pause but a halt. But it went on and on.

Lucy glared at me. 'Bullshit. You did it for yourself. You're a coward, you can't stand to see illness or suffering . . . You run away!'

'I know. I do.'

'You disgust me, with your evasions and your sophistry.'

Gone, out of control, tied to the rails, irretrievably crushed. From such a death, what resurrection? And how to explain? That I had found myself – we poor humans all the time find ourselves – trapped by what is on offer. By the available choices. This, or that. Well, I chose. Was I wrong? I still don't know. No. Yes. Damned if I can figure it out.

Clear discriminations are for lawyers and priests and moralists. Lawmakers of one sort or another. Logicians.

This-ers or that-ers: this is legal, that illegal. Moral, immoral. Godly, or sinful. Whereas in real life . . .

Useless to argue, useless to explain. If I exonerated myself, I blamed myself equally. Lucy would not have understood this. I hardly understood it myself.

'I disgust myself . . . I have hidden myself away like a wounded animal in the darkness. It hurts my eyes to be in the light, it bruises me to be back in the world.'

'You could have counted on me! Been with your family. Been with your grandchild who loves you!'

'I couldn't.'

'It's weak, pathetic, self-indulgent. It's, it's . . . solipsistic stewing.'

It was rather a good phrase, and I felt a quick impulse to congratulate her. 'Guilty as charged. Call me names. Be angry. You cannot find me as culpable as I have found myself, and I hardly find any route to self-forgiveness, save for the single fact that I believe myself to have done a brave thing.'

'You're not getting forgiveness from me, why should you?'

Sam gave a little encounter-groupy sort of cough, and we dutifully subsisted. No sense merely recriminating.

'I helped her to die. That's right. I got hold of the right tablets and stirred them into some sweet tea and she sipped it all down. Then she fell into a sleep, then a deeper sleep. I sat with her all night, holding her hand.'

'Oh, great! That's more than you did when she was conscious. Then you couldn't get away fast enough, could you? She didn't need your assistance, she was doing just fine by herself! That doctor said it would only be a week or two. What right did you have to make that decision for her?'

'Well, she couldn't make it for herself. I think if she

hadn't been so weak she would have ended it. That's why she stopped eating and drinking, to hasten the end.'

'That was her prerogative, not yours. Who do you think you are, God?'

If she'd saved up the line, I'd saved up an answer. 'Somebody has to be. To take charge. To act kindly and firmly and respectfully. Lovingly.'

There was another long and necessary pause, and all of us respected it. It was a fruitless conversation. Lucy hunched into herself, crouched with her head in her hands, perhaps listening, or merely blocking me out.

I was happy to let it linger. I didn't want to yield to the imperative for me to defend myself, to plead that we give too one-sided a privilege to the needs of the dying. Everybody dies, after all. But not everyone has to witness a death, sit through it, be dragged into the abyss by it. The lucky thing about dying is that it is over and done, you don't have to worry about its effect on you. But witnessing a protracted and horrible death infects the soul, the images implant themselves, root and flourish, you can never look at yourself or others in the innocent light – you are tarnished, uncleanably darkened.

Lucy rose so quickly, her face twisted and tears pouring from her eyes. I thought for a moment that she was going to hit me. 'How can you? I sat through it too. My mother! And unlike you, I faced it, didn't turn my back. Men cannot do this. They cannot care or put themselves out. When the going gets dirty, they are selfish and squeamish and cowardly.'

'That's not fair.'

What to say? In fact Lucy was hardly there most of the time – and I told her nothing of it – when life in our bedroom was a maelstrom of shit and tears and vomit and blood, when I spent hours on hands and knees, cleaning and puking, while Suzy rested between bouts of expulsion.

'*You put her down!* Painless and humane, so that's it? She got treated like a dog!'

'She was lucky. Vets are kinder than God, and better at their job. Do you remember that little Shih Tzu, Milly?'

'Who?'

'One of your friends owned her when you were little.'

'No, I don't. Why do you ask?'

'Never mind.'

Sam, his coffee long finished and a second slice of cake dispatched, rose from his seat. 'Can I suggest we take a break? This is heavy stuff.' He put his arm around Lucy as she rose, still sobbing, and pulled her to his chest, looking at me over her shoulder. A love hug. Was I next?

I rose quickly and stretched.

'I did some grief counselling courses, Dad, and yours is a classical case. Don't you think it might be useful to talk to someone? After all, there are both psychological and moral problems here – even legal ones – and it would be healing to talk them out.'

I stood up so abruptly that it made me giddy. 'I think I'll have a stroll in the garden. Perhaps smoke a cigar. Excuse me.'

They didn't, they followed me through the plastic conservatory that was attached like a boil onto the backside of the house, with its white plastic table and chairs and a square bright-blue plastic box filled with balls and toys.

The garden was overlooked on all three sides, separated by a wooden fence which had seen better days. Most of it was laid to lawn, which had been mowed recently, while along the perimeters were beds with various colourful flowers, planted a bit thinly, or maybe just immature, ready to fill in slowly.

I wasn't allowed, even, to light up in the breeze-free environs of the conservatory, and it is difficult to get decent draw off a cigar fired up in the open air, the tip rarely burns evenly. The key to this, as any aficionado knows, is that you have to smoke an outdoorsy cigar, smaller, narrower gauge. A Montecristo No. 4 will light easily enough even in a breeze – no cigar lights properly in a wind – whereas a No. 2 will not. I took the pack of five from my inner jacket pocket, selected one, rolled it in my fingers, snipped off the end, and got it lit. Satisfying enough for something that is too small.

'Just as long as you are finished with it when Rudy gets home. I don't like him to see you smoking, it upsets him.'

'Been brainwashed at school, has he? Right little dictators, kids are these days, full of self-righteousness.'

Sam took a noisy deep breath. 'Perhaps he is merely aware that his Granny recently died of lung cancer? And perhaps he might be frightened . . .'

'Enough, you're right. I promise. I'm just a bit desperate because every time I smoke one in the Parks some stringy spinster gives me the evil eye and begins to wheeze.'

Lucy took my arm. 'Come and walk round the garden. I don't mind the smoke. It smells lovely really, though Rudy will notice it on our clothes and give us a lecture. Isn't it looking terrific out here? Rudy and I planted it after Mum died. He says it's his Granny garden. He picked the flowers himself at the garden centre. He remembered a lot of them from last spring when we came to London that day. He even knows their names.'

'Good for him!'

'Do you?'

'Hmm. Not very good on flowers. I prefer them in vases really, or I did until Suzy got ill . . . But let me try . . .'

I peered downwards myopically, walking along the border that skirted the rear of the house, taking my time, hoping to establish a new tone, find a way to let her feel superior. *Dad is a foolish old git who doesn't even know his flowers*. It beats *And he murdered my mother!*

'These ones – primulas?'

'Close. Primrose.'

'Not bad. At least I didn't say hydrangeas. And I do know these! Small and yellow with a bright orange centre. Daffs!'

'Almost. Narcissi.'

'Same thing Mum used to say. Same family.'

'I'm surprised you listened.'

'And these gorgeous ones are tulips, right?'

'They're called Queen of the Night.'

'Lovely purple black colour, like a Rothko.'

'What's a Rothko? Is it variety of tulip?'

I must have looked startled. She laughed.

'Gotcha! You did keep Mum's garden up, didn't you? It was so gorgeous and she'd worked so hard on it. She used to love having her coffee there in the morning, listening to the birds, reading the papers . . .'

'What would have been the point? I'm no gardener. I never even went into it.'

'You could have hired somebody.'

'Why would I do that?'

'It's called respect. It's a form of love.'

'How did you know?'

'It was pretty obvious. Both of you were at breaking point. I could see the thought in your eyes every time Mum took her morphine. And what appals me is that I wanted you to do it. Sort of. Part of me. Wanted you to. I feel so ashamed. What right do I have to castigate you?'

'You didn't do it, though, did you?'

'No.'

Sam, bless him, had removed himself, off to fetch Rudy from school.

'He knows you're here, he's so excited,' said Lucy.

'How could he know that? I could easily have left by now.'

'I texted him. I said "Great news! Gampy is here!" He missed you terribly, you know. Did you get his letter?'

'Letter?'

'Oh. Anyway, you'll stay for tea, won't you?'

Rudy insisted on sitting on my lap to eat his plate of sausages with red sauce and round bits of spaghetti. The grown-ups got oven chips with theirs, and frozen peas.

'I'm afraid we're used to kiddie food, Dad. I could have done better if I'd known we were having company . . . But to tell you the truth, I prefer it this way. This is who we are. Every time you and Mum used to come for dinner, I'd have a nervous breakdown over my Nigella cookbook, trying to dish up something up to your standards.'

'It was always delicious.'

'No, it was always crap. I can't cook a roast without burning it, or boil a potato without it going all mushy. I know I'm hopeless. I actually prefer sausages and fish fingers now.'

'So do I,' said Sam. 'Proper food!'

Following the conversation, wriggling deeper into my embrace, Rudy was watching a children's programme on the telly as he ate.

'Let's turn that off, shall we? Then I can talk to my little Rudy better.'

Rudy looked hurt, but didn't object.

'You know Gampy was ill, don't you?' said Sam. 'That's why he went away for a while.'

Rudy looked at me wisely. 'I know. Mummy says I forgive you. Cos you forgot my birthday.'

'I'm very sorry, but I'm back now.'

'Do I still get a present?'

'Of course you do. I'm just sorry it's late. What would you like most? Do you fancy going to the Natural History Museum again? Remember? You loved that, they have all those handles and switches you can pull to make things happen.'

He took a spoonful of spaghetti loops, many of which went into his mouth. 'That was cool. But Gampy, can I really have what I want most?'

'Of course you can.'

'Cool! Can we go see the Blades?'

'The Blades? What are they?'

'I'm a junior blade! Did you know?'

'No . . . Do tell!'

'It's my football team, silly! Anybody knows that! From Sheffield!'

'Well, that's a long way to go.'

'They come to London, Gampy! We can see them. We can get tickets! Please! I've only ever been to one game, cos Daddy says they are so expensive, and just for special treats.'

'Perhaps we could do that. Because it is a very special treat to be with you again.'

'I'll see what fixtures there are. My iPad is upstairs, I'll go and get it.'

'Not now, love, you know the rule about iPads during meals.'

'Oh, Mum, just this once? It's so exciting!'

'I'll tell you what,' said Lucy, 'why not go over to the fridge and take down one of your drawings to show Gampy? He'd like that.'

'I would like that. Are they of Captain Blade?'

'No, that's silly.'

He walked into the kitchen and pulled a drawing from under a fridge magnet, and walked over to hand it to me.

'Why that's lovely! Aren't you clever! When did you do this?'

'After Granny died. It's an angel!'

'I can see that – it's a very good angel. Very life-like.'

'I learned how to draw them. Mrs Goddard teached us. Do you want to see? Then you could draw one too! They help you to do the grieving. Angels can make you cry, which is good if you're very sad.'

'That's a nice thought,' I said. 'I'm sure that's right.'

In a few minutes, I rose from the table to say thanks and goodbye. I stumbled slightly as I pulled my chair out.

'I must go,' I said, I fear a bit hastily. 'I need to get back.'

'Where are you staying?'

'You know, the Old Parsonage. On the Banbury Road. It's very comfortable.'

'The Old Parsonage! But Dad, that's so expensive! And now you're here you must move in with us. Your old room – yours and Mum's room – can be ready in a jiffy. I'll just go and put on some sheets.'

'No, Lucy. Thanks. It's good for me to have a little time on my own, helps me make the transition.'

'But it's so expensive! And renting that fancy car! How long have you been here?'

'Only a couple of days. And they upgraded me to a suite! They're taking good care of me.'

'Not as good as I can.'

'Of course not, love, of course not. But I'm like a bear coming out of a cave – ' (Rudy laughed) – 'and I keep blinking at the light. I'll get used to it soon, but after you've spent so long in the darkness it's hard to acclimatise. Especially at my age.'

'OK, suit yourself. But can we see you again tomorrow?'

'I hope so. I'm rather exhausted. I'll need a lie-in.'

Rudy came over to take my hand. 'I have a good idea, Gampy. Tomorrow is Saturday and Daddy is home. Can we all go to visit Granny's grave? We go at the weekend some-times. I bring flowers for her from my Granny garden.'

'Isn't that nice? I'll tell you what, I'll ring in the morning, see how I feel.'

'Please Dad, that'd be so good.'

'Yes,' said Sam, 'and not only that but – '

'I'll see,' I said, opening the door.

Suzy was buried in a country churchyard, twenty minutes from Abingdon, that we'd once discovered when hunting for country pubs. There was a perfectly pleasant one oppo-site, with good beer and a sign recommending their home-cooked food, though why 'home-cooked' is a recommendation is unclear to me. Plenty of bad cooks about, making noxious food in their own homes. But the Plough provided a passable cottage pie, and the 'vegetables from our own garden' – another dodgy category – were fresh and rarely over-cooked.

After lunch, all those years ago, we'd wandered into the church opposite, a run-of-the-mill Saxon edifice, with a squat tower, some not very good post-Dissolution stained glass and the pleasing chilled austerity that characterises the interior of English churches. But if the building itself was unprepossessing, the churchyard was magnificent, over-looking a wooded dell, with several yews around the western perimeter and a profusion of daffodils on that grey day in May.

Suzy wandered about reading gravestones, computing the ages of people when they'd died, finding a considerable number of infants who had died in the middle of the eighteenth century. 'There must have been some sort of local epidemic,' she said, kneeling down to try to read the chipped mossy headstone of a little girl's grave. 'Eliza . . . something . . . 1756. Beloved daughter of Samuel and Mary . . . Butler, I think it is.'

I knelt down to look at the faint inscription.

'It makes you wonder who they were, and what sort of lives they led. And this is all we have of them – maybe something in some registry or public record office, but nothing else. They're gone. It's so final, isn't it, and cruel?'

'I don't know. I suspect they weren't very interesting . . .'

'Everyone is interesting!'

'You might be. I'm not. I'll be quite happy to be forgotten. I don't even want a grave.'

'I do! And you know what? I'd like to be buried here. Right by those yews. There's even some free space . . .'

'Hold on, you're a long way from dead! And I thought . . . you know . . . that you might want to end up in Dorset, in the family plot.'

'Family plot? Don't be daft. Mummy and Daddy were the first-generation Moultons to live there, and they just bought up some premium space in the cemetery. Hardly anybody to bury except them, and I suspect Daddy fanta-sised about being interred in Westminster Abbey, poor sap. I can hardly think of anything worse than spending eternity lying next to them.'

'Bit dreary, what?'

'Of course. But now you know what I want.'

'I'll probably die before you. You're so hearty, and I'm – '
She chortled, unwilling to supply an appropriate adjective.

'Anyway, to get buried in a churchyard you have to be a member of the congregation, don't you?'

'Well,' she said, to my surprise, never having evinced the slightest interest in religion as anything other than a universal aberration, 'let's join.'

She wasn't entering the Anglican communion, she was putting a down-payment on a piece of property, as a long-term investment. The next day we wrote to the vicar to introduce ourselves, and said we were looking for a local congregation as we were resident in Oxford and preferred a quiet country setting.

We got a charming letter in reply, went to a service, reserved Suzy's chosen plot for that fateful future day, and tried to remember to make a contribution to the church appeal every year.

But when the time came, the vicar had moved on, and one who didn't know us from Adam had arrived. He was young and very modern. He probably didn't know Adam from Adam either.

Suzy was gravely ill, but still mobile enough to look after her affairs, and insisted that we drive up to Oxfordshire to ensure that the plot that we had earmarked was still ours. We hadn't bothered to keep track, busy with our lives, intimations of mortality brushed easily aside.

'I'm pleased to meet you both,' the vicar said a little strictly, wondering why he had never encountered us before.

'We moved to London, you see. But I believe we've kept up our contributions to your – I mean, our – restoration fund. I think you'll find we have reserved a plot in the south-west corner, near the yews.'

'Yes,' he said, drawing out the word as if it had several syllables. 'I have a note here that we wrote to you several years ago, to say that we now require a yearly stipend for reserved plots. Just a token amount, but it enables us to keep in touch with – '

Suzy leaned forward fiercely. With the loss of weight, and the disastrous effects of her chemotherapy, her visage had grown hawk-like, and when roused she was quite a frightening prospect.

'Are you about to tell me that I no longer have a reserved plot? That you have sold it – that's what I'd call it! – sold it to a better customer?'

'Now Mrs Darke – '

'That's Miss Moulton. I go by my maiden name.'

'Suzy . . . Moulton. You're not *the* Suzy Moulton, are you?

'I suppose I am still, just.'

'The writer?'

'Yes! What about it? Are you now going to scold me and tell me that you have no places available for sinners and free-thinkers?'

'Not at all. I read your novels. I thought them the work of a very clever girl, young and anxious to shock, who was likely to do some good work in her maturity. Why did you stop writing?'

'I never stopped writing. I stopped finishing.'

He nodded gravely. 'I see.'

'You don't. Now, do I have my burial plot or don't I?'

'I am afraid to say you don't. I regret causing you this distress . . .'

I took his arm, a little firmly perhaps, and turned him

in my direction. 'Suzy, perhaps you could take a stroll. I need to talk to the vicar for a minute.'

She wandered off, still seething, but knew that I was more likely to negotiate a settlement than she was to force one.

'Now, Vicar, I am sure we can come to some arrangement. I notice that you have an appeal out for special funds for the restoration of the roof? How's that going?'

He caught my drift immediately. 'Not so well as we had hoped, we're still some ways from our target.'

'I see. Would £2,000 help?'

'Of course it would! Thank you so much.'

Seeing us amicably engaged, Suzy came back.

'I think we can see our way to reinstating your name on our list, Miss Moulton, thanks to your husband's kindness.'

'What kindness?'

'He has agreed,' said the vicar smoothly, 'to give £3,000 to our restoration fund. It is like an answer to our prayers, and exactly the amount we needed before work on the roof can begin. With a little luck, it will be done by the end of the summer.'

'That was generous indeed,' said Suzy.

'Extremely,' I said.

Sam was a bit sniffy about the Mercedes – if one had to buy German, he was an unregenerate Beetle man – but Rudy was enchanted by it.

'It's like an aeroplane, Gampy! You're like a pilot! Can I sit up front with him, Mummy? Then I could be a co-pilot with all the instruments!'

It was easier to give in, and Rudy joined me in the cockpit, gazing at the controls intently. Once we were on the road, he subsided somewhat, peering over the edge of the window in the hope that one of his school friends might see him. In a Mercedes! In the front!

As we pulled into the dirt lay-by in front of the church, Rudy started to giggle.

'I did something,' he said.

In a second it was clear enough what, as a foul smell filled the car.

'Rudy!' said Lucy. 'There's nothing funny about that. Push the button and let down your window.'

'It was a smelly one,' he announced happily.

'It's no wonder you're named Rudy, is it?'

'Why, Gampy?'

'Because you are rude.'

'Like the BFG, right? He's always doing farts! He's funny. And you're called Gampy because you are – ' He thought for a moment. 'Grumpy! You know, like Mr Grumpy in my book! Grumpy and Rudy like in a cartoon. You know, like Itchy and Scratchy!'

'I suppose so.' I pulled the car over and opened my door gratefully.

'Rudy, enough!' said Lucy crossly. 'That's quite enough of that.'

As Rudy ran off into the churchyard, with Sam in his wake, Lucy took my arm. 'I'm so sorry, this is hard on you. He's very over-excited, he's not usually this demanding. I guess he feels he has to catch up on all that lost time.'

'It is rather exhausting. I'm not used to it. Not used to anything really. Bit like putting a mole on the beach – everything is too bright and intrusive.'

'Like Rudy.'

'He is very bright, isn't he? Never mind, he'll settle down, and I'll settle in, just bear with me, please. I'm not as young as I used to be.'

'Dad! Why do you keep calling yourself old? You're basically still middle-aged.'

'I won't argue the semantics of it. I feel like an old man. I am an old man.'

'That's ridiculous! It upsets me when you say that.'

'For Christ's sake, I have a Senior Railcard!'

'But you're still in your sixties! That is not *old*!'

'We won't argue about it.'

There was a stone vase, filled with withered flowers for Rudy to take away and replace with his cut Queen of the Night tulips. As if in an Italian cemetery, they had placed framed pictures on the graveside: one of Suzy in her Indian parrot shirt, another with one of Rudy's angels with '*Granny*' in his handwriting underneath. Another had a framed quote from Kahlil Gibran, done on creamy parchment paper in thick black type:

> For what is it to die
> but to stand naked in the wind
> and to melt into the sun.

'Sam chose it,' said Lucy quietly. 'He loves that quotation.'

'Mum would have loved it too,' Sam said, proudly and solemnly. 'She was arty, wasn't she?'

'It's very striking, and it moves me,' I said. 'Might I take it home with me? I know just where to put it.'

'Of course you can,' said Sam heartily, pleased that his choice had my approval.

We stood there for some time, Lucy at my side, hand in hand, while Rudy renewed the flowers and filled the vase from a plastic bottle of water, with great care and gentleness.

I left him standing there, helping Sam to clip the grass

around the headstone, and walked abruptly round to the other side of the great tree.

'Mummy,' I heard Rudy ask, 'why is Gampy crying?'

I tried to still my tears, and failed.

'Because he misses Granny.'

Rudy was quiet for a few moments.

'So do I.'

Sam walked towards me quickly, a bashful look on his face, and took me in his arms. I allowed it, surprised and inexplicably moved.

'It's all right, James,' he said. 'It's going to be all right.'

'Thank you,' I said, releasing myself gently from his arms.

Lucy came closer and put her arm on my shoulder. 'Dad,' she said, 'Sam and I have something to tell you.'

'Yes, Gampy! Listen, it's so exciting!'

I'd collected myself by then. 'Yes, darlings, what's that?'

'You! You'd never have guessed, would you?'

'Yes, Gampy! Guess! Guess!'

'I'm terrible at guessing games. I always get things wrong. Even when we used to play charades in Dorset, I was always the one – '

'Oh do be quiet, Daddy,' said Lucy. 'You're right, you'd never guess.'

'So what's the big news?'

'I'm pregnant,' she said.

Rudy gave a whoop. 'We're having a baby! I'm going to be a brother!'

Well, I'll be damned. Never saw it coming, never expected it. Thought she'd got fat, let herself go. I fear my response was insufficiently enthusiastic.

'That is a surprise! Are you sure you can afford it?'

'Dad!' said Lucy, perhaps more crossly than she would have wished. 'We thought you would be thrilled.'

'Yes. Of course. I am. Yes. I just want to make sure it's practical. Can you extend your leave of absence from the Housing Department?'

'No. When I knew I was pregnant, I decided to quit.'

'Are you sure that was wise?'

'Well, we'll have the money Mummy left me, after we finish that probate stuff. We'll be OK.'

'Please let me help. I know you won't let me hire a nanny after the birth, but could I help you out during the – '

Sam put his hand on my arm, and I came to a full stop. 'Dad,' he said. 'This is an emotional moment, not a financial one. Can't we just celebrate together? After all, since Mum died – '

'You can produce an immediate replacement? Call her Suzy if it's a girl, right? Well, I'm not at all sure that – '

'Stop,' said Lucy. 'Stop right now. It's time we got home. No more talking.'

'Can I be co-pilot again? Please, please!' said Rudy.

'Whatever,' said Lucy, who turned and walked to the car stiffly.

I dropped them off without going back into the house myself, conscious after the silent ride home from the church-yard – even Rudy had subsided, aware of the cool air flowing around the car – that we were all anxious to be done with the experience. It had been too much, too soon, and, whatever Lucy felt about my relative youthfulness, had made me feel doddery and bruised.

I have never entered the lobby of a hotel more gratefully and, ignoring the greetings – 'Good afternoon, Dr Darke!' – retreated to my room, drew the curtains – darkness, blessed gloom – and lay down on the bedspread. Within a few minutes I was asleep.

When I woke, my head ached as if filled with cotton

wool infused with cayenne pepper. I tried to go back to sleep, but failed, then got up, took three ibuprofen and staggered into a hot then cold shower. I dressed myself in fresh clothes, crisper and cleaner after the hotel's laundering – jacket, tie. No reason, save to feel more presentable.

To whom though? Myself? It was pitiful, making this kind of fatuous effort after the fiasco we'd been through. I ought to have known better. I was never a good father, barely a willing one at first. And when Rudy was born, I left all the feeding and burping and nappy-changing and cuddling and bonding to Suzy, who loved it even more than she had when she was a young mum. Presumably she'd missed that nurturing stuff, though she was relieved that it had time limits imposed on it, that she could hand the baby back after a few hours, arise, and go home.

I have no memories, no sense traces even, nothing in my brain or skin or heart can recall having been cherished in such a fashion, and so it didn't come naturally to me. It didn't come at all, really. I was a stiff father, who tried hard not to be, and only seemed more so.

As a grandfather I was quite prepared to beam and nod, I rather liked that. I felt distinctly beamish and noddish, like an Edward Lear character, but anything more visceral made me recoil. Not with disgust, though there was some of that in the face of the shit and mucus storm of the new-born, but simply because I was being tried out for a role which didn't fit me, for which I hadn't auditioned, and which I could not ad lib with the slightest degree of confidence.

As he grew older, and became a toddler, little Rudy sensed this, and with the perverse generosity of the rejected, favoured me more than his adoring grandmother, as a cat or dog will inevitably hurl itself upon a visitor who dislikes cats or dogs.

'It has no significance,' I said. 'He adores you, does everything with you, goes out in the pram to the park, smiles up at you . . .'

'Fickle little bugger!' said Suzy. 'I wonder why I bother? This always happens to the woman. You give everything, put your own concerns comprehensively to the side, and they still head for their fathers and grandfathers as if they were magnetised. No wonder God is such a shit . . .'

'I'm not quite sure I follow that.'

'Of course you fucking can't. No man could.'

That was all right. It was manageable. She was. She adored Rudy, and the pleasure of his company sustained her until she grew too weak to tolerate more than a brief smiling glance, no longer even a cuddle. Then no smile at all.

But she is gone, and if anyone is going to do some grandparenting, it will have to be me. I fear I am not up to it, not now.

The Mercedes is gone, thank God. I never bonded with it, nasty, cramped taxicab. I have instructed my classic car dealers to pick up the 3.8 and do what's necessary. Full service, valeting: get that beautiful British racing green back to showroom condition. I might just be ready to take it for a spin.

It's a relief to be home again. I'm as light-averse as ever I was: the curtains stay closed, occasional lamps light my way. I made a resolution, strolling around Oxford, home of the clever and the industrious – though fewer of either than might be supposed, most dons being indolent and self-satisfied – that I might just return to my Dickens monograph. Though I have been 'at work' on it for years, there is nothing to show for it. At all. George is aware I am a little blocked on my *jeu d'esprit*, and Suzy encouraged me regularly until I begged her to shut up. But the mono-graph itself is as unwritten as it is over-contemplated.

I don't even know, quite, what to call it, aside from a pain in the arse. *Charles Dickens and the Rhetoric of Indignation* is still at the top of the page, whatever snappy alternative title George may have foisted on me. Best to write the damn thing first, that's the usual way. In the meantime I might return to the works, making notes, finding examples, seeking and citing, though I feel no inclination to do so. I have a notebook full of examples of whatever they are: indignations, outrages, disgusts. What I care about, after all, is how angry he is. I admire that – he's a perfect role model. He is angry because his heart is breaking, constantly, it's a capacious heart and there is an ocean of good in it. In that respect we are different. I'll settle for more anger and less goodness. Can't have everything, can I?

I suppose I have Bronya to thank for this, after our conversations in the kitchen? Or rather, *not* Bronya but Lucy. Because – as Lucy explained to me at exasperated length – Bronya's apparently gratuitous discovery of Dickens, and her sly enquiries about him, were prompted by Lucy, who had introduced herself one Thursday afternoon as Bronya walked to the Tube.

'I knew you would need a cleaner. So it would be on Thursday, because you know that's my therapy day, so I can't go to London. And I know how fastidious you are. You might be knee-deep in despair, but you'd still want your hoovering and dusting done. I'll bet you got dressed elegantly every day, never missed a shower or a shave. You never let yourself go, do you? Just Mummy – and me and my family. You're like the captain of the *Titanic* dressing formally, waiting to drown.'

It was hard to deny any of this, from the trivial to the damning.

'I told her why you were behaving so peculiarly, boarded up in your mole-hole, and she was interested and sympathetic. Told her that you'd had a breakdown, and that since she was the only person who had access to you, perhaps she could help in some way? But she couldn't imagine what she could possibly do, given that you barely came out of your study when she was there.'

I was astonished to hear this, but as Lucy went on, it began to make sense.

'Well, I hardly knew what to suggest. It was going to have to be a gradual thing. I knew that you would try to walk all over her and that, if she allowed it, she wouldn't last long. She had to put up some resistance, establish herself as someone with rights. Even tiny ones, that's how you cope with bullies. She suggested that she insist on opening the curtains while she worked, even if you came down to close them. That wouldn't be too threatening, but it would establish her as someone with a will of her own, and rights. Otherwise she was prepared to act the ninny, to make you comfortable.'

'Ninny? What do you mean?'

'Oh, all that cod Bulgarian ignorance. The crema on the coffee, the funny tomatoes. I'll bet you thought her a right idiot.'

That was unfair. Isn't it appalling how wrongly people can perceive each other? I remonstrated briefly, as Lucy refilled my tea cup, but she flicked me off with what sounded rather like a harrumph.

'The key was that she had to get you engaged. You were not likely to be interested in her – her country, background, education, travels, life in England, plans and dreams – none of the above. No, she would have to get you going, subtly, on one of your enthusiasms. Cooking? Hardly. Wine or cigars? Nope. Vintage Jags. Hardly. But what about reading? What about *Dickens*?

'Bronya is not stupid, she's actually well educated in the sciences, but she is relatively new to England, and had never heard of Dickens. But I assured her she would like him, and offered to lend her the books, and perhaps also a biography. Her reading English is much better than her spoken. Dickens? Duck! Water! She loved it all, and now and again we would meet to have a discussion. I decided she should start simply, with *Oliver Twist*, and then to slowly tempt you with themes from Dickens's life: what he got angry about. How he tried to do good. And then, for the *coup de grâce*, which would draw you out and her in, the final playing card. What a total shit he was to abandon his wife and children. Bang! You have enough opinions on this topic to fill a bathtub, and you're a top-class abandoner!'

Throughout this sad and seedy disclosure I went entirely quiet. Inert. I ceased to sip from my tea as a signal of my disapprobation, though Lucy did not notice. I tinkled the cup in the saucer to draw her attention to its untouched plenitude. She didn't look. She was enjoying this, all of it, full disclosure: her clever intervention, Bronya's studious beneficence, my gullible predictability.

'Well,' I admitted, 'I fell for it.'

'Hook, line and sinker.'

'I think it was impertinent of you. I cannot see what right you have to – '

'Dad,' she said, 'fuck off!'

I was astonished to be addressed with such disdain. When her mother told me to fuck off, it had the merest trace elements of contempt, mostly it was just a reflex, a harmless trope that meant *stop bothering me*. It was almost fond. Lucy's iteration was a step well beyond casual disrespect.

'I object to being manipulated like some sort of a puppet.'

'Come off it. You're not as smart as a puppet. Manipulated! What, you think you're subtle? Mummy used to run you like a train, she'd say. She knew how to make the schedule, where to make you stop and go, what speed you could run at, how tired you would get if you ran out of steam . . . She used to laugh about it. *Oh, don't you worry*, she'd say, *I can manage him!*'

So they managed me. Then, Suzy. Now, Lucy. And Bronya the cleaner. It was a plot worthy of Dickens himself, which is to say, not all that subtle, a trace sentimental, a wee bit melodramatic, that any reader of the slightest prescience could see through quickly enough.

It had taken a few days to let this settle in and down, and I was no longer angry, only a little humiliated to have been so malleable. Mostly I was impressed − by Lucy's ingenuity and Bronya's good will. Bronya − how clever of her. How stupid of me. It's rather touching to have been duped so felicitously.

'And he is bad man, Dickens. Leaves poor wife and childrens.'

The line, Lucy happily acknowledged, originated with her. She knew I thought poor fat Catherine a walking baby factory, unworthy of any part of Dickens, save the one. It is astonishing he stayed as loyal as he did, though I rather suspect that his fascination with prostitutes was not entirely unresearched. Call it field work perhaps.

For a moment I had an impulse to try to get back in touch with Bronya, perhaps to resume our talks about Mr D. Her interest was not feigned, and perhaps we might read together . . .

I know, I know. The time had passed, the incidents stuck in their right time and place. But if Bronya was gone, Lucy was most certainly present, and threatening a visit. I could no longer hold her off – she had my phone number (but I don't answer) and my email (and I have to, eventually). She knows I am sometimes out, and that gives me some leeway in responding. And she is pleased that I am slowly re-entering the world.

It had been less difficult than I had imagined. The 3.8 was back, purring and glistening. It missed me, and I took us out for little trips, avoiding too much strenuous contact with my fellow creatures. I made a visit to Kew Gardens, and had a light and indifferent lunch at their café. If they can make good plants, why can't they make vegetable soup? Or a decent *salade niçoise*? In general I prefer eating plants to visiting them, but I have – like so many of my kind, or perhaps I should say sensibility – rather a weakness for orchids. *Orchidaceous.* A lovely term coined by Cyril Connolly. In reference to Ronald Firbank, I believe.

There's a better café at Sotheby's, cliented by the well-heeled and odoriferous, which makes a lobster club sandwich on an adequate toasted brioche, though the amount of lobster in it just about gets them through the Trades Description Act. If you poke about amidst the lettuce and tomato accoutrements, you will find a bit of that elusive hard-nosed crustacean, minced beyond recognition by tongue or eye. You may not taste its presence, but you pay for it. But before an afternoon auction, there is nowhere more convenient.

I'd come to preview some mid-level Victorian watercolours, a market that is almost as depressed as I have been, and found – somewhat to my surprise – that even the better ones felt flat on the paper and dead on the wall. Perhaps am growing out of them? Next thing I know I will be buying a Howard Hodgkin, something messy and cheerful.

The second reason for my visit was to ask one of the 'experts' to value and hopefully to offer for sale Suzy's Rimington (S.), which I had photographed, it being too large for ease of transport. It just about fitted in the back of the 3.8, but I did not want to be seen in its company on Bond Street.

The 'expert' was a stylish young woman in a dark navy suit and – rather butch and sexy, a bit of the old transgenders – sporting a bright red silk tie. Like all her generation, she used too much make-up. You could see a plaster film on what remained of her face. I wanted to touch her cheek, scrape away at it, reveal the pristine beauty of the skin, the youth beneath. Why go around looking like a pancake?

Suzy didn't. Just a little touch here and there, a daub of her characteristic scent behind her ears. For years I supposed she didn't wear anything save the perfume, though she would apply various touches of something or other at her dressing table. I never took it in. What did I think she was doing? No idea, just gazing in the looking-glass, I suppose.

Pancake Madeleine's field was contemporary art, and she was *delighted* to see the Rimington (S.), which was apparently from 'just the right period'. It's rather depressing to think of him having been around long enough to have periods, but the implication that prices and quality – and I hope he – have declined in recent years was cheering, whatever the 'good' period collaborations were worth.

'We haven't had one of these in the rooms for five or six years,' Madeleine said, 'and that one was neither as big nor as important as yours. Did you buy it from the original show?'

'I didn't buy it at all. I hate it. My wife, my late wife, constructed it and then purchased it, and I am anxious not to pass it on to my daughter.'

'I see. Well. That's good provenance. Do you have the original documentation and receipts?'

'Of course.'

'The next Contemporary Art sale is in four months, and there is plenty of time to get it catalogued, if you wish to consign it.'

'I do, once you tell me what it might fetch.'

She nodded happily, and got out the relevant forms.

'Let's get the estimates and terms clear first,' I said.

I have no faith in experts, or in auctioneers. Anyone who tells you that they can represent both buyer and seller in the same transaction is not to be trusted, but their publicity machine and social caché is so great that people fall for it. *Sell at auction! Get the best price! Buy at auction! Get a bargain!* And as for my pretty piece of Madeleine, if she were actually an expert she'd be dealing on her own, or swanning about at a top gallery, making real money. As it is, she dresses up, is mildly patronising to her clients, and takes home just enough to supplement hubby's income. He will be working in the City.

'Yes, of course. In the light of previous results over the last ten years – you know of course that he has a big reputation in the States?'

'A reputation? What as?'

She smirked. It was rather sexy. 'I would confidently expect between £60,000 and £80,000.'

'If you are right, that would be satisfactory. We'll reserve it at the low estimate. I will pay 6 per cent, not 10 per cent, because you can gouge the big money out of the buyer, and I will not pay for either insurance or for an illustration in the catalogue – though of course you will provide both.'

She stopped for a moment, and her smirk widened and then transformed into a look, if I may flatter myself, of mild admiration. 'You've done this before.'

'Do we have a deal?'

'We do,' she said, and shook my hand, rather too firmly for my taste.

We finished the paperwork, and I returned to the café to risk a coffee. By the time I left I felt pretty pleased with myself, a result of exposure to my tasty Pancake and coffee, and the impending loss of the Rimington (S.).

A bit of high life in the heart of Bond Street, a few mildly flirtatious moments (were they?) with a sexy woman, the cut and thrust of commerce, a chance to feel superior to pictures from two different centuries – that should have lifted my spirits. I used to love this sort of thing – dealers, pictures and first editions, buying, selling, haggling, but it left no taste other than that of not-lobster and ashes.

There was a book sale in progress, and I peered into the room where the auctioneer was plodding on, anxious to awaken some enthusiasm in a torpid and largely empty saleroom. I didn't bother to go in. Auctions are dull, with a few quick moments of action when there is something to bid on. And even then, you either buy the lot or (more frequently) you don't. Big deal. When I was younger and first chasing my Dickens, this was exciting, romantic even, and I looked forward to auctions for weeks, made strategies, prioritised my various interests, and generally came home with a treasure or two.

I retrieved the 3.8 just a few minutes before the time expired from its parking place in George Street and made my way home, feeling deflated, garaged it, and walked up the street to buy milk at the corner shop.

'Oh, and might you have a few empty cartons – you know, cardboard boxes – that I could take home?'

The uninterested boy behind the counter pointed down

the left aisle, where a few boxes were unevenly deposited in the corner.

'All yours.'

'Thanks.'

'Saves putting them out.'

Spared the task of even this minimal degree of effort, he managed a weak smile and a nod of the head.

It was a bit difficult, the boxes being of the same size, to get more than four into my hands, once the milk carton was deposited in one of them.

Milk in fridge. Boxes into my study. Pause. I had so little reason to come in here now, other than the task – was it a task or an obligation or a purgative or a relief? – of writing all this journal stuff. I hadn't looked at my collection for ages, save to confirm that Bronya hadn't damaged any of the books. Suzy had no interest in them at all, and was scornful about Dickens, who, she maintained, had the soul of a peasant. She meant this unconditionally as an insult. (She thought the same thing of Rodin. *The Kiss.* Ugh!) As far as I am aware, Suzy is the only person since Thomas Hardy to take the category 'peasant' seriously. What she meant, I think, was that Dickens lacked both subtlety and fineness of feeling *and* of discrimination. And I am beginning, reluctantly, to agree with her.

Who cares any more? The Rhetoric of Bloody Indignation. The project really lost impetus (if it ever had any) with the coming of the internet, and the multiplicity of sites offering quotations from chosen worthies. One such has over 500 citations from Dickens. What had taken me years of reading, note-taking, considering and filtering, could now be done by a diligent undergraduate in an hour for his weekly essay. And when I entered such sites and poked about, something became clear that I had been aware of in a subliminal way, but had never entirely labelled. Yes, Dickens can be testy, Dickens can be irate, Dickens is occasionally indignant:

> Dignity, and even holiness too, sometimes, are more questions of coat and waistcoat than some people imagine.

You can locate a number of such instances, and ponder which of the sub-categories of anger they might be placed in. But most of these sentiments, when you roll them around in your mouth, aren't angry at all. They're cutesified, smug, as unconvincing and self-satisfied as an epigram by Oscar Wilde. For every instance of a sentiment inspired by pity for the dispossessed, and disgust that they should be ill-treated, there are a score of homilies, bite-sized bits of sugar sweets. The instances will come to mind without my needing to go through them. Brush your teeth with Tiny Tim!

> I will honour Christmas in my heart . . .
> I only ask to be free. The butterflies are free . . .
> A loving heart is the truest wisdom . . .

Dickens is a slobberer. Anyone who can so insistently recommend the goodness of the heart and the primacy of love is never, quite, to be trusted. Bronya knew this instinctively, for when she began interrogating the man she looked beyond the works and emerged on the other side shaking her head wearily. Had she access to the term 'shitslinger', she might have used it.

Of Dickens? My dear Dickens? Could that be true?

And who gives a damn any more? I'm sick of books, they've begun to make me slightly nauseous. Time to have a purge, a proper clear-out. When I used to go into our school library, which had a significant collection dating back to early editions of Chaucer, and a First Folio, covering in depth the great writers in English – or perhaps I mean England – I was often depressed by the sheer number of volumes. And these were only the best ones by the best writers, in a (relatively) tiny holding. For someone trying to hold onto a simple premise – that books matter, that literature guides and teaches and consoles us – there was simply too much of it. I had supposed that one day I could read my way through a substantial chunk of the genuinely serious books, but it keeps piling up, and every year so much more is published, that I get incrementally less well read as time goes by. Too many books, too great and too unrewarding a challenge lurking on the shelves.

If you are escorted into the stacks of the British Library, left free to wander for a few minutes amidst the miles of shelves and millions of volumes, you are struck not by the extraordinary range of human endeavour, but – as book follows book towards some unimaginably distant biblio-horizon – by the sheer fatuousness of it all. The vast percentage has been untouched since they hit the shelf, save when reshelved in a yet more capacious venue. They are worthless. No one reads them, or cares about them. In the long term – the term of suns and galaxies and black holes – all shall be lost, books, libraries, readers, our puny civilisation. Soon enough, in cosmic time, no one will be around to read, or to care. Goodbye, immortal Shakespeare.

FATUOUS

Silly, foolish, inane, childish, puerile, infantile, idiotic, brainless, mindless, vacuous, imbecilic, asinine, witless, empty-headed, hare-brained, pointless, senseless, ridiculous, ludicrous, risible, preposterous, fucking absurd

Sotheby's can come and pick him up. Goodbye Charlie! I'll be visited by one of the young men in the Books and Manuscripts Department, who are quietly efficient and rarely known to do anything other than smile. Bit bland? Not at all, they are sharp as tacks underneath the smooth exteriors and decent suits. But pleasant enough to deal with until something goes wrong, which it often does.

Five days later, Lucy arrived. She noticed neither the missing Rimington (S.) nor the absent Dickens first editions. I'd replaced the picture with an almost pleasing watercolour, which had been in a cupboard for years, and my glass-fronted bookcase was as full as ever. Nothing to notice, unless you knew what you were looking at or for. And Lucy didn't. She had scant interest in art, and thought books were objects of utility.

As soon as she had come in, sniffed a bit, looked round disapprovingly, opened a few curtains and windows, and generally fuss-potted about, I told her about the forthcoming auctions.

'Why would you do that?' she said sharply. She hates change, and it was insensitive of me to impose it so soon after her mother's death. I had no right, not yet, to alter my environs, or my possessions, much less Suzy's.

'Well,' I said, 'I have enough money to see myself out, given my advanced years. I can live off capital if necessary, and can make it to ninety if I do. I intend to be frivolous. I might even buy a little place in Italy . . .'

'In Italy? You? You've so got to be kidding. Where did that come from?'

'Just because your mum was rude about Chianti-shire doesn't mean I would hate it. I could eat wonderful simple food, look at buildings and pictures, listen to opera, read, invite friends.'

'You don't have any friends.'

'I do. At least I think I do. I seem to have mislaid them.'

She peered at me intently. 'Oh my God . . . you don't have a girlfriend, do you?'

'Heaven forfend! Anyway, maybe I will go on cruises. I'd like that. Lovely and indolent.'

She peered at me more intently. 'I think you need to see a doctor. This isn't you. Italy! Cruises! What're you, crazy?'

'Perhaps. But before I go a-squandering, I thought I would put aside some money for a trust fund for little Rudy.'

'Dad, no! You know my feelings about this, and Sam would be livid. Next thing I know you'll be laying down port.'

'I did that when he was born.'

'Dad!'

'Anyway, it's not that much – might come to a quarter of a million, but it will grow over fifteen years.'

It is hard to silence Lucy, but this did for almost three seconds, during which her jaw dropped and only slowly realigned itself upwards.

'That is more money than Sam and I made together in four years! I hardly need a son who is richer than we will ever be!'

'I just want him to have a nest egg when he turns twenty-one, maybe enough to buy a nice flat, get him set up.'

'Oh, grand! Offer him a life free of genuine adult responsibility. A copy of you?'

'No chance of that.'

'Well, I never had a trust fund, nor has Sam. He hates that sort of thing, you know that. Believes in the equal distribution of capital – '

'Lucy, stop! Don't be disingenuous. You will inherit

millions when I die! Is Sam going to donate it to the
Socialist Workers Party? If so, I – '

'Enough, please! You're simply trying to buy us out of
our class!'

'On the contrary, I'm trying to buy you back into it.
Anyway, let's stop,' I said. 'We've been over this too many
times. Of course I won't insist on my little idea. More
money for me! More cruises, a better Italian villa!'

'Whatever,' she scowled. 'You always do what you want
anyway. But not to me, or to my family.'

I pulled her to me, and she resisted for a moment, then
melted into my chest, allowing my arms to enfold her. There
was a sound of sniffling from someone or other.

'Let's not,' I said. 'I do love you so much.'

There was no sense confronting her head on, any more
than there'd been when she was three and had a tantrum
when asked to wear a red garment, or anything with buttons.
The objects and issues had changed over the years, but the
resistance had become more sophisticated and prolonged,
and could no longer be deflected by the offer of a walk to
the newsagent's for a handful of sour sweets.

Suzy had rather welcomed the confrontations: win or
lose, conflict with Lucy animated her, and to my naive eye
it appeared, incomprehensibly, to make them closer. I
avoided such conflicts. I'd been rather frightened of Lucy,
over-respectful of her moodiness, for as long as I could
remember. She knew this, and used it.

'Come and see something, will you? I have a surprise.'

She allowed me to take her hand. In the kitchen I put
the kettle on and made a pot of strong Darjeeling, put a
jug of milk on the tray, and led her outside.

It had taken a gardener a full day to cut the grass, edge
and weed the beds, trim and prune this and that. I'd set a

table with tea crockery, plates and cake under the tree at the rear, amidst the late-season tulips.

I leant over, pretending to smell the blooms.

'Tulips don't smell, silly! Come and sit. Shall I be mum?' she asked, as she picked up the strainer and began to pour.

'Please,' I said. 'Fancy some lemon drizzle cake? I made it this morning, it's rather good, I think. Sweet, but sourlicious.'

She took a bite, and pursed her lips. 'It is! What was that you called it?'

'Sourlicious?'

'Yeah, that. Cute term, I like it.'

Neither of us had been in Suzy's bedroom since the night they carried her away – her body away. As I opened the door, fearfully, I felt physically sucked into the space, as if by a current of stale air, inwards into the gloom. Lucy followed behind me, clucking and fussing, opening curtains and windows, turning on table lamps against the fading, dusky light.

She turned on the bedside lamps, too, where we had spent so much time drawing chairs up to the sides of the bed, sitting and waiting, fewer and fewer words between us as the time passed, and the end approached. Left with nothing to say.

I pulled the armchair from its place under the window, plumped the cushions – dust rose into the air – and sat down, uncertain of my footing for those moments. Lucy walked around the room slowly, taking things in, hesitating before her self-appointed task of going through Suzy's things, dreading it.

'Why are you putting yourself through this?' I said. 'You can hardly want her clothes . . . wrong size, wrong styles.'

'You mean, I am fat and dowdy? No style at all?! That's what it's like when you're pregnant. Oh and thanks for asking.'

'Asking what?'

'Oh, Lucy dear, how is your pregnancy going? When is the baby due? What plans are you making for its arrival? That sort of thing!'

'I'm sorry, I — '

'Not half as sorry as I am!'

Animated by her anger, she opened the walk-in wardrobe, turned on the overhead light and began shuffling through the racks of clothes — so many clothes — pushing hangers aside brusquely, as if they resented her presence.

I could see her — Suzy — in the bed in those final days, her final body. As I sat beside her, dying, her first youth too was in my eyes and heart. Limbs breasts brow lips legs. The easy perfection and the ruins lay side by side in my mind, my wasted angel lying beside me, my fallen one. Young Suzy, wife Suzy, dying Suzy, mum Suzy — mingling, sometimes distinct, sometimes intertwined.

She was more present than Lucy and I were, for a time she dominated the space, then slid away to let us in: Lucy with her polka dots and sour sweets, me and me and me. Time present and time past, passing together. And our human swarm gathered in the still air and smiled and remembered and communed as the afternoon sun warmed the room, and I wept.

Hearing this, Lucy came out of the wardrobe, looked me over, hunched amongst the cushions, still angry, unable or unwilling to come over. I dried my tears and tried to look interested.

'You know what drives me crazy? What I find so hard to forgive? You liked it when you were locked up, with us locked out. It made you feel in control, didn't it? It made you feel alive.'

'I don't know what you mean. I felt lifeless, inert, incapable of — '

'No, you didn't. You do now. You are just going through the motions, without much interest or enjoyment or engagement.'

'I'm sorry to be listless and tearful, I know I am. I'm coming round. It takes time. But there is a film between me and the world, a kind of mist, and I have to peer through it, and it still doesn't come into focus.'

'Well,' she said. 'Well, you have to make an effort, don't you? No sense wallowing. Time has passed, there's no reason – '

'I do. I have. It helps me when I write.'

'Write what?'

'I've kept a sort of journal.'

I didn't expect her to understand, and she wouldn't have been sympathetic to the paradox. Grief doesn't merely dull the senses, it enhances them, because if, like me (and unlike Lucy), the words *matter*, then grief demands utterance, accuracy, aptness. Misery requires a voice to express, to refine, even to heighten: that's why neurotics talk so much and so articulately and so compulsively. Why the grief-stricken remember obsessively.

But happiness? You can say whatever, anything you like: who gives a damn? Glow away, stupid. No need for reflection, utterance, formulation. No need to compose oneself when so comprehensively composed. Happiness makes language unnecessary, has no need of it.

Not that I'm happy. Thank God.

Lucy was waiting impatiently, but there was nothing I could say that wouldn't make things worse, and yet I had to try.

'I'm not sure how to put it . . . The words were keeping me afloat. Like buoys.'

'Boys! What are you talking about?'

'No – buoys, as in the sea.'

'You mean swimming?'

I grimaced, and she paused a moment to think. 'Oh, I get it: words. Buoyed you up, right. But I don't *really* get it.'

'They mattered. More.'

I couldn't put it better than that, though it hardly made sense even to me. She was right. Eating a not-lobster sandwich at Sotheby's or walking in Kew made me feel less alive than when I was cursing and damning, sunk in grief and commensurately articulate. When what I could compose was all that I had, all that was me. When I had to think before I wrote. That's what I missed. For that you need – I need – suffering, and guilt.

Now I am out of that claustrophobic space, no longer entombed in self, letting a little light and air in, things had become less intense, and less real. It hardly mattered how I noted or denoted, any old words would do. When I was suffering, it demanded careful articulation, as if, in the absence of consolation, only words could console, whereas now I just did this or that, one thing or another, who cares, what's the difference?

She finished in the wardrobe after a few minutes, unready for the job, too many of the clothes freighted with recollection: a midnight blue silk dress that Suzy wore once or twice to fancy literary dinners, the russet cashmere cardy that kept her warm when she first took to her bed. Lucy had intended to make a pile of things for herself, but all that she'd managed to find was a few pairs of simple flat shoes.

She looked defeated, as she sat down on the bed. She'd rummaged amidst the objective correlatives of the differences between her mother and herself, and could find no points of contact.

'I think I've had enough,' she said wearily. 'I can't go on. It's too sad. Let's get Oxfam in.'

I don't remember much about the next few months, not without an effort, as if trying to recall what I ate for breakfast last Thursday. Seeds and a flat white. Bad example. But the point remains: re-entering the quotidian was only to revisit the way in which one damn meaningless thing superseded another. I suppose I was recovering, and while it would be damnable to yearn wistfully for my acute grief – God forbid – I nevertheless felt less alive, less attuned to the movement of my own heart. It was less necessary now for me to write, an obligation rather than a necessity. It would soon be over.

I didn't go to the Sotheby's sales. There is something pathetic about sitting there abjectly with crossed fingers, hoping for one bid to follow another, and another. What will be, will be, and what will be, was. The Rimington (S.) sold for £68,000, a confirmation of how idiotic the art world had become. My copy of *Great Expectations* doubled the high estimate, and the rest of the books did as one might have expected. I intended to put the money – just over £275,000 – into a trust fund for Rudy, and say nothing. When the time comes, Lucy and Sam can cluck away, I won't be there to hear it, but Rudy will be thrilled.

Over those months I saw more and more of Lucy, often in London, which I preferred. We'd go out to lunch, catch a matinée at the theatre, and she could still be home in time to put Rudy to bed. Sometimes I would stay overnight with them, take Rudy to the Parks after school, give him his tea at the Covered Market. We loved that.

The Blades were not in London until late November, for they had fallen so far that few London teams were still in their league, the First Division, which Sam informs me is actually the Third Division. The only London side in this group was apparently Brentford. I looked this up, being vaguely aware of it only as some West London suburb. Hardly London at all.

The details of our outing took some negotiating. I was to pick Rudy up in Abingdon on the morning of the game, drive to Brentford, and then to London afterwards. Rudy was determined to stay with me overnight, after which I could pop him back to Oxfordshire.

'I'm not sure he's ready for this, Dad. He's only once tried a sleep-over with a friend, and after dinner I had a call saying to come pick him up. He hasn't tried since, and also – '

'You're not sure that either of us is up to it?'

'I guess not, really.'

I was as uneasy about the prospect as Lucy. I enjoyed Rudy's company in small doses, but was always relieved to give him back.

'Let's try. He has his heart set on it, and the worst that can happen is that he will be anxious. Nothing so terrible about that. It might be good for him to see that he can do things that he thought he couldn't.'

'It might be good for you too.'

Rudy was looking through the window when I drew up. He'd been there for an hour, hoping that I might have hired a Mercedes for our grand occasion. He hated the 3.8. It had no air conditioning, no satnav, no CD-player, no computers telling you what mileage you were getting and what the temperature was. It didn't even have electric windows. And it made a funny noise when it started, and sounded like a gruff animal on the road. He was ashamed to be seen in it.

By the time he was strapped into the back seat, we were all desperate to get the departure over with. Rudy was sucking his thumb, slumped in the rear, a little tearful, his backpack at his side. In the front, I was armed with a full set of instructions, a bag of sweets (for emergencies only!), my fully charged mobile at my side.

I wasn't feeling very confident either. I have learned by experience how much Valium I can take and still drive safely. I'd taken it. Consulting the printed instructions that would get me to the M4, we drew away from the kerb. In the rear, Rudy was silent, playing some small computer game, which seemed not so much to calm him down as to put him into a trance.

By the time we reached Brentford, parked the car (which was much admired by various passers-by, though Rudy didn't notice) and made our way to the ground – you just follow the people dressed for the occasion – both of us had perked up. Rudy was snugly bundled into his parka, his red Sheffield United scarf wound twice around his neck to keep him warm. I was clutching our bag of provisions: thermos of coffee, packets of sarnies and sweets and Valium, extra socks and sweaters in case it got too cold, and small folding umbrellas.

'We'll win, Gampy! You'll see! We're a real good team!'

We didn't. Brentford scored in the first few minutes, and again half an hour later. With twenty minutes still to go, Rudy announced glumly that he'd had enough. 'Can we go now, Gampy? We're going to lose.'

'Maybe just ten more minutes? We might get a goal – and you haven't touched your sandwiches.'

'We won't win! I want to go now.'

At least we would miss the post-game traffic. We trudged back to the car, which to my surprise hadn't been scratched by some envious yob, and made our silent way home.

He was tired, overwrought, fidgety. And hungry, no doubt.

But he refused my offer of fish fingers and oven chips –
pre-ordered from Waitrose by Lucy.

'I want pizza!'

'I'm sorry, love,' I said, 'we don't have pizza.' When I was
six, I ate whatever I was given. I'd learned better than to
refuse. Leaving a clean plate was a sign of gratitude and
good manners, a military virtue. Children did not have
many choices then, and it was good for them.

'We always order it in! From Domino's. Look them up.
You can do it online! I like it with mushrooms and sausage.'

'I don't know. I've never done that. Is it good?'

'It's my best! I love it! And can we have Coke too?'

'Mummy says no Coke.'

'OK, I'll just have some juice.' Lucy had ensured adequate
stocks of apple and cranberry juice.

Rudy took his iPad out of his rucksack and started it
up. 'What's the password for your wifi, Gampy?'

'I think the man who put it in entered a code, so I've
never needed to do it.'

'Never mind. I've got five bars. I can get it on the phone
line!'

I had no idea what this meant.

He was studying his screen, pushing the little letter
buttons. 'What sort of pizza do you want, Gampy?'

'I'm not very hungry, love. I might just have some toast
and marmalade.'

'But Gampy, you have to! You'll love it!'

'OK. I'm sure you're right. I'll just have a plain one, then.'

The pizza arrived twenty-five minutes later. We'd set out
plates and knives and forks on the kitchen table, with a
glass of juice for Rudy and of Chianti Classico Riserva for
me.

It wasn't as bad as I'd feared – it was worse. Even the

smell was intolerable. I struggled to eat a bit, cutting small pieces off the crusty end. I cut a tomato into small pieces, drizzled some olive oil over them, and ate them with the crusts.

Rudy picked off his pieces of sausage and ate them separately, then folded his slices in half and wolfed them down. I'd remembered to tuck a large piece of kitchen towel around his neck, which intercepted much of the overflow.

When he'd finished – God knows how he could eat a whole one – he looked up expectantly. 'Have we got any pudding?'

'Well,' I said, 'I might just rustle up some Cherry Garcia ice cream . . .'

'Cherry Garcia! It's my best!'

'Is it? That's lucky!'

We stacked the dishwasher together, rinsed our hands and went upstairs. It was almost eight, and he'd had a long day. I'd made up a bed on the divan in my study, remembering the rubber under-sheet that Lucy had given me, in case Rudy had an accident.

'Make sure he doesn't see it, though,' she reminded me, 'or he'll be embarrassed. Just tuck it in firmly and cover it with the light under-blanket, then the regular sheet and the duvet.'

Once he had washed and brushed his teeth – he was too tired for a bath – and got his jim-jams on, I tucked him in and got a book off the shelves, and joined him on the bed.

'Darling Rudy, you'll like this. It's *Winnie the Pooh*. Shall we read the story about Eeyore and the balloon? It's funny!'

He turned away. 'I don't like it. I don't like talking animals.'

I was profoundly shocked. 'But darling, all children's books have talking animals! Pooh and Piglet! *The Wind in the Willows*, *Peter Rabbit*, *Alice in Wonderland*!'

'I don't like them.' He was starting to pout.

'*The Hobbit*, *The Lord of the Rings* . . .'

He put his hands over his ears. 'Stop, Gampy! We don't like them. Daddy says they're stupid, and bad for you.'

I didn't think it was possible to lower my estimation of Sam's judgement, but it positively plummeted. I must beard him about this. What an ass! A talking ass! Talking out of his ass. To deprive Rudy of the classics of children's literature because of his bumble-headed father's righteous views . . .

'I brought my own book, Gampy, it's in my backpack. If you get it, I can read it to you!'

It was a tattered paperback by Roald Dahl. *The BFG*, with illustrations by Quentin Blake.

'What does BFG mean?' I asked.

He took the book from my hand happily, and began to find his place. 'Big Friendly Giant, silly! Haven't you read it?'

'No, but I like the pictures.'

'They're ever so funny. I tried to copy one, but it was too hard. Let me read it to you. You have to settle down and close your eyes.'

I moved over on our mattress, straightened the pillow and tucked him into the crook of my left arm.

'It has a lot of hard words. You might have to help me, but I know most of it by heart. I read it all the time.'

'Just you carry on, darling, we'll be fine.'

He read it slowly but well, until he got to his favourite bit, when he had no need to look at the book at all:

'A whizzpopper!' cried the BFG, beaming at her. 'Us giants is making whizzpoppers all the time!

Whizzpopping is a sign of happiness. It is music in our ears! You surely is not telling me that a little whizzpopping is forbidden among human beans?'

He laughed. 'Whizzpoppers, Gampy! They're what he calls farts. That's funny, isn't it? Whizzpoppers!'

'Very funny, my angel. I like that. Whizzpoppers!'

He read on for a page or two before he began to nod off, the book soon lying against his chest. I unhooked my arm from him gently, stood up and turned off the lamp. The nightlight glowed its golden reassurance warmly in the corner as I tiptoed out of the room.

I retired at much the same hour as Rudy, unable to use my study. I lay reading on my bed happily enough, turned on Radio 3 at low volume, anxious in case I heard sounds of distress from the room next door. I got up to check him several times, and he was sleeping soundly.

It had been a hard day, unused as I was to the neediness of a small child. I'd been lucky that he'd spent much of the time strapped in the back of the car with his machine, then in a seat at the arena where he struggled to be heard above the noise of the crowd. But I was as unused to children as to crowds, even small ones, and the effect was surprisingly exhausting. I would remark that I'm too old for all this, if I wasn't worried that Lucy would telepathically hear me saying so.

I popped 5 mg of Valium, thought again and had 5 more, and soon enough fell into as deep a sleep as that narcotic can facilitate. I'd remembered to keep a lamp on in the corner, in case Rudy needed me in the night.

He did.

I was awakened by the sound of whimpering, and a hand on my shoulder, shaking me. Hardly aware of where I was, and forgetting entirely that Rudy was staying the night, I was frightened and sat bolt upright, remembering too many scenes in the night-time with dear Suzy. Too many broken dreams, too many memories, too fresh. The images began to swarm, and I had to bat them away, shaking my head violently. Which frightened him, and he began to cry.

'I called you,' he said in a quavery voice. 'But you didn't come.'

'I'm so sorry, darling. I was sleeping.'

He cried harder. 'I want Mummy! I need her!'

'Of course you do. Why don't you get in bed with me first, and try to get back to sleep?'

'I can't.'

'Of course you can, I'll budge over and you can pop in – '

'I'm all wet.'

I got out of bed, and fetched his spare jammies from his backpack.

'Let's get you changed. Do you want a bath, to get all clean?'

He'd stopped crying by now. 'No!'

'That's OK then. Let's just get you changed.'

I dried him as best I could with his favourite fluffy towel, put him into his fresh pyjamas, and coaxed him into the bed. Lay down beside him, as he snuffled and tried to get comfortable.

'I have an idea!' I said.

'What?'

'Let's play Rudy and Grumpy! You can be Rudy – you know – rude. Maybe make some whizzpopper sounds?'

He giggled. 'Can I really?'

'Do your best!'

He pursed his lips and made a modest farting sound, and laughed.

'Not rude enough! You're supposed to be really Rudy!'

'And you're supposed to be really Grumpy!' He made a much louder series of mock-farts.

'What a disgusting sound! You are a very rude boy!'

'I am,' he said, settling down. 'Very rude! And you're a very grumpy Gampy!'

'I am.'

He was quiet now, and soon half-asleep in my arms.

'Goodnight, my love,' I said softly, kissing his cheek.

'Goodnight, Gampy,' he murmured.

We woke at seven, and stumbled downstairs for juice and cereal, flat white and seeds.

'I have a good idea,' he said. 'Maybe I could stay a little more and we could go to that museum that I like. The one with things you pull.'

'You mean levers. That's the Natural History Museum.'

'Yeah, that one! Can we, Gampy, can we?'

'I'm not sure. Mummy will be missing you, and she expects you home this morning.'

'She won't mind, silly. She'd be glad. She likes museums. Daddy does too. She'll say yes! I bet she will.'

'I'm sure that's right,' I said.

It was Suzy who'd taken him to the Science Museum, a month or two after she started chemotherapy. She insisted that she have Rudy on her own, on the fairly observed grounds that I would be bad company, and that Rudy would fawn on me anyway.

'At least this way I get him to myself,' she said, which rather overestimated her strength.

Rudy had a whale of a time, rushing about madly, pulling anything with a handle on it, whooping and laughing, until he knocked himself out, began to cry and insisted that Suzy buy him a rock crystal that cost £295 from the museum shop. He settled for an ice cream instead.

Suzy came home exhausted. 'I loathe show-and-tell museums. They dumb things down, and wind kids up, like some sort of fucking culture playground!'

'Poor you,' I said.

'This'll be the last time. I'm not up to it any more. I love him dearly, but I can't keep up now. It's going to have to be you soon enough . . .'

'Don't,' I said. 'Please don't.'

'Shhh,' she said, touching her finger gently to my lips. 'You'll be OK, you always are.'

I kissed her finger, sucked at the tip of it briefly. 'I won't,' I said. 'I don't know how to bear it.'

She smiled, her old smile, and withdrew her finger. 'You'll think of something. You always do.'

Acknowledgements

I don't know where James Darke came from. His voice simply popped into my head and he wouldn't go away. His first phrase, on insinuating himself, was 'fucking T.S. Eliot!', which was for some time the opening line of the novel. I was inhabited by him for months – I didn't yet know who he was – and inhibited by him as well: I lost confidence in my own voice and my native cheer was fading demonstrably in the face of his constant presence. The only way to get him out of my head, I eventually reckoned, was to write him down. It didn't work, not entirely, for the more I wrote, the deeper he insinuated himself. During the height of this infestation, a friend told me, rather strictly, that I was becoming rather curmudgeonly, and that it wasn't very congenial, or indeed very like the 'me' he was used to.

Of course James Darke would have laughed at this, for it is one of his firmest beliefs that the 'I' we all so simplistically think we are – *my* voice, *my* disposition, *my* likes or dislikes – is actually the uneasy and unacknowledged outcome of competing voices, introjected over a lifetime, many of which have lost their original sources and become constituent parts of ourselves. Indeed, James, passionate reader and teacher that he has been, is a bit of an echo chamber of other people's voices – writers, largely – whose words have become his own. (He thinks this is undesirable, but I disagree.) Sometimes he acknowledges his sources, but most often the phrases and sentiments of the great writers slip into his thoughts and feelings unannounced, and unacknowledged.

I have not put such instances into quotation marks, nor indeed have I noted them in any way. This kind of casual appropriation – not plagiarism, but also not unlike it in a minor key – is central to his way of constructing himself, and his distinctive voice is an amalgam of other distinctive voices. Though he might claim that the osmosis is largely unconscious, I'm not sure we should believe him: after all, he refers to 'composing myself in painstakingly extracted bits', which suggests time spent in his library, or (even) on Google.

Attentive readers will note interwoven phrases from many writers. The ones I am aware of include: Edward Abbey, Arnold, Beckett, Blake, Conrad, Donne, Flaubert, Dr Johnson, Joyce, Kafka, Larkin, Lawrence, Milton, Pope, Pound, Sartre, Swift, Dylan Thomas, Twain, Updike, Wittgenstein and Yeats. There are probably others that I have either forgotten or of whom I am unaware, because, like James Darke, I am myself a bit of a compendium of borrowed felicities, or what he shrugs off (in another context) as 'the odd casual insertion'.

But if James is sometimes lax in acknowledging the wisdom of others, I do not wish to be. For this book could not be as it is without the patient benignity and high critical intelligence of a number of its early readers. Of these, as ever, the most important is my wife Belinda. I had feared, rightly, that James Darke would not be a congenial presence in her life, and certainly on first introduction she didn't like him one little bit. She had her reasons, and after a struggle I listened to them. The James of Part I of this book is – can you believe it? – considerably toned down from his first and darkest incarnations, in which his disgust with himself and his fellow humans was more pronounced. My friend and literary agent Peter Straus also felt this overdone, and under pressure from his formidable judgement a number of major changes took place in the later drafts of the novel. Peter's colleague at Rogers, Coleridge & White, Rosie Price, lent an intelligent young sensibility to her reading of the penultimate draft, which profited greatly from her acuity.

In that period of intense revaluation of the early drafts, I was sustained and encouraged by the very enthusiastic readings I had from my friends (and former editors) Rosalind Porter (Granta) and Andreas Campomar (Constable and Robinson).

I'd also like to thank my son Bertie, daughter Anna and son-in-law Steve Broome and nephew Matthew Greenberg for their support and critical input. My sister Ruthie and my friend Jonathan Strange have been, as ever, eagle-eyed proofreaders. I am also most grateful for the medical information offered by my doctor friends Sandra Goldstein and James Scott.

When Canongate, to my immense pleasure, bought this book, I was lucky to have the enormous enthusiasm and critical acumen of Jamie Byng, Jenny Todd and Francis Bickmore to spur me on during the final revisions. I couldn't have asked for better publishers.